# A Day to Pick Your Own Cotton

## Other Books by Michael Phillips

*Destiny Junction*
*Kings Crossroads*
*Make Me Like Jesus*
*God, A Good Father*
*Jesus, An Obedient Son*
*Best Friends for Life* (with Judy Phillips)
*George MacDonald, Scotland's Beloved Storyteller*
*The Garden at the Edge of Beyond*
*A Rift in Time*
*Hidden in Time*

CALEDONIA

*Legend of the Celtic Stone*
*An Ancient Strife*

THE SECRET OF THE ROSE

*The Eleventh Hour*
*A Rose Remembered*
*Escape to Freedom*
*Dawn of Liberty*

THE SECRETS OF HEATHERSLEIGH HALL

*Wild Grows the Heather in Devon*
*Wayward Winds*
*Heathersleigh Homecoming*
*A New Dawn Over Devon*

SHENANDOAH SISTERS

*Angels Watching Over Me*
*A Day to Pick Your Own Cotton*

03B

# A Day to Pick Your Own Cotton

Michael Phillips

Bethany House Publishers
*Minneapolis, Minnesota*

*A Day to Pick Your Own Cotton*


Cover photo of girls by David Bailey
Cover design by Kirk DouPounce, UDG DesignWorks



Uncle Remus stories are the creation of Joel Chandler Harris (1848–1908).

Published by Bethany House Publishers
11400 Hampshire Avenue South
Bloomington, Minnesota 55438
www.bethanyhouse.com

Bethany House Publishers is a Division of
Baker Book House Company, Grand Rapids, Michigan.

Printed in the United States of America

---

**Library of Congress Cataloging-in-Publication Data**

Phillips, Michael R., 1946–
A day to pick your own cotton / by Michael Phillips.
p. cm. — (Shenandoah sisters)
ISBN 0-7642-2706-8 (hardback : alk. paper) —ISBN 0-7642-2701-7 (pbk.)
1. North Carolina—Fiction. 2. Female friendship—Fiction. 3. Plantation life—Fiction. 4. Race relations—Fiction. 5. Teenage girls—Fiction. 6. Reconstruction—Fiction. 7. Orphans—Fiction. I. Title. II. Series: Phillips, Michael R., 1946- , Shenandoah sisters.
PS3566.H492D396 2003
813'.52—dc21 2003001434

---

MICHAEL PHILLIPS is one of the premier fiction authors publishing in the CBA marketplace. He has authored more than fifty books, with total sales exceeding six million copies. He is also well known as the editor of the popular George MacDonald Classics series. Michael and his wife, Judy, have three grown sons and make their home in Eureka, California.

# Contents

# Civil War Sisters

## 1

I reckon it'd be almighty presuming of me to guess what was going on inside the brain of the lady who ran the general store and post office in the town of Greens Crossing in Shenandoah County, North Carolina. But I do know what was going on inside mine. *If we can't fool Mrs. Hammond, we'll go hungry. Or worse—they'll come and take us away.*

Elfrida Hammond wasn't the kind of lady a body could draw a good bead on just from looking at her. Except for one thing, that is. She had a grum expression set permanent-like on her face. Suspicious, that's what I'd call the lady, her eyes a little squinty. I'd only seen her once before, and that was from an upstairs window, where I hid when she came to the house. But just from listening I could tell that hers wasn't a cheerful kind of voice.

It wasn't my house. I'll explain that later. But what I was about to say was that she wasn't smiling then, so I doubted she was smiling today. Fact is, I don't know if Elfrida Hammond ever smiled.

Who can say what she was thinking, or whether she saw the wagon pull up in front of her store, or what went through her mind when the door opened and the little bell above it tinkled to announce that she had a customer. But I do know that when she turned to greet the young lady who had just walked in, her eyes narrowed yet a little more.

"Kathleen . . ." she said in a slow, worrisome tone that trailed off and then went up at the end like a question.

"Good morning, Mrs. Hammond," said the girl. She was only fifteen, and had only turned that about a month before. But she had a special reason for trying to sound more grown up than her age.

"I see your mama's not with you."

"No, ma'am. She couldn't come to town today. So I came instead. I want to get some supplies, Mrs. Hammond. Here's the list of what we need."

She handed a piece of paper over the counter. The lady took it and looked it over like a schoolmarm grading a test.

"There are a lot of things here, Kathleen," she said.

"Yes, ma'am."

"Did you tell your mother what I told you about her account?"

"We talked about it, ma'am. She said to tell you she promised she'd get it taken care of real soon, and asked if you could just help her out a little longer."

"I declare," said the lady, "I don't know what she expects me to do."

Mrs. Hammond looked at the list again, then at Katie,

then glanced outside her shop where the wagon sat. Her eyes narrowed a little more.

"Who's that darkie you got with you?" she asked.

"She's my—er, one of our house slaves."

"I've never seen her before. Is she Beulah's pickaninny?"

"No, ma'am."

"She's ugly as sin."

"Not when you get to know her, ma'am. And she's real smart."

"Well, she doesn't look any smarter than she does comely," huffed Mrs. Hammond, who didn't like anyone telling her anything, especially a young girl. She took *any* statement by someone else, especially if it expressed an opinion on just about any topic under the sun, as grounds for contradiction. "No, she doesn't look like she has a single brain in that little black head of hers," she added after a minute. "I'm not sure I like the sound of it one bit."

"We'll be back when we've done our other errands," said Katie, "when you've got our order ready." Then she turned and walked back outside.

The black girl they were talking about, sitting in the wagon outside, was me. 'Course I couldn't hear everything from where I was sitting, but Katie told me all about it later. This is our story. Hers and mine together.

I'm Mary Ann Jukes. But folks call me Mayme, which I figure you might as well too. The girl inside the general store and post office was named Kathleen Clairborne. Folks called her Katie, at least her friends did. That's what I called her, or Miss Katie.

Katie and me were in a pretty bad fix 'cause the war had

left us all alone in the world. That's what we were doing together.

I reckon I ought to tell you a little about it.

You see, Katie and me had found ourselves together about a month and a half before, when some real bad men called Bilsby's Marauders had come through Shenandoah County after deserting from the army.

When the marauders came through, they killed people at both my master's plantation and at Katie's. I'd been fetching water and was away, and that's why I didn't get shot. And Katie's mama had hidden her in the cellar of their house, so they didn't find her either. But they killed both of our families.

I left as soon as I'd finished the burying. After wandering a spell, I found myself at Katie's plantation. When we first saw each other, neither of us knew what to do. But gradually we started talking. I spent the rest of the day there, figuring at first that Katie needed someone to take care of her for a spell until she got used to what had happened. But she wanted me to keep staying. So I did, and gradually a week, then two, then finally three passed.

All that time the two of us just lived there in that great big plantation house all alone, milking the cows and making bread and taking care of ourselves. Katie showed me books and gave me one of her dolls and taught me how to read better. And I taught her how to do things like chop wood and sing slave revival songs. She read me stories from books, and I told her stories from memory.

But all the while I knew I needed to be getting away from Rosewood—that's what Katie's folks' plantation was called. If anybody found me, a colored girl and a runaway, sleeping in a white man's bed, I knew they'd skin my hide or hang me from a tree or something else pretty bad. I didn't know what had happened to my own master. He might be alive or dead for all I knew. But mostly I was worried about what would happen to Katie. I tried to get her to think about her own future and what she oughta do. She had three uncles and an aunt. The aunt lived up north somewhere, but Katie had never seen her. One of her uncles lived not too far away, and after Katie told me about him, I was afraid he might try to get his hands on the plantation. Another of them had gone to California hoping to find gold, and Katie figured him for dead. The third was a ne'er-do-well that came around sometimes when he needed money from his sister—which was Katie's ma. Katie didn't seem to like any of them and didn't cotton much to the notion of going to live with any of them either.

One day some rough men came looking for one of Katie's uncles. We hid and managed to scare them away by shooting guns over their heads. After that, I knew Katie was in danger and that she had to do something. Eventually I figured it was the best thing for her if I left. And I did leave, too, but not for long, because Katie came after me and begged me to come back. She had just discovered a girl hiding in the barn! The girl was about to have a baby and Katie needed my help with the birthing.

That girl was Emma, a halfwit slave girl who was running away from some trouble we couldn't get her to tell us about.

It was while we were trying to figure out what to do with Emma and the newborn baby, and when I was thinking about leaving again, that Katie came up with her crazy scheme.

Her scheme was just this—for us to keep living at Rosewood alone like we had been, but to pretend that we *weren't* alone, to make like her father and brothers hadn't come back from the war and that her mama and the slaves were still there.

And that's why we were together that day, orphans and Civil War sisters you might say. This trip into town, leaving Emma and her little baby boy, William, alone at Katie's house, was our first try to see if we could make people believe everything was normal and how it should be back at Rosewood.

# The First Test
## 2

KATIE CAME OUT OF THE STORE AND WALKED toward the wagon, glancing up at me with a little smile on her face. Behind her I saw the hawk eyes of Mrs. Hammond staring at us through the open window.

"Don't say nothing, Miss Katie," I whispered, trying to keep my lips from moving. "She's watching!"

Katie started to turn around.

"Don't look!" I said.

Katie turned back toward me. As she climbed up and sat down, I stared straight ahead, trying to keep the kind of look on my face that white folks expected out of colored slaves—dull and expressionless, like they aren't thinking of anything, like they don't even know how to think.

But inside, my mind was racing. *If we can make Mrs. Hammond believe everything is fine,* I thought, *we oughta be able to make anybody believe it!*

Katie took the leather, released the wheel brake, then

flicked the reins, and we bounced into motion along the street. I knew we were both dying of curiosity to look back. But we couldn't yet, 'cause we both knew Mrs. Hammond was likely still watching us.

"I did it, Mayme!" Katie finally said softly. "I think I made her believe Mama sent me into town."

"Don't forget, Miss Katie," I said, "we gotta go back and see her again."

Suddenly I heard someone speaking to us. I nearly jumped out of my skin!

"Mo'nin' to you, Miz Kathleen," called out a friendly voice.

I turned to see a tall, lanky black man on the side of the street tipping his hat and smiling broadly.

"Hello, Henry," said Katie, pulling back on the reins, then stopping the horses.

The man approached. I saw his eyes flit toward me for a second. But I still kept looking straight ahead. It was a little hard, though, 'cause sauntering up beside him a couple steps behind was a black boy just about as tall who looked about the same age as Katie and me. I could feel his eyes glancing my way too.

"How's yo mama, Miz Kathleen?" he said.

"Uh . . . everything's just fine, Henry."

A funny expression came over his face, like he'd noticed Katie's stepping sideways to avoid answering his question directly. But before he could say any more, Katie spoke up again.

"This is Mayme, Henry. She's going to . . . uh, work for us."

"Dat right nice—how 'do, Miz Mayme. Ah's pleased ter make yo 'quaintance."

He paused briefly, then looked to his side and then back. "I don' bleeve you two ladies has eber made 'quaintance wiff my son Jeremiah.—Jeremiah," he added, looking at the boy, "say hello ter Miz Kathleen an' Miz Mayme."

The young man took off the ragged hat he was wearing, glancing down at the ground and kind of shuffling like he was embarrassed, then looked up at the wagon.

"How 'do," he said. "Glad t' know you both."

"I . . . I never knew you had a son, Henry," said Katie as the boy looked down again. "Did . . . I mean, does my mama know?"

"Can't ermagine she could, Miz Kathleen," replied Henry. "I neber talked 'bout him much on account ob how much it hurt ter 'member him. 'Twas all I could do ter keep from cryin' downright like er baby. Him an' his mama, dey was sol' away from me, you see. Dat be when Jeremiah bin jes' a young'un. An' after I bought my freedom, I dun search high an' low ter fin' 'em, but I neber foun' so much as a tiny noshun where dey might hab git to. But after der proklimashun, Jeremiah dun come a-lookin' fer me. His mama, she dun tol' him enuf where fer him ter make his way here ter Greens Crossing."

Once or twice while he was talking, I could tell that Henry's son was looking at me out of the corner of his eye. I could feel my neck and face getting hot all over, but I just kept staring down at my lap and pretended I didn't notice.

"Is your wife here too?" asked Katie.

"I'm sorry t' say she ain't, Miz Kathleen. She din't make it through der war."

"Oh . . . I'm sorry."

"Dat's right kind er you t' say, Miz Kathleen.—Say, hit seems ter me dat bridle er yers is frayin' an' 'bout ter break. You don' want ter hab no horse runnin' loose wifout a good bit in his mouf. Why don' you two come ter da livery an' let me an' Jeremiah put on a new piece er leather? Won' take but er jiffy."

"Uh, we don't have time just now. We've got to get back. Well . . . good-bye, Henry," said Katie, giving the horses a swat with the reins.

We continued on again, and for some reason I was glad to be done with Henry and his son. As we rode off down the street I was dying to glance up, and I almost did too. But I'm glad I didn't, because I could feel that he was looking at us and watching us ride away.

We didn't have anything else to do in town, but when we'd made our plans to come in, we thought it might be good for folks to see me and Katie, just to get used to the idea of seeing us together. So in spite of what she'd just said to Henry, Katie led the team through town, greeting a few people she saw that she knew, pretending to be about some business or other, though we weren't. Then when we reached the end of the street, we went around behind a few houses and headed back the way we'd come.

"You want me to come in with you, Miss Katie?" I asked when we stopped in front of Mrs. Hammond's store for a second time. "To carry out what you're buying? She'll think it a mite strange if you carry it yourself."

"I wouldn't have thought of that, Mayme," she said. "Yes, come in with me."

We got down and walked into the shop. I kept a step or

two behind Katie and kept my eyes down. I wanted to look around, and especially to get a good faceful of Mrs. Hammond, but I didn't dare.

"I see you're back, Kathleen," said Mrs. Hammond, glancing over at me for a second with a look like I had some kind of disease. "I have your mama's things ready. Tell her to take them out," she added, nodding her head in my direction.

Katie looked over at me. "Take these things out to the buggy, Mayme," she said.

"Yes'm, Miz Katie," I answered slowly, taking a step forward.

At the words, Mrs. Hammond spun around with fire in her eye and glared at me.

"Watch how you speak to your betters, girl!" she said, almost yelling at me. "Didn't Mrs. Clairborne tell you how to address her daughter? You are to call her Miss Clairborne or Miss Kathleen."

"Yes'm," I nodded, feeling stupid for forgetting something so simple.

All of a sudden the door banged open behind us and a man stormed in. He walked straight up to the counter and started talking to Mrs. Hammond. I snuck a glance at him and his profile seemed familiar. And if there was a white man that I knew or that knew me, that couldn't help be anything but bad. So I quickly turned away from him.

"You seen a runaway nigger girl anywhere?" he said to Mrs. Hammond. "I figured you'd know if there'd been any talk."

"Why, no," replied Mrs. Hammond, though I saw her

hawk eyes dart my way and narrow slightly as she said it. "Whose is it?"

"One of our brats is missing. She might have a baby with her."

At the word, I saw Katie start to glance my way, but then she stopped herself.

"A baby—gracious," said Mrs. Hammond. "Did she steal it?"

"Naw—it's her own. Since all this commotion with Lincoln's proclamation . . ." he went on, then paused.

Now for the first time he seemed to notice me standing on the other side of the store. I kept my head down but knew he was looking me over. Apparently satisfied because I had no baby and was too thin to be carrying one, he turned back to Mrs. Hammond.

"You know how it is now," he said. "The girl wouldn't give me a day's work, and now she's up and disappeared."

"I'm sorry," said Mrs. Hammond. "I've heard nothing."

"All right then, guess I'll be going. You keep your ears open, though, you hear."

He turned and walked out, throwing me a scowl as he went by that worried me a bit, like I might be familiar to him too but he didn't know why. I let out a breath of air when the door closed. Whoever he was, I didn't like him!

As soon as he was gone, I walked forward and took the two packages off the counter and slowly walked toward the door. As I passed by her I saw that Katie's eyes had gotten all wide again. She looked at me, and I looked at her, but neither of us said a word. I think we were both thinking, *We'd better get out of here before anything worse happens!*

A minute later I walked back in and picked up the last

of the three packages wrapped in brown paper. Then we left the shop together. I was conscious of Mrs. Hammond's scowl staring at our backs the whole way out to the street.

We were both mighty relieved to get up on that buggy and finally start back toward Katie's home. We felt like laughing, but we couldn't yet because we were still in town.

"Hello, Reverend Hall," said Katie as we passed the church at the edge of town.

The minister, who was walking toward the church from town with his back toward us, turned and then when he saw who it was, beckoned toward Katie. At first Katie didn't slow up, intending to keep on going. But he ran toward us and called out, so that Katie had to rein in the horses.

"Good morning, Kathleen," said the minister, walking up to the wagon, puffing a little. "I wanted to ask a favor of you—tell your mama to come see me, would you?"

"Yes, Reverend Hall."

"Your father and brothers aren't home yet?"

"Uh . . . no, sir."

"Well, some of the men are having a hard time of it when they come home after so long at war. There's a man on the other side of town who is drinking so much that his wife and daughter are sometimes terrified of him."

"My daddy doesn't drink like that," said Katie.

"I'm sure not, Kathleen, and I am glad. But there are other problems too. Men change from war and I just want your mama to be prepared. Tell her to come see me when she can."

"Yes, sir," said Katie, flicking the reins.

Relieved again to be on our way, eventually the last of the houses disappeared out of sight behind us. What the minister had said sobered Katie for a minute. But pretty soon we both started thinking about Mrs. Hammond again.

Finally we couldn't help it. I started to giggle and Katie burst out laughing so hard I thought she was gonna scare the horses into a gallop.

"That was the beatenest thing I ever saw!" I said. "—with Mrs. Hammond. You were acting like a regular grown-up back there in her store, Miss Katie."

Katie was still laughing too hard to say anything.

"One thing for sure, you knocked poor old Mrs. Hammond into a cocked hat!"

"What about you?" said Katie as she laughed. *"Yes'm, Miz Katie,"* she said in a gloomy voice, trying to imitate how I'd sounded. Then she started laughing again. "And with that long face and staring down at the ground. You were doing more playacting than I was!"

"Except for my mistake of calling you Miss Katie! That just about put her on to us."

"It didn't, though."

"But did you notice that look on that fellow Henry's face? He didn't seem too altogether pleased with your answer after he asked about your mama."

"He's always been nice to me, nicer than just about anyone. But I didn't really notice Henry too much with his son standing there. I can't believe it. And to think that they haven't seen each other in all those years."

I didn't reply. I didn't know what to say about Henry's son. But there's no use denying that I couldn't help thinking about him for the rest of the day. But Katie's voice interrupted my thoughts.

"Do you think that man in the store was looking for Emma?" she asked.

"I reckon," I said. "Leastways, that seems likely."

"Should we tell her?"

"That's up to you, Miss Katie. But it'd likely set her into an almighty panic—as if she isn't in enough a one all the time as it is."

"You're right, Mayme. I don't suppose there's any reason to tell her . . . not unless something comes of it."

Neither of us said anything for a spell, then slowly a smile spread across Katie's face as we rode along.

"Mayme," she said excitedly, "we did it!"

"You did it mostly yourself, Miss Katie," I said.

The thought sobered her up some. She stopped laughing and got a funny look on her face, like she realized I was right and was almost proud of herself for it.

Then she smiled. "I guess I did at that, didn't I?"

"You sure did, Miss Katie . . . I mean Miss *Kathleen*."

We both burst out laughing again.

# MAKING PLANS

# 3

WHEN WE GOT BACK TO KATIE'S MAMA AND papa's house, Emma was in a fix of excitement and worry waiting for us. We'd been talking excitedly and laughing all the way back from town. Having Emma running outside the moment she saw us, going on and on about how she thought we were never going to come back, reminded us right quick that no matter how much we might have fooled Mrs. Hammond, we still had problems of our own right here.

By then we were tired and hungry. We went inside and sat down and tried to eat something while Emma kept talking without taking a breath.

"William was fussin' real bad, Miz Katie," she said. "I cudn't git him ter stop no how."

"What did you do?" asked Katie, speaking softly to calm her down.

"I fed him, Miz Katie, an' den he went ter sleep, but I thought you was neber gwine git back."

"Well, we're back now, Emma," said Katie. "And we won't have to go back into town again for a good while yet."

After we'd had something to eat and drink, we set to unloading the supplies and taking care of the buggy and horses.

"We gotta start making plans, Miss Katie," I said later that day.

"What kind of plans?" she asked.

"We gotta figure this whole thing out and decide what's to be done. We can't do everything around here, so we gotta decide just what we can do and what we should do, which fields to tend and which parts of your mama's plantation to keep up."

"But I don't know anything about tending fields, Mayme."

"I do. I been working in the fields since I was eight. But besides the fields, we gotta tend to other stuff to make it look like your mama's still running the place."

"Like what kind of other stuff?"

"You gotta try to think back to everything your mama did."

"All right, I see what you mean."

"So tomorrow, Miss Katie," I said, "here's what I think we oughta do . . . that is, if it's to your liking. I don't want to tell you what to do, but—"

"Mayme, please don't talk like that," interrupted Katie. "I could never do any of this without you. I've told you that before. You're smart, Mayme, just like I told Mrs. Hammond. You have more common sense than me."

"You been showing a heap more smarts about Emma than me."

"I don't know—we'll help her out together. But I don't know what to do about so many things. So I want you to just keep saying what you think and telling me what we ought to be doing."

"But it's *your* plantation, Miss Katie. I don't wanna be presuming too much and—"

"For now, Mayme, it's *our* plantation . . . yours *and* mine."

"That can't hardly be, Miss Katie."

"If it's mine, like you say, then right now I'm giving half of it to you."

Her words silenced me on the spot. I didn't know what to say.

"All . . . all right, then, Miss Katie," I said, fumbling for words. "If that's the way you want it, I don't reckon I can keep arguing with you."

"It *is* the way I want it, Mayme. So what were you getting ready to tell me?"

"What I was gonna say a minute ago is that I think you oughta show me all around to everything. We'll saddle a couple of horses, and then we'll ride everywhere and you can show me your mama's plantation."

"*Our* plantation now."

"All right, then, our plantation . . . the fields, the slave cabins, what's growing where . . . everything."

"I don't know if I know where it all is, or exactly which fields were my mama and daddy's."

"Well, do the best you can, and probably you'll remember as you go places where you saw your papa or his slaves working at one time or another. But we gotta try to figure out what's yours and what we oughta do with it."

# Rosewood
# 4

After breakfast the next morning, when our chores with the cows and pigs and chickens were tended and we had Emma and William taken care of for a spell, we saddled up two horses. Then we set out for a ride around the farm, with Rusty and the other two dogs barking and chasing along with us.

First Katie led me down the sloping hill toward the colored cabins about half a mile from the main house.

"This is where our slaves lived," she said as we rode up, then slowed to a stop.

We sat on the horses for a few seconds just looking at it. Everything was so quiet. There wasn't much to say. One colored village looked about the same as any other. This run-down collection of cabins could have been where I lived, or where any slaves lived. I had the feeling Katie was seeing it through different eyes now, after being to where I'd lived. It was probably hard for her to think that these shacks had once been people's homes, people just like me, people that her own daddy had owned and who he had likely treated no better than my master had treated us.

Both of us were looking at the world through different eyes than we had just a short time before. Just the fact of slavery was dawning on Katie more than ever, I think. And I was seeing things different too, 'cause now I *wasn't* living in a place like this anymore.

After a while we continued on.

"That field there," Katie said, pointing to the right, to a stretch of land behind the cabins. "I know that's our main cotton field."

I looked where she was pointing. The field was full of growing cotton. It was just like our cotton fields, and I had hated them. The field was getting full of weeds between the rows too, now that there was no one to hoe and cut them down. How many hours had I spent in fields just like this, from when I was so young I could hardly remember.

"I'm not sure about the one beyond it, over past those trees. But those woods over there," she said, "that's my secret place. I don't think any of our fields are past it. I don't remember ever seeing our slaves or mama going out past there."

We rode on to the second field Katie had pointed to beyond the one growing with cotton. It took us about five minutes to get there. It was full of stalks of green that were about three feet high by now. I figured it was probably wheat.

We kept riding to the left, in the opposite direction from Katie's woods. We crossed a little stream and then came to the river and passed along its bank on our right, which Katie said was one edge of Rosewood's boundary.

We crossed over the road leading toward town and gradually made a great big circle going to the left all the time. As we went Katie showed me several other fields—some large, some small—all with crops growing in them, mostly cotton.

"I think I remember seeing our slaves working here," she said. "And over there I went with my mama once when she had to talk to Mathias."

"That's corn there," I said. "We could pick that easy enough when it's ripe and have plenty to eat for a long time."

"What's that growing there?" asked Katie, pointing off in another direction.

"I ain't sure," I said. "I don't recognize it, though it might be tobacco. Your mama and daddy have a tobacco drying barn?"

"I don't think so. You mean a barn different than for cows?"

I nodded. "I reckon you'd know if you had one. I ain't seen anything that looks like one. It must be something else. Or maybe this field belongs to someone else."

That thought seemed to startle Katie and the two of us looked around, half expecting to see someone staring at us, wondering what two girls—and one of them colored—were doing in his field. But we saw no one.

Eventually we came back behind the house from the opposite direction from where we'd started by the road leading to Mr. Thurston's.

"That's one of the other fields where we take the cows," said Katie, pointing off toward our right.

"The grass is getting tall," I said. "Doesn't look like it's been grazed for quite a spell. We'll bring them over here tomorrow."

We got back to the house and walked around there. I wanted to see everything else I hadn't noticed or paid attention to before.

A well house sat to one side of the barn, though with the pump inside the kitchen, we only used the pump there to keep water in the troughs for the pigs and cows and horses. There were two wooden troughs connected to each other but angling off into two different directions, one that the pigs could get to from their fenced-in pen, the other for the horses and cattle at the edge of the pasture that sat next to the barn. When the cattle were out grazing in the fields for the day, they drank from the stream that ran through it, the same stream that went through Katie's woods on its way to the river.

Besides the well house, there were several other little wood buildings and sheds I hadn't paid much attention to—a tool house, a gardening shed, the smoke house, and a little shed that sat on top of the ice cellar. Besides the main big barn, there was a smaller barn that housed more tools and equipment and the blacksmith shop. Connected to the main barn were the stables for the horses. The horses came in and out by themselves, usually staying out in the field that the stables opened to when it was sunny, and coming in under cover of the stables and barn when it rained. The horses took care of themselves pretty much, though we fed them oats every day.

There was so much equipment, and so many different parts to the plantation that neither of us knew about, I didn't see how we could ever make it seem like things were *really* normal.

# EMMA'S STORY

# 5

I KNEW WHAT WE NEEDED TO DO WAS GET A WORK routine established to make it seem like Rosewood was really a plantation with folks running it and taking care of it. I doubted Emma would be much help, 'cause she needed all her strength just to keep her baby fed and cared for. So I figured me and Katie were likely gonna have to work the plantation ourselves.

The next morning when I got up, I went outside and walked around for a bit, just looking at everything.

Then something struck me. It was like one of those things you suddenly notice, and then you can't think of anything else, and you can't imagine why you didn't see it before.

This whole place didn't *look* right. It looked run-down and abandoned. There was stuff lying around. Several windows of the house were broken—the one Katie'd shot out with the rifle and a few others that must have been broken by the marauders who had killed her family. There were a few boards lying around, and the pile of broken dishes I'd cleaned up that first day was still there on the ground outside the kitchen door. A little flower garden was growing beside the wall of the house, but it was getting full of weeds. Nothing looked kept up.

And it was too quiet. Except for baby noises coming from the house every once in a while, it all seemed deserted. If anybody was to come and take a look around, they'd figure nobody lived here, though having Emma around would keep it from ever being altogether quiet!

We had to figure out a way to make it look more full of life. Somebody would come again as sure as anything, and we had to make it seem like a normal place where people lived and were doing things.

After Katie and Emma were up and as we fixed our breakfast, I told Katie what I'd been thinking.

"We gotta make the plantation *look* right, Miss Katie," I said. "Sometime more people are gonna come, and eventually somebody's gonna realize it feels all wrong."

Talking about people coming around set Emma right off.

"Dey be lookin' fer me too, sure as sin! What's gwine become ob me when dey come?"

"Nothing's going to happen to you, Emma," said Katie. "We'll hide you if we have to."

"Who do you think's gonna come for you, Emma?" I asked, still hoping to get to the bottom of what her predicament was all about. We'd asked her questions about it several times, but she hadn't ever been too eager to tell us much. But for some reason, on this day she started talking more than before.

"Some frien's er da master's son."

"Was one of them the father of your baby?" I asked.

"No, none er dem. It was der master's son himse'f. When he come back from da war an' foun' me fat wiff his baby from wen he'd come visitin' one time, he took one look at me an' I knew what he wuz thinkin', 'cause he was 'gaged ter be married ter some rich white lady from some plantation roun' 'bout dere somewheres. An' I knew dat da wedding wuz supposed ter be soon 'cause everyone wuz talkin' 'bout it in da big house. I don' know what dey thought 'bout me gettin' so fleshy, but nobody said nuthin' till he came home."

"What did he do?" I asked.

"He figgered me fer a loose-tongued fice, dat's what I heard him say ter his frien's. He said dat if his father—dat's da master—wuz ter fin' out, he'd cut him off wiff no money or lan' nohow, dat's what he said, an' dat dere'd likely be no weddin' either. So he tol' his frien's ter git rid er me. He said not ter hurt me none, but I knew dose frien's er his wuz bad. But all dere talk din't matter, 'cause den da master, he foun' out anyway. Somebody musta tol' him I was fat wiff his son's baby. He dun flew inter a wrathy rage. Dey din't know I wuz listn'n, but I heard 'em from da other room. Dat's when I heard what dey wuz fixin' t'do ter me."

"What did they say?" asked Katie, her eyes getting big as she listened.

"Der master, he was shoutin' at his son, callin' him a fool fer rapin' a dumb nigger girl, an' den he say, 'You git rid ob dat nigger an' her bastard baby!' Wen I heard dat, I got plumb skeered outta my wits."

"What were they going to do to you?" asked Katie.

"I listened real careful da next day, skeered fit ter faint," said Emma. "I wuz in da house 'cause I wuz a house slave, an' I heard William say dey gwine preten' ter take me down ter da colored town ter clean up after what had happened, though all da others wuz dead by den—"

My ears perked up as I listened. What had she meant—that all of the others at the colored town were dead! Had it happened to more plantations than just where I lived?

"—an' on da way," Emma continued, talking fast and excited, like she was scared all over again just from remembering, "his frien's wuz gwine nab me an' take me somewhere far away. But I knew dat dey wuz gwine dump me in da river in a sack full er rocks, in a deep place where nobody'd eber fin' me. But dat night, I got up an' snuck outta der house, an' I hid in a wagon full er some cotton from las' year's crop dat wuz headin' fer town da nex' day. An' jes' when da wagon pulled outta da yard in da mornin', I heard someone callin' my name. I wuz skeered dey'd stop the wagon and search it, but dey din't. An' when we got close ter town, I jumped out an' ran fer da woods. An' I kep' runnin' an' runnin' fer my life. I knew dey'd be after me come midday wen dey hadn't nobody seen me. An' so I ran an' ran an' kep' hidin' in da trees, an' I got wrathy hungry so I cud hardly keep goin', an' skeered too—I wuz so skeered. An' two or three days went by, an' I hid in da woods an' drank water when I foun' it. An' I thought I's a goner when dat dog er yers came a'chasin' me dat mornin' wen you two wuz walkin' across da field an' I was hidin' in da trees an' here come dis ole dog barkin' up a racket."

Katie couldn't help laughing to hear her tell it.

"I remember that day," she said. "I thought Rusty was

after some critter in the woods."

"Dat critter wuz me, Miz Katie!" said Emma. "An' den I stole yer bread, 'cause I wuz like ter starve, an' snuck inter yer barn. I'm sorry 'bout dat bread, Miz Katie."

"Don't think anything of it, Emma," said Katie. "I'm just glad we found you, that's all."

"An' den you came ter da barn totin' dat big gun, an' my heart wuz poundin' so hard I thought you wuz gwine ter kill me yerself."

Now I couldn't help laughing. Katie'd told me about it, but I still had a hard time picturing her with that gun!

After she and Katie talked awhile more about when William was born, I tried to ask Emma more about where she'd come from. I was mighty curious as to how far she'd wandered and how likely those men she was talking about were to wind up at Rosewood looking for her. But she said she didn't know where it was or how far she'd come. And trying to squeeze information out of Emma was like trying to squeeze meat drippings out of a turnip, and so I finally gave up trying.

# Making Rosewood Look Right

# 6

LATER THAT DAY, AFTER HEARING HER STORY, I got to feeling real guilty for being so hard on Emma when she'd first come. She was in the same fix as I had been. I was glad Katie'd taken her in and was ashamed of how I'd behaved. But all that was behind us now.

"How's you gwine make dis place look right, Mayme?" asked Emma that evening when we got back around to talking about what to do next.

"I don't know," I answered. "First thing, we gotta clean everything up so it looks more tidy—the junk that's around, the weeds in the garden."

"Elvia used to weed the garden," said Katie.

"All right, that's good," I said. "And you gotta try to think back to other things your mama and the others did. We gotta do things to make the house look lived in too, like making sure a fire's always burning. On warm days we don't even build a fire. But maybe we should have one burning every day so there's smoke coming from the chimney. And the slave cabins all looked deserted too."

"But no one's there. How can we make it look any different?"

"I don't know, maybe building a fire there too, so it'll look like somebody's cooking."

"Just build a fire for no reason—we can't do that every day."

"Why not?"

"It seems like a waste of time."

"Not if Mrs. Hammond comes again, and it keeps her from getting too nosy."

"Who's Miz Hammond?" asked Emma.

"A busybody white lady from town," I answered. "She's a suspicious type who we don't want asking too many questions."

"I don't think she'll come again, Mayme," Katie put in.

"But she might. Didn't you see how she was looking at us when we were in her store? She was mighty curious, I know that much. And she didn't like me no how."

"I don't think she likes anyone who's black."

"That's all the more reason we gotta be careful. You never know about somebody like that."

"Then we'll put clothes out on the line to dry and maybe have a horse tied in front . . . I don't know, Miss Katie. It was your idea to pretend to make the plantation look like your mama and the slaves were still here. And I'm telling you it looks mighty deserted. So we gotta find things to do to start pretending, like you said that night you thought of it."

Katie was quiet a few minutes.

"You're right, Mayme," she said, starting to look around herself. "I hadn't realized how much work it would be. We'll have to start doing those things every day."

"What else do we needs ter be doin'?" said Emma, already starting to think herself one of us and getting excited too as she began to catch on to Katie's scheme. "I kin help. Please let me help!"

"You need to get yourself strong again," said Katie, "and take care of William," she added, nodding to the little bundle asleep in her lap. "When the time comes, you'll get to do plenty of work around here—won't she, Mayme?"

"I reckon so," I said, smiling over at Emma. "Don't you worry none, girl—there's gonna be plenty for us all to do."

"I kin work, Miz Mayme. I'll work real hard!"

I turned again to Katie.

"You lived here with your mama, Miss Katie," I said. "You know what it was like. So you have to remember the things we need to do."

"I'll try, Mayme."

"We're gonna have to go into town again too. We're gonna need things, and we need to keep Mrs. Hammond thinking that everything's normal."

"The first thing I'll start doing is to weed the flower garden," said Katie. "I'll do that today."

"And I'll clean up the broken dishes. You'll have to show me where you put the garbage."

The next day we both worked pretty hard. Emma tried to help some but was mostly in the way, pestering us with her scatterbrained talk all the time. I must admit, she tried my patience! But we were a little excited now that we had a plan and knew what we needed to do. It wasn't much, but even by the end of that day I thought the outside looked a little tidier, and Katie had made the flower garden look real nice.

Every once in a while the old Katie would suddenly erupt from out of nowhere.

"I hate all this work and this dirt and sweat!" she burst out once in the middle of the afternoon.

Usually I didn't say anything and she'd calm down and remember that everything was different now, and then slowly start in working again. Or she'd take a look at Emma and then she'd realize that we had a new mama and her little baby to take care of and that was even bigger and more important than just keeping Rosewood functioning.

It had to be a lot harder for the other two than it was for me. I'd had to work hard all my life. But tragic circumstances had thrown us together, even though we were from two different worlds—maybe even three different worlds—and now we had to learn to survive together. As Katie seemed to recognize the fix we were in, knowing that we had to depend on each other and help each other, she'd seemed to grow up again all of a sudden, like she had when Emma had come and William had been born. She was turning into a grown-up girl who was ready to take charge.

We were tired by the end of the day. But as we worked and talked, more ideas kept coming to us. Pretty soon I found myself thinking that maybe we could make Katie's plan work after all.

# The Old Pages

# 7

I WAS STILL PRACTICING MY READING AND WAS GETting better. I was reading more in the McGuffey Readers. Sometimes Katie would read to Emma just to settle her down, especially in the evenings, almost like she was reading to a child. I reckon she was doing just that after all. I don't think Emma had ever had anyone treat her so kindly as Katie treated her, and before long when she was nursing little William at her breast, she'd ask Katie to read to her, which she always did. I'd never seen anyone as devoted to another human being as Emma was to Katie. And Katie was *so* loving and patient to her that it just couldn't help making me respect Katie in a new way. Whatever Katie might have said about herself when I'd first come, about not being as smart as me, I'd never seen anyone with a heart that was able to love as much as her. I think I'd heard somewhere about tragedy making a body more capable of love. I don't know if that was true, but it sure was with Katie.

And when Katie and me were alone at night, after

Emma was asleep, we still read and told stories to each other after getting ready for bed. I found myself wondering if we could teach Emma to read too. Black folks had to get started learning how to improve themselves sometime, and maybe if Emma learned to read, then William could grow up reading himself, and by the time he had children of his own, they would take things like reading and writing for granted, just the same way white folks did.

One day I remembered my old diary papers that I'd found under my mattress back at the McSimmons place. I thought that now I was ready to look at them again.

I went and got them out of the drawer where I'd put them and sat down on the edge of the bed and started to read them. I hadn't looked at them once since that day. Now as my eyes fell on the old, smeared, tattered pages, so many feelings swept through me. It was like reading words that somebody else had written. They looked so awkward and crude, like a little child had written them, which I reckon was the truth. I had been a child.

Maybe I hadn't realized how much I'd changed till that moment. All of a sudden, I saw how different my life was now. I guess that was pretty obvious. I was living like a white person! But sometimes you realize something in a whole new way. And even if it's a little thing, the realization seems big and changes you inside. I guess it makes you grow up a little more just in realizing it. And this was one of those times for me.

I had grown up in other ways too. I was thinking about things for myself, thinking about things maybe a little like a grown-up would think about them. It had only been a couple of months. But in another way it seemed like years since

I'd run away from the McSimmons colored village, where I'd lived the first fifteen years of my life.

I looked down at the gray writing from a dull pencil in my hand and started to read.

*Wee pikt kotin today. Roes a kotin iz soo long. I got whipt cuz I fell down. I tol Rufus a storee bout to foxs chasin chikins. Master kame an lukt at me en stuk his han in my mouf. I lukt at him an hated him, but dint say nuthin. Mamas sik an babys cryn all nite. Had to git up in dark agin to pik at da weeds all day. Im soo tird. Sumtimes I wunder whats gonna happn to me an ef masters gonna mak me have a baby to an ef itl hurt, but I git skeered an don think bout it. Why is white men soo meen. Granpapa got whipt for just wakin to sloo. I hated da man dat dun it, but I lukt da other way so I wudnt see granpapas teers cuz I nowd deyd mak me cry to see em an den Id git whipt fer cryn.*

A sad smile crept over my lips and tears filled my eyes and I sniffed a few times. That life seemed so long ago.

Who was the girl that had written these words? Had it really been me? Those years had been so long. I thought they'd never end. One day out in the fields seemed like a year sometimes, every minute going by seemed like an hour.

But then all of a sudden . . . it was gone.

Now here I was pretending to be helping to run a great big plantation with a white girl I hadn't even known three months ago and a slave girl who likely wouldn't even be able to keep alive without Katie and me helping her.

How quick things could change!

I couldn't keep from crying as I sat there, even though I was still half smiling too as I looked at my words. Finally I took a deep breath and put the pages away.

*Good-bye, little girl of my past,* I said quietly. *I don't think I'll ever be you again. Whatever my future holds, I gotta look ahead, not behind. Whoever I'm going to be, whoever I'm growing into, it's somebody I don't know much about yet. But it's not that little girl anymore. I'll try to make you proud of me . . . and Mama, I'll try to make you proud too, and to grow up to be a woman that's worth something mighty fine.*

I closed the drawer.

*Good-bye, little slave girl,* I whispered again.

I turned around back into the room, wiped at my eyes, then took a deep breath and let it out slowly.

That was my past. But now was now. I would keep those pages as a reminder of that life. Not a good life, but a life that had made me who I was, and even a life I could be a little proud of in a different kind of way. I guess it wasn't only happiness that went into making you who you were. Maybe sadness made better things inside you than being happy all the time. I didn't know. I felt good about who I was anyhow. But I didn't know if I'd read the pages again.

Just looking at my old writing made me realize how much I'd already learned just in this short time. I could read a lot better. I wondered if that meant I could write better too.

I would try. I would get some new paper and start writing again about *now,* about what me and Katie were doing, and about who this *new* me was who was changing from the little girl I used to be.

In fact, I thought, I would try it right now!

I got up and went to find Katie and told her what I

wanted to do and asked if she had some paper and a pencil I could use.

"I have something better than that," she said. "I have a journal you can have."

"I don't want to take your journal, Miss Katie," I said.

"It's an extra one my mama gave me."

"But don't you need it?"

"Not yet. I have two others already. I use one for my poems."

"What's the other one for?"

"Thoughts and things I want to write down and remember. But there's not much in it. Here, I want to give you this one," she said. She took a brown book down from a shelf and handed it to me. It looked just like a regular book, but when I opened it I saw that all the pages were blank.

I held it a minute, thinking how beautiful it was.

"I want you to have it, Mayme," Katie repeated. "It will make me happy for you to write in it."

"Thank you, Miss Katie," I said, smiling and trying to keep from crying. "You're too nice to me."

"You'll need a pen too," said Katie, turning and looking over the desk. "Here's one . . . and a bottle of ink."

"I've never used a pen like that before," I said.

"I'll show you," she said. "It's a little hard to get used to. Practice on another piece of paper first before you write anything in your journal."

She made me sit down, then showed me how to hold the pen and how to dip it in the ink. I made a mess at first, spilling a big splotch of black over the paper.

Katie and I laughed. But she kept showing me and I

moved it around on the paper, pretending to make some words. And slowly I got the hang of it.

That night I sat down at the desk in the room I was using and opened to the first page of my new journal. I sat there a long time thinking what I should say. Finally I dipped the pen into the jar of ink and started writing.

This is what I wrote.

*My name is Mary Ann Jukes. People call me Mayme. Im fiften yeers old an I grew up as a slave on a plantashun. But to munths ago all my fambly was killd by some bad men ridn on horses wif guns. I hid an then ran away an came to anoder plantashun calld roswood. I been here about to munths. I met a white girl calld Katie Klarborn. She let me stay an were friens now. I been tryin to read the Bible cuz wen we went back to where I lived before we foun my mamas an grandmamas Bible an Katies been helpin me lern to read. I also ben tryin to pray an Gods ben answerin some to an that makes me know hes takin care of us. Anoder black girl came here to whos in trouble. We helpt her have her baby an theyr stayin wif us. Katie an mes tryin to preten to run the plantashun so nobodyll know were jus three girls an a baby all alone here.*

I set down the pen and looked at what I'd written. It wasn't a whole lot better than what I'd written when I was younger. But it was a good start. And right then and there I said to myself that I'd keep writing, and would make this book Katie'd given me the story of my life, whatever came of it.

# Putting Our Plan to Work

# 8

AFTER A WEEK OF KEEPING FIRES GOING ALL THE time in the main house and in one of the slave cabins, Katie said to me, "This is too much work. We're going to run out of wood and kindling and matches. Why do we have to keep doing this and putting clothes out on the line if nobody's watching?"

" 'Cause we don't know when somebody might be," I said.

"Why don't we just get it ready, then, and do it when we need to?"

"Because by the time they come, it'd be too late. We couldn't do it after they were already here."

Then suddenly it dawned on me that we had a big problem—what if anyone caught sight of Emma and William in the main house? Then we'd be in a fix for sure! The crazy way Emma carried on, no one would ever believe her for a house slave.

"Miss Katie," I said, "what are we gonna do about Emma if someone comes?"

"Why can't she just hide in the house?" said Katie.

"What if William starts fussing or crying? Or what if Emma gets scared and starts yelling and babbling like she sometimes does and we can't shut her up?"

Katie thought a minute.

"I don't know, Mayme," she said finally. "But you're right—we'll have to do something with her if anyone comes."

Our talk put an idea into my head a little while later. We could set a fire all ready to go in one of the slave cabins and maybe in the blacksmith's shop. Then if anyone came, I'd run down and light it and then come back pretending to be coming from the colored village. If and when Emma got her strength back, she'd be a big help too.

"And we can do the same with a basket of laundry," said Katie. "And let's hitch up a horse and buggy outside so it'll look like my mama's fixing to go someplace."

For the next several days we thought of more things like that, making plans and practicing what we would do the next time we had a visitor. We planned and practiced other stuff too, thinking of what we would do when somebody came, how we'd explain ourselves.

"But, Mayme," said Katie after a while, "we're going to wear ourselves out."

"Emma will be able to help us directly," I said.

"Not very directly. She's still so scrawny and weak and needs all her energy just to keep William alive with her mother's milk."

"I reckon you're right," I said. "She ain't likely gonna

be much help till we manage to get some meat on her bones, and who knows how long she'll be here anyway with those men she says are after her."

It was a good thing that we'd come up with a few plans, though we still didn't know what we'd do with Emma and William.

One morning I was coming back from the barn and heard a bee buzzing around up in the rafters. *Probably a bee's nest,* I thought, looking up wondering where it was. Then the words came back into my mind from the old poem I used to hear the men singing. Pretty soon I was singing it myself as I walked toward the house.

*"De ole bee make de honeycomb,*
*De young bee make de honey,*
*De niggers make de cotton en' co'n,*
*En' de w'ite folks gits de money."*

I smiled to myself. I sure wasn't making any cotton or corn, and Katie wasn't getting any money!

*"De raccoon totes a bushy tail,*
*De 'possum totes no ha'r,*
*Mr. Rabbit, he comes skippin' by,*
*He ain't got none ter spar'."*

But I didn't have time for any more of the verses.

Because just like we knew would happen, all of a sudden I heard a sound. I looked behind me and saw a covered wagon with painted writing on the side coming slowly, rattling along the road from the direction of town.

Two people were sitting in front. The minute I saw

them I forgot all about bees and cotton. I ran straight for the house.

"Who's that?" I said as I ran inside, then turned and looked out the window. Katie ran to my side.

"It's the ice delivery man, I think," she said, squinting to look.

"Will he come to the back door?"

"I think so."

"There's no time for me to get there going out the back," I said. "I'll run out the front where he can't see me and go light the fire down at the cabin. You do like we planned and pretend your mama's upstairs!"

"But, Mayme, what about Emma?"

"Put her somewhere out of sight and tell her to be quiet!"

I turned away and dashed through the parlor.

I was out of the house from the front, a direction where nobody could see me, while inside Katie hurriedly hid Emma and then ran upstairs herself. Then she waited for the man in his wagon to pull up and walk to the kitchen door while the boy who must have been his helper sat in the wagon. She had already opened a window looking right down over the kitchen door. When he got near enough, and trying to make her voice a little deeper like her mother's, she called out loud enough so he could hear.

"Katie, Mr. Davenport's here with the ice," she said in the pretend voice. "Will you go down and tell him we need four blocks."

"Yes, ma'am," said Katie, changing her voice back to normal.

Then she ran down the stairs, through the house, and opened the door.

"Hello, Mr. Davenport," she said.

"Good morning, Kathleen. I'm sorry I wasn't able to make it last month. I take it you need some ice?"

"Yes, sir. Four blocks please. You can put it in the ice cellar."

He walked back to where he had parked the wagon next to the ice cellar.

By then I was just getting to the slave cabins. I hurried inside the one we'd got ready and lit the fire we'd set. It only took a few seconds for the smoke to start drifting up through the chimney. I watched and waited about five minutes till the man and his boy had finished unloading the ice and taken them down the steps. When the man was walking back to the house, then I walked that way too. He and Katie were just starting to talk again when I came up. Katie looked toward me.

"Oh, there you are, Mayme," said Katie. "Mama wants to see you. She's upstairs in the sewing room."

"Yes'm, Miz Kathleen," I said, keeping my head down as I walked into the house.

"How much is the bill for the ice, Mr. Davenport?" asked Katie.

"Sixty cents for the four chunks."

"I'll go ask mama about it."

Katie went inside, ran up the stairs, exchanged a look with me, got a few coins, and went back downstairs.

"Here is half of it. Mama wants me to ask if we can pay you the rest when you come next month."

"Tell her that will be fine."

"Thank you, Mr. Davenport."

The ice man took the money, kind of looked about, saw the smoke coming from the fire I'd just lit, seemed to hesitate a second or two, then started walking back toward his wagon.

"Uh, Mr. Davenport," said Katie. "I just remembered. Do you know who might be able to fix our windows . . . who my *mama* might be able to get to fix them for us?" she added.

He paused, turned, and looked back. "Why, Mr. Krebs, the glazier—your mama knows that," he said.

"Uh, yes . . . could you wait just a minute please?"

Katie ran back inside. Mr. Davenport likely thought he heard voices talking from the open upstairs window. A minute later Katie returned.

"Could you please tell Mr. Krebs that my mama would like him to come out and fix these four windows that got broken?"

"All right . . . yes, all right, Miss Clairborne—I'll talk to him. But—"

"Thank you, Mr. Davenport," said Katie, then turned, went back inside, and closed the door.

By then I was nearly laughing to split my sides. Katie was some actress!

I had been peeking out of one of the windows from behind a curtain. I watched as the man just stood there a few seconds watching Katie come back inside, then kinda shook his head with a puzzled expression, and finally went back to his wagon, got up, shouted to his horses, then rattled off toward the Thurston place.

As soon as he was gone, I came running down the stairs laughing.

"You did it, Miss Katie," I said. "You really made him believe your mama was right up there all the time!"

A sheepish smile crept over her face. Then she started laughing too.

We talked for a minute, then suddenly a startled look came over Katie's face.

"Oh, oh—I forgot about Emma!" she exclaimed.

I'd forgotten too. "Where is she?" I said.

But already Katie had turned and was running into the parlor. She threw up the carpet and opened the trapdoor in the floor leading down into the cellar. The instant she did, the sound of a baby crying came up from the blackness below.

"You can come up now, Emma," said Katie, taking two or three steps down the ladder. "Here, hand William up to me."

"Miz Katie," I heard Emma calling from below, "it was so dark down dere, I wuz skeered."

"I'm sorry, Emma. It all happened so fast. But next time we'll put a candle or lantern down there for you."

"You gwine make me go down dere agin, Miz Katie?" wailed Emma as she climbed up out of the dark hole.

"Only if we have to, Emma. Only if someone comes again. But it will be better next time, I promise."

# A Talk About God

# 9

One day after we had just finished the milking, we were taking the cows out to pasture. As the two of us were walking along the road I glanced back. There were the eight or ten milk cows following lazily along, stretching out behind us in ones and twos. And I realized that we were doing it, we were getting up every morning and keeping things going. It might not have been much of a plantation, but at least the animals were still alive and we were surviving, although we were sure drinking a lot of milk. It was good for Emma, though. She was starting to fill out a little and was looking a mite less scrawny. And in time I reckoned William would start drinking some cow's milk directly from a bottle instead of his mama's breast.

I glanced back again.

The cows behind us didn't care how old we were. They just went where we led them and ate the food we gave them and let us milk them. They didn't care if we were black or white or young or old.

A wave of happiness surged through me as we walked. I ain't sure quite what caused it. But with the sun shining and the cows clomping along and me and Katie just going about the day like it wasn't so unusual and like we actually knew what we were doing, it was just a good feeling.

I snuck a glance over at Katie beside me. She had a contented, almost happy, carefree look on her face too. She had already changed so much from when I'd first come. I could see it in her expression, just in the way she walked and talked. She was so much more confident already. She didn't look like a frightened little girl anymore. I think taking care of Emma had matured her more than anything. It made her feel useful and needed. She knew how much Emma and William depended on her for their very survival and that couldn't help but make a body feel more grown up about things.

"Miss Katie," I said as we walked along, "do you ever wonder why God let all this happen—our families getting killed I mean?"

"Do you think He let it happen, Mayme?" she said.

"I thought He made everything happen," I said. "I thought that's what God's will was, everything that happened."

"I don't see how something as bad as that could be God's will," she said.

I thought about what she'd said a minute.

"I see what you mean. I guess I don't see how it could be either, if He's a good God," I said. "But I thought everything was His will."

"I don't know," said Katie. "My mama and daddy didn't teach me too much about God."

We walked along a while more. My mind was turning the thing around and around.

"Do you think He is a good God, Miss Katie?" I said after a bit.

"I don't know. I just thought He was . . . God."

"But what's He like?"

"I don't know. But doesn't it seem like He'd have to be good?"

"Why's that?"

"Well, if He's God, He'd *have* to be good, wouldn't He?"

"I don't know. I don't reckon I ever thought about it much before."

"What else could He be?"

"Why do you think that?"

"I don't know. It just seems that way. I mean, life is a good thing, isn't it? So if God made it, He'd have to be good."

"Life ain't so good if you're a slave," I said. "And life ain't been so good to you and me and Emma. How can life be good when there's so much killing?"

Katie thought about that a minute.

"Maybe God made things good at first," she said. "I bet there weren't any slaves back then."

"I reckon you're right," I said. "It sure don't seem like God could want one person owning another and being mean to them and with folks of all colors being able to kill each other."

"So if God doesn't like people being slaves," said Katie, "maybe He's still good, even though people do bad things, like those men who killed our families."

Again I thought for a minute. It was hard to get my brain to grab hold of the idea all the way. The harder I thought about it, the more it moved around, like the idea was trying to squirt out of my hand.

"But it still seems like He'd have done something to not let it happen, if He's good like you say," I said finally. "Why wouldn't God make good things happen instead of bad things?"

"Maybe He can't," said Katie.

"Why couldn't He? If He's God, can't He do anything?"

"I don't know. Maybe He can't make people be good if they don't want to."

"Hmm . . . I suppose that could be."

"Maybe He doesn't want to make all the bad things in the world go away, things like your being a slave, and those marauder men."

"I wonder why not."

"I don't know," said Katie. "But I see what you mean—why can so much bad happen if God is good? It seems like He ought to do something to keep it from happening."

"Yet as much bad as has happened to us," I said, "God's taken care of us too. I think He cares about us, don't you, Miss Katie?"

"Yes, I think He does."

"So maybe there's good and bad all mixed together, like it's been for us. Even though terrible things have happened, God still loves us—at least we're pretty sure He does. So that part of Him must be good. Though I admit, it's still a mite confusing."

We walked for a couple minutes just thinking.

"I wonder how you find out," I said finally.

"Find out what?" asked Katie.

"What God's like."

"Isn't that what the Bible's for?"

"I don't know, I just thought it was stories about olden times."

"I suppose you could ask Him what He's like."

"You mean ask God?" I said. "Like we did before, when we asked for His help?"

Katie nodded.

"But how would He tell you the answer?"

"I don't know," said Katie.

"Maybe by how you feel," I said, "like when I thought He was telling me to stay here. It was a mighty strange but good feeling to think that God was talking to me."

We were just about to the field by now. We led the cows through the open gate, then closed it behind them. They frolicked for a few seconds in the thick, tall green grass, if something as big and clumsy as a cow can frolic. Then they got down to their business of the day, which was to eat as much of it as they could.

We turned and walked back toward the house. Neither of us said anything more for four or five minutes. We were about halfway back by then. I'd been thinking the whole way about what Katie had said a little while ago about asking God.

"Why don't we, then?" I said.

"Why don't we what?" said Katie.

"Ask God what He's like. We prayed that other time in the house, when we were reading the Bible and asked Him to come live in us. And then I prayed that He'd show me what to do about staying. So it seems like when we pray, He answers, doesn't it?"

"It seems like it," said Katie.

"So why don't we ask Him this?"

"Okay," said Katie. "I guess if He wants to live in our hearts and answer our prayers, then He'd want us to know what He's like."

"I reckon He would at that," I said.

*"God, please show us what you're like,"* said Katie without even a pause. We kept walking, and she just prayed so natural, with her eyes still open. I was always surprised at how natural she was with God, as if He was right there with us and there wasn't anything to be afraid of or feel funny about by just talking to Him like you'd talk to anybody. But I reckon if you can't be comfortable and natural with Him, who can you be comfortable and natural with at all?

*"I ask you to show me too, God,"* I said. *"We want to know what you're like, and if you're good, even though so many bad things happen."*

## Back Home
## 10

Even though I'd agreed to stay at Rosewood with Katie, I couldn't keep from thinking once in a while about what would become of us . . . later, I mean. I was still concerned about Katie's uncles. I'd agreed to stay for now. But I knew I couldn't just stay forever.

And I couldn't help thinking from time to time about my own status too. I was a runaway slave just like Emma was. Like I'd said to Katie, there wasn't any two ways about it—bad things happened to runaways. I wondered what had happened to my master and the rest of the plantation. Had they been killed too, like my family? When Katie and me had gone back, I hadn't seen or heard anything. But I hadn't felt like getting none too close to the plantation house to find out. I didn't want anybody to see me. But now I found myself wondering. If they hadn't been killed, and if they found me, I'd be in big trouble. For all I knew Mr. McSimmons knew who'd been killed and who hadn't and was out looking for me.

So I decided to go back to the McSimmons place again. I reckon it was a stupid thing to do, because if they got their hands on me, they'd put me to work or into some bed with a man. I'd heard about some of the McSimmons boys, and I didn't like the thought of that one bit. But I had to know what had happened to the rest of them, and what was likely to happen to me. I couldn't think straight to help Katie know what to do unless I had some idea about myself.

I thought about it for a week or more. Part of me was terrified to go back again. Somehow I think I knew I'd get seen. Another part of me didn't want to do that to Katie. But finally I couldn't hardly think of nothing else. I had to find out if anybody was alive or not.

So finally one day I told Katie that I was going back to my old house again.

"But, Miss Katie," I added, "I need to go alone."

Her eyes started getting big like they did. All of a sudden she was a little girl again.

"I'm sorry, Miss Katie, but I got to do it," I said.

"But what if they make you go back to work, Mayme," she said in a shaky voice. "What if you never come back . . . what will I do then? How will I take care of Emma?"

"If that happens, I promise I'll get word to you somehow," I said. "But I'll be real careful."

"Please don't go, Mayme. I'll be afraid without you. Why do you have to go?"

"It's just something I think I'm supposed to do. I gotta find out if they're looking for me. I don't think I could stand having that over my head all my life."

"How . . . how long will you be gone, Mayme?"

"Just a day."

"When are you going?"

"Tomorrow."

Katie looked away. I knew she was starting to cry.

"I'll hurry as fast as I can, Miss Katie," I said, facing her back.

"You'll . . . you'll ride, won't you?" she said, still looking away.

"If you want me to, Katie."

She only nodded, then got up and left the room.

I got up early the next morning. Katie got up with me. We hadn't told Emma. There was no need to. Neither of us said much. When the horse was saddled and I was ready, Katie reached out and took my hand and held it tight.

"Mayme," she said, and her voice was stronger now and she had gotten over her crying from yesterday, "you come back." She looked straight into my eyes as earnestly as I'd ever seen her. "I can't do this without you, Mayme," she said. "I'm afraid. So you come back."

"I will, Katie," I said. "I promise."

She let go of my hand. I saw her take in a breath, a little quivery, but she tried to smile. I got up on the horse and smiled down. Then I turned and rode away along the road toward town.

"Be careful!" she called out behind me. "Don't let anyone see you. And hurry, Mayme!"

The idea in my head was to sneak up close to the plantation house and see what I could see. I kept to the road but didn't hurry. I was thinking about a lot of things and I didn't care if it took me all day. I just walked the horse slow, and whenever I saw somebody coming I got off into the woods to hide, waited till they were past, then continued on.

I went first to the slave cabins like we had before, and tied the horse a little ways away. It was still mostly deserted, but now I saw a little activity and heard voices. Somebody was living in one of the shacks now, but I didn't recognize the voices.

I kept out of sight and snuck up to the big house, coming toward it from the side away from the barn, where I thought I'd be most out of sight. I was just gonna look around and see who I could see.

I crept toward it until I was pretty close, then ducked down and hid behind the well shed. I saw people. There was the overseer and the master's two sons walking behind the barn. I didn't see any coloreds, but the white folks looked like they were working as usual. Then gradually I saw some other people I didn't recognize, both white and colored.

All of a sudden I heard a voice behind me.

"Hey, girl, wha'chu—why, *Mayme*!"

I spun around at the sound of the familiar voice.

"What'n tarnashun . . . dat really you?" There stood the ponderous form of Mistress McSimmons' housekeeper and cook, who we all said ran the whole plantation.

My heart skipped with joy to see a familiar face!

"It's me, Josepha," I said, smiling.

"We thought you wuz dead wiff da others . . . how in tarnashun . . . but where you been all dis time, chil'!"

"I ran away," I said.

She waddled toward me, her round black face beaming, and took me in her arms. It was all I could do not to break out bawling.

"Den it muster been you dat buried yo family—dat wuz

what none ob us could figure, why some ob 'em wuz buried an' not da res'."

I nodded with a sad smile at the thought of that horrible day.

"Come in da house!" she said, standing back and running a scrutinizing eye up and down my frame. "You al'ays wuz a scrawny one, but wherever you been, dey ain't been givin' you enuff food. You needs some vittles in yo tummy."

She started half pushing, half leading me toward the house. But I hesitated.

"I can't stay, Josepha," I said.

"Wha'chu mean . . . you ain't fixin' ter run off agin?"

"I can't come back here, Josepha," I said. "The master'll whip me but good for running off. I've got another place that's home to me now that my kin's gone. Please don't tell them you saw me."

"You set yo min' at ease, chil'," she said. "Jes' come wiff me. I'll take care ob you, chil'. Why, I wuz dere when you wuz borned. . . ."

She paused a moment, and an odd expression passed briefly across her face as she looked me over—a little strangely, I thought.

"What I's sayin' is dat you's always been a mite special ter me. 'Sides, no white man ain't gwine tell you what ter do no mo, no how."

"Why, what do you mean?" I asked.

"Ain't you heard? Ain't no mo slaves. We's all been dun set free."

"Free," I said, not understanding what she meant.

"Dat's right—you's free now, chil'. Dere's sumfin called er 'mancipation proklimation what's done made it against da law ter own slaves. Some feller named Lincoln done it. You's a free black girl. Da white man kin't do nuthin' ter hurt you no mo."

We had heard talk from some newspapers we'd read about Lincoln's proclamation, but I never really believed it could be true. Leastways, not for me. I couldn't see how some fancy words from far up north ways was gonna change Master McSimmons' mind about slaves.

"But what about the war?" I asked.

"Dat's all over, Mayme, chil'. Dat's what dey wuz fightin' 'bout, near as I kin tell. Da norf won an' da souf had ter set us coloreds free. Leastways, sumfin like dat's what da master done tol' me."

My brain went numb at what she was telling me. It was hard to imagine any white man fighting for colored folks, let alone a whole army. While I was still trying to make sense of it all, she put her great big arm around me and I found myself walking up the steps into the house with her.

I'd never been inside the big house before. As we went through the door I kept looking around nervously. After what she'd told me, and after being in Katie's house and acting like it was my own, I don't know why I should have been nervous now. But I couldn't help still being afraid of the master. It hadn't been so long that I'd forgotten what his whip felt like.

I was still jittery when Josepha put a plate of bread and cheese on the table in front of me.

"Wha'chu gwine do now, chil'?" she said. "Da master'd likely keep you on like he dun me."

"You mean, stay here like before?" I asked.

"Dat's what I mean. But not like no slave. You'd git paid

fer yo work now. You could stay here in da house wiff me, an' be a house girl an' work wiff me."

"What do you mean, get paid?" I asked.

"Jes' what I mean. Dey gots ter pay us now, since we ain't slaves. I's be gittin' five cents er day ter stay an' work fer master McSimmons. I don' know what's ter become er me effen der young master marries dat lady what don' seem ter like me none. But fer now I gots me my same room ter sleep in, an' you can see wiff yo own eyes dat I ain't sufferin' from not havin' enuff ter eat."

She broke out in a chuckle that shook her huge frame. I could feel rumbling on the floor under my chair. The idea of a colored person getting paid real money was more than I could imagine.

"And . . . and you *want* to stay here?" I said.

"Where would a fat ole black woman go, chil'? I reckon I'm free, but I gots no place else t' go. I been here all my born days, so I figure dis'll be my home fer da rest of 'em."

I took a bite of bread and thought about what she said.

"No . . . no, Josepha," I said. "I don't think I can stay. And so I reckon I oughta be going."

I stood up from the table.

"Wha'chu gwine do den, effen you don' plan ter stay here?" she asked, looking up at me from where she sat like I was a little crazy.

"I . . . I don't know exactly," I said. "But I know I don't belong here no more. After what I saw happen to Mama and Sammy and Grandpapa and the others, I don't think this could ever be my home again. I'm sorry, Josepha, but I just gotta go."

I started walking slowly to the door. Josepha stood and

just watched me for a second or two, like she was really sad that I was leaving.

"Well den, chil', jes' a minute," she said. I stopped and turned. "You jes' wait dere," she added.

She turned and trundled into another room and disappeared for a minute. When she came back she was holding something in her hand. It was a piece of white cloth. She took some more of the bread and cheese and wrapped it inside it, and gave it to me.

"Don' open it till you's gone," she said. "Dis is jes' from me ter you. I know it won' make up fer losin' yo mama, but maybe it'll help some."

Then she took me in her arms and held me for a long time. I'd forgotten that folks you've known a long time are important. I cried as I felt her holding me against her. I reckon Josepha was just about as close to a mama as anyone I had in the whole world anymore. And she was colored too, like me. All at once part of me thought that maybe I should just stay here with her, thinking that she'd keep me safe, and wondering if they'd take Katie in too, and then we'd both be safe. But then I remembered that Katie was white, and there'd be a lot of questions, and then likely something would happen to her house that might not be good for her and she might lose everything. And from what I knew of the master's sons, I didn't want Katie anywhere near them.

Slowly I stepped back, then looked up into her face.

"Thank you, Josepha," I said. "It was real good to see you."

"An' God bless you, chil'," she said, and I could see great big tears starting to drip down her face. "Now dat I knows you's alive, I ain't gwine be able ter keep from thinkin' 'bout you. Anytime you want, you come back an' see Josepha, you hear?"

I smiled. "I may do that," I said. "I reckon you'll see me again."

She walked me back outside. I walked slowly down the steps from the porch, then away from the house. I glanced back one more time. Josepha was standing there sniffling and wiping her eyes with the back of one hand, her other hand half raised waving at me. I waved back, then turned and kept walking.

All of a sudden from around the side of the house, the master came walking straight toward me. He slowed as he saw me, then stopped.

I froze. My heart started beating with terror. I don't reckon a black girl's face can go pale when she gets scared like a white person's. But I could feel my insides jumping all over themselves and my knees going weak. I didn't know if I could run faster than him, but I was about to find out if he tried to grab me.

At first I don't think he recognized me. I reckon if Katie had changed, maybe I had too. There used to be a saying among the slaves that all coloreds looked alike to a white man's eyes. Not being white, I never knew if that was true. I'm sure nobody'd ever confuse me and Josepha, 'cause she was huge and I was thin as a rail. But I could tell from one look at the master's face that he was confused seeing me walking away from the house. He knew I didn't belong there. But at the same time, a little look as his eyes and forehead wrinkled slightly told me that he recognized me, even though he didn't quite know why.

Then slowly a light came over his face. He said, "You're old Henry and Lemuela Jukes's kid, ain't you?"

I nodded, my feet still nailed to the ground.

"You didn't get killed?"

"No, sir."

"Where you been all this time?"

"Over yonder."

I don't know what he thought I meant by that. I'm not sure what I meant myself. He didn't seem to question it, or wonder how I'd kept myself alive for two months.

"Well, don't matter now, I guess," he said. "I reckon what you do's your own business. You ain't mine no more. Well . . . talk to Josepha—she'll put you to work."

Then he kept going the way he'd been walking and disappeared around the other side of the house.

Josepha looked at me from the porch, like maybe she thought now I'd change my mind. But I just waved again, then kept going the way I had been.

I didn't look back again. I didn't want to cry, and I knew that if I saw her big tear-streaked face again, I would.

# A Remembrance of Freedom

## 11

I WALKED BACK DOWN PAST THE SLAVE CABINS TO where I'd tied the horse. I gave one last glance toward the little house, empty now, where I'd lived most of my life. This time I didn't even want to go back and look inside.

That part of my life was over, especially after what Josepha had told me. That part of this world was gone. If I'd have known what I know now, I might have lingered a moment longer, just thinking how slavery was something that was now gonna fade into the history books. But I was still a girl, and I didn't want to linger. History was the last thing on my mind. I just wanted to go.

*Good-bye, little girl,* I said again like I had a week before. *You ain't a slave no more!*

I got to the horse. Now that I was alone, for some reason, even though I wasn't hungry, I decided to open the cloth Josepha'd given me. I sat down on the grass and put it in my lap and unfolded it.

My eyes shot open wider than Katie's! There were six

pennies and another coin that was a silvery color sitting on top of the piece of bread. I just stared at them a minute, then took them in my hand. I'd never even felt money before in my life, much less had any of my own.

Josepha . . . the dear old lady! I didn't know how much this was, but however much it was, she'd had to work more than a whole day for it, 'cause it had to be more than five cents. My first thought was to run back and thank her. But I decided I'd better not, 'cause with as much love as I was feeling for her right then, and knowing I didn't have to be afraid of the master, she might talk me into staying!

I wrapped the coins back up and put them in the big pocket of my dress, then got on the horse and rode slowly away the way I'd come. I was hardly thinking about where I was going or what I was doing. My mind was so full of new thoughts. It's impossible to describe to anyone who's never been a slave what it's like to suddenly realize you're free. I would never forget what I felt like that day as long as I lived.

Suddenly everything had changed. *Everything!* I didn't have to wonder if someone was gonna grab me and make me a slave again. I wasn't a runaway anymore!

But then . . . who was I? Who was I now that I was free?

I felt like the same Mary Ann Jukes . . . but at the same time I didn't feel the same at all. I felt like yelling for joy and screaming at the top of my lungs, *I'm free! I'm not a slave!* and crying all at once.

So who was Mary Ann Jukes . . . now? What kind of worth did she have?

Always before that moment, any worth I'd had was just

measured by being a slave, by how much work I could do, how many babies I would have, what kind of price I could fetch my master.

Now all of a sudden . . . did this mean that I might have worth . . . just as a *person,* not because I could fetch some white man ten dollars, or thirty, or fifty? Who owned me now?

For the first time in my life, I wondered who that person was. Did I own myself?

While I was still thinking about it, I came to a place on the road where there were two signs. I looked up at them kind of absently, and all of a sudden I realized that I could read them. I could read what they said!

One of the signs said, *Greens Crossing—3 miles.* That was the road I'd come on. The other that pointed in the opposite direction said, *Oakwood—2 miles.*

It was getting on in the afternoon by now. I don't know what got into me, but suddenly I found myself leading the horse in the opposite direction from the way I'd come, toward the town of Oakwood. I'd heard of it but had never been there in my life.

I think my brain was swirling so fast around the idea of being free that inside I just wanted to *do* something to show it was really, really true. There had never been a time in my life when I'd just been free to do *anything* I wanted. Even when I was running away after the men had killed my family, I hadn't been actually thinking of what I was doing, I was just trying to get as far away as I could. And for the last couple of months, I didn't do anything without thinking how it affected Katie.

But when I sat there looking at those two signs, I was

really free to go either way I wanted. It wasn't so much that I wanted to go to Oakwood, I just wanted to see what it was like to do something I had decided just for myself.

I came to the town about twenty minutes later.

As I rode through the streets, I started to get afraid again. For a minute I thought about turning around and galloping away. But something inside me wanted to see if I could go into town, as a free person, and see what would happen. I'd never been in a town by myself in my life.

So I kept riding through the main street. A few people looked at me, but I pretended not to notice. I just kept going.

I was doing it! I was alone and free and nobody was trying to stop me!

Up ahead I saw a great big sign painted on a building. I recognized it from being in Greens Crossing with Katie. But again it made me feel good to realize that I could read the two words painted there . . . *General Store* . . . and knew what they meant.

I went toward the building, got off the horse, and tied it onto the rail outside, then went up onto the boardwalk and into the store.

I was trembling from head to foot. For a colored girl to just go into a store like that, all alone, that was a pretty bold thing to do. But if I was free now, why shouldn't I?

I tried to pretend I wasn't nervous as I looked around at all the pretty things. The man at the counter stared at me and didn't look none too pleased about having me in his store.

I wandered slowly around, nervous but trying to pretend I wasn't. The whole time the man was watching me like a hawk, as if he thought I was gonna steal something.

Some pretty lace handkerchiefs caught my eye, a little like the ones I'd seen that were Katie's and Katie's mother's. But now that same feeling I'd had looking at the signs filled me, the feeling that maybe I could do anything I wanted because I was free now.

And besides that, I realized I had money in my pocket!

People bought things with money, I thought. And what if . . . what if I could actually really buy something pretty like this *for myself*!

I reached out and touched one of the lacey handkerchiefs.

"Hey you!" the man called out to me. "Don't touch the merchandise if you aren't going to buy."

I jerked my hand back. But then I thought about the money again.

"Maybe I *am* going to buy," I said. My voice came out like a little squeak.

I was trembling inside as I said it. I wasn't trying to be a white person. I just wanted to know that I could do the same thing a white person could do. I was scared to hear my own timid voice talking back to a white man. But what business did he have to talk that way to me if I was free? I wasn't his slave. I wasn't anybody's slave.

So I got my courage up, then reached out and touched the hanky again.

"How much does this one cost?" I asked.

Gruffly he came over to where I was standing.

"Nine cents," he said after looking at it and then scowling at me like he was mad I'd asked.

"Please, sir, could you tell me how much I have?"

I opened my hand and held the coins toward him.

"What kind of a question is that?" he said in the same voice. "You have eleven cents—a nickel and six pennies."

"I want to buy it, then."

He looked at me as if to say, what could someone like me want with a pretty handkerchief? Then he took it and walked back to his counter. I followed him.

"How much is that pretty red ribbon hanging up there behind you?" I asked.

"Half a cent a foot," he answered, "or two feet for a penny."

"Then I would have enough for two feet of that too, right?" I asked.

"Of course you would. You must be a simpleton, which is exactly what you look like! You would have one penny left over."

"Then please give me that too," I said.

He sighed, then cut off a piece of ribbon and put it with the handkerchief, wrapped them up in brown paper, and handed the little packet across the counter to me. I handed him all the coins except one of the pennies. I reckoned all storekeepers must be like him and Mrs. Hammond. Maybe people who didn't know how to smile ran general stores. He didn't say anything else to me, and he didn't seem none too pleased about making a sale.

But I didn't care. I turned and walked out of the store, beaming with pride.

I'd actually bought something . . . just for myself!

I sat down on the ledge of the boardwalk with my feet in the street next to the horse. There was a bench next to the store, but it didn't even occur to me to sit down there.

Slaves might have been set free by some man named Lincoln, but coloreds were still coloreds, and I knew my place. It was a white man's world, whatever the man called Mr. Lincoln had done. I'd just gone into a white man's store 'cause I had money to spend. But I knew he'd more'n likely chase me off if I sat down on his bench.

I opened the packet and unfolded the handkerchief on my lap, then took the last penny Josepha had given me and set it in the middle of it. I folded the lace handkerchief around the penny and tied it together with the red ribbon, and tried to make a little bow out of the ends that were left over. I had to do it several times till the end of the ribbon came out even. Then I held the pretty little package for a long time just looking at it.

A pretty little white lace handkerchief tied with red ribbon.

I reckon it was kind of a silly thing to buy. But it was *mine*. Only mine. I had bought it with my own money all by myself.

I just sat and held my little bundle with the penny in it for a long time, looking at it and thinking more about being free.

I can't even remember exactly what I was thinking. At first I felt like yelling and jumping and screaming. Now I was quiet inside. I don't know if I was exactly thankful. I don't even know if I'd say I was happy. It was more like a place was opening up inside me that had never been there before. I don't know how to say it other than that.

There ain't no way to describe the feeling of having that word *slave* lifted from your shoulders, like a great big chain that had been around your neck all your life. And as I sat there staring at it, I knew that this little white handkerchief with the penny inside would always be my reminder of this day. A reminder of something special that had happened to me, a reminder that I was a new person from this day on . . . a reminder of freedom, and the freedom to do something just for myself.

I would never forget this moment for all the rest of my life. I would always remember this as the day I found out I was free, the day I walked into a white man's store all by myself and bought a white woman's pretty lace handkerchief.

# Sign in a Window
## 12

FROM WHERE I WAS SITTING, I LOOKED UP AT THE horse standing there patiently waiting for me.

Finally I got up. But instead of getting back on the horse, I stepped back up on the boardwalk and started walking along it and looking into some of the other shops. My mind was still full, and I just wanted to know what it felt like to walk through town along a boardwalk like white people did, just taking my time and seeing what was in the store windows.

I passed a linen store. Two ladies were just coming out. Not knowing what to do, I half smiled at them as I walked by. They seemed surprised to see me and moved away to the other side of the walkway, as if they didn't want to get too close to me. I reckon I had been riding all morning. Maybe I smelled bad, though I couldn't tell myself. They said a few unkind things as they walked away. But I didn't mind. They couldn't hurt me and I was free, so what did I care what they said?

There were other people about as I walked too, and most of them acted the same, either saying something like, "Get off the walk, girl!" or "This ain't no place for you!" or else just moving to the other side to avoid getting too close to me. I pretended not to notice and just kept going, but after a while it kinda stung to hear what they were saying. Even when I was a slave, nobody said those kinds of things to me. Maybe the white folks were mad to think that I was now free just like they were and could walk anywhere I wanted, even right through a town full of white folks.

I passed a baker's shop, and for the first time almost wished I hadn't spent the nine cents on the handkerchief. There were some mighty good smells coming from inside!

But I kept going and came to a store with some equipment in it, then walked past some offices, and then a bank. Across the street was a saloon with music and loud voices coming from the open swinging doors. I had no interest in getting too close to it, so I turned at the bank and went along the walk in the other direction from it.

People kept staring at me and sometimes saying rude things. I still hadn't seen any other coloreds. Maybe I was the only black person in this town. Maybe that's why none of them seemed to like me being there.

Up ahead I saw a hotel and restaurant. There were people walking in and out of it. I started to turn around, but then I saw a notice in the window and for some reason it drew my attention. I walked toward it, curious to see if I could read it. I stopped in front of the window and slowly tried to make sense of the words. I was surprised at how easy it was. It only took me a few minutes before I knew what the whole thing said:

*Wanted: white maid, 25 cents a day plus room and board.*

*Wanted: colored girl for cleaning, 10 cents a day plus r & b.*

I turned and slowly started walking away on the boardwalk back in the direction of the bank. But the words from the sign kept repeating themselves over and over in my mind.

*Wanted . . . colored girl . . . ten cents a day . . .*

What if—my brain was spinning around and around with the thought of it!—what if I was to . . . could someone like me really get a job? One that actually paid money? That was more than Josepha got in a day. If I took a job that paid ten cents a day, would *that* be what I was worth?

All of a sudden I found myself turning around and walking back, and then I was walking into the hotel, walking right past the white ladies in fancy dresses and hats, and past the white men in black suits. I walked up to the counter and stood waiting there till the man behind it noticed me. I reckon the work dress I was wearing wasn't none too pretty, and maybe I did smell, for all I knew. But I didn't care. They weren't asking for somebody who smelled nice and was dressed pretty, but for someone who knew how to work. And that's something I knew how to do all right.

Finally the man looked over the counter at me. He just stood there and stared.

"I . . . I want to ask about that sign you got in the window," I said, "saying you're wanting a colored girl."

"I'll get the manager," he said, then turned and left.

My heart was pounding, but I stood there and waited and tried to calm my insides down.

A minute or two later the same man appeared again from through the door where he'd gone. He was followed by another man, a little older and half bald and kinda fat, though nowhere near as large as Josepha. He was wearing a shiny black vest and a funny-looking thin string tie around his neck and down the front.

"What's your name, girl?" he said when he got to me. He was just like all the white people in this town—he didn't seem to know how to smile.

"Mary Ann," I said.

"Mary Ann what?"

"Jukes."

"Where you from? Who was your master?"

"Master McSimmons, sir."

The man nodded.

"You still living there?" he said.

"No, sir."

"Where, then?"

"Uh . . . somewhere else . . . where I went after I left Master McSimmons," I said.

The man looked at me a little suspicious. "Well, I don't suppose that matters. You know how to work?"

"Yes, sir."

"You know how to keep your mouth shut and mind your betters?"

"Uh . . . yes, sir."

"And do what you're told?"

"Yes, sir."

"Come along, then, I'll show you the room."

He came out from behind the counter and walked through the hotel. I followed him. We walked through a long hallway and pretty soon came out at the back of the building and outside. I kept following until we came to a little building out at the back. We went through a door into another dark hallway, walked almost all the way to the other end, turned a corner, went up a narrow stairway, and then stopped. He opened a door and walked in.

"This is where you'll stay," he said. "You got any things with you, put them in here. Then come to the front desk and I'll put you to work."

I glanced around. The room was so tiny, there was only room for the bed against the small wall and a tiny table and chair. It didn't look too clean, and from where I was standing I thought the mattress on the bed was stuffed with straw, like my old one had been at the McSimmons colored town. The place didn't particularly strike me as where I wanted to live for the next few years, even for ten cents a day.

"I don't know if I want to take the job yet, sir," I said.

"What! An uppity one, are you? I should've seen it in that ugly face of yours. What are you wasting my time for!"

"I'm sorry, sir. I just wanted to know about it."

"Get out of here, and don't show your face around this hotel again unless you're ready to go to work."

He huffed out of the room and down the stairs, leaving me to find my own way back out to the street in front.

# DECISION 13

I WALKED OUT OF THE HOTEL, FEELING THE SCOWL of the manager's eyes on my back from the counter, where I knew he was watching me.

I came out onto the boardwalk and started back the way I had come. As I retraced my steps from earlier, all kinds of new things to think about were swirling in my brain.

*A job!*

A real job, a room of my very own . . . and real money! It wasn't much of a room, and maybe the ten cents a day wasn't even half what the white person's job got. But it would be mine . . . my own room, my own money.

I could buy things, clothes for myself, a pair of shoes . . .

I looked down at the white handkerchief I still had clutched in one hand. If I took that job I could buy all the lace handkerchiefs I could ever want. I could buy a dozen of them if I wanted to! With every kind of colored ribbon I could think of!

All at once my future was full of so many possibilities and opportunities. Not only wasn't I a runaway slave . . . why, I could be and do anything I wanted to!

I was walking slow, thinking about so many things.

Did I . . . did I really want to take that job? Even with the gruff hotel manager and lumpy straw mattress and dinky little room.

What a change it would be!

Once I started getting paid, maybe I'd even have to open an account in that bank, just for me, in my own name—a bank account that said *Mary Ann Jukes* on it.

But then the question came to my mind—did they let black folks have bank accounts? I didn't know the answer to that. And I was still just a girl, I wasn't even a grown-up black yet.

Well, if they didn't . . . then I'd keep my ten cents a day someplace else. If I worked long enough at that hotel, I could get rich!

My steps slowed, then came to a stop. I had come to the corner again by the bank where the saloon was across the street.

I stopped right at the corner. Down the street past the baker's and offices and linen store, there was the horse still standing in front of the general store waiting for me.

Still thinking about the money, I looked inside the bank. Just thinking about having a bank account with my own money in it was so exciting a thought!

Then I glanced back down the street behind me at the hotel.

I just stood there for a whole minute or two. I knew I had to decide. It was nobody's decision but mine. I was free.

I could do whatever I wanted. I could take that job if I wanted. Or—

A sound disturbed me out of my daze as I stood there on the corner of the boardwalk next to the Oakwood bank. I don't know why I noticed, 'cause there were people about and horses and a few buggies clomping and rattling along the street. But in the midst of all the noise and movement and activity, I heard the sound of a man's voice calling out to a team of horses from the middle of the street coming behind me from the direction of the general store.

I knew instantly that it was a black man's voice, 'cause there's a difference and you can always tell. And instinctively I turned around to look.

There was a wagon loaded with hay and some other supplies being pulled by two horses rumbling along the street toward where I was standing. And sitting up on the buckboard lashing the reins and calling out to the horses was Katie's friend Henry from Greens Crossing!

I don't know why I didn't want him to see me. Seeing a familiar face suddenly filled me with the feeling that I shouldn't be there.

I started to turn away and duck behind the corner wall of the bank building.

But it was too late. He had seen me too.

Our eyes met briefly as he came even with me in the street. I had the feeling he might be about to rein in or say something.

But before he had the chance, I looked away and started walking. I hurried along the boardwalk past the door of the bank and on toward the general store.

I got to where I'd tied the horse. I stopped and looked

back. Henry was gone. I could see the roof of the hotel beyond the bank.

I thought again about the job and realized I still hadn't made my decision.

Money . . . a room of my own . . . a bank account with my name on it . . . and maybe even ten dollars in it someday . . .

But what did any of that matter?

I had a friend waiting for me. And a friend was worth even more than a hundred dollars!

What had I been thinking? My home was with Katie now! She didn't care if I was black or white or ugly or smelly. She needed me and looked up to me. So maybe that's what I was worth—I was somebody's friend.

I smiled, gave the street one last look, then untied the horse, got up into the saddle, and rode out of town without wasting any more time.

I still didn't want Henry to see me again, and I didn't slow down until the houses and buildings had completely disappeared behind me.

# Surprise at Rosewood
# 14

I rode for a while but suddenly realized I was really tired. I suppose emotions tire you out as much as hard work or anything else, and I'd sure been through a lot of them today. First being nervous about sneaking back to the McSimmons plantation, then seeing Josepha and what she'd told me, then encountering the master, and then everything that had happened in Oakwood.

All at once I was plumb wore out. And hungry and thirsty too. I thought I could do with a rest.

I didn't want to wait till I came to the river, which was about halfway back. I had seen a stream following the road on and off, so I started looking for it and it wasn't long till I came to it again. I led the horse off the road and down toward it where there was a little clump of trees and some grass for the horse to eat.

I found a nice spot. Both the horse and I had a long drink from the stream. Then while he was munching away at the grass, I got out Josepha's little cloth with the bread and cheese in it. I sat down and had as pleasant a meal as anyone could imagine.

When I was through I glanced about. It was pretty late in the afternoon by now. Katie was probably fixing her supper by now and the sun was on its way down. I figured I had another good two or three hours of daylight left, plenty of time if I cantered part of the way and didn't waste any time.

But stopping and sitting down and eating had made me so sleepy I couldn't imagine getting back up on that horse's back again. Maybe I'd just take a short little nap to get my energy back before going the rest of the way.

I lay down in the soft grass, feeling about as happy and content as I had felt since my family had been killed. I got drowsy and then slowly closed my eyes.

I must have been more tired than I realized, because when I woke up it was the middle of the night sometime. I sat up suddenly, remembering that I needed to get back home. But I knew instantly that there was no use of that. It was pitch black. There was no moon anywhere in the sky, and I didn't want to risk trying to find my way in the dark. I didn't know the way well enough and who knew where I'd wind up.

There was nothing to do but go back to sleep, which I did easily enough, even though I was hungry again and a mite cold.

The next thing I knew, a snorty, fleshy nose was sniffing around at my face. It woke me up with a start. The sun was back up and Katie's horse was letting me know that it was time to get started back toward home where his trough of oats was waiting for him.

I got myself up and stretched out the kinks. By now I was *really* hungry, but there wouldn't be anything to eat till I walked into the kitchen back at Rosewood. So there wasn't any sense wasting any more time. I took a big drink of water, and then we got back on the road.

I pushed the poor horse a mite harder than maybe I should have, but I knew we were both anxious to get back. I was mighty relieved when I finally saw the buildings of Rosewood up ahead.

"Miss Katie!" I called as we galloped in and stopped at the back of the house. "Miss Katie . . . I'm back!"

I ran into the kitchen, expecting to find her there. But it was empty.

"Miss Katie!" I hollered up the stairs. "Miss Katie, you up there?"

There was no answer. The whole house was quiet, so I knew she wasn't inside. But from the fire and the look of things, it hadn't been long since she'd been there. Then all of a sudden I realized something else—I didn't hear Emma and William anywhere either!

Then I really started to get worried. What could have happened to them?

They must have all gone someplace . . . but where?

I walked back outside. Maybe she was out in the barn, I thought, and hadn't heard me ride in, although I didn't know how that could be.

I led the tired horse across the entryway and to the stables, looking all around as I went.

"Miss Katie!" I called into the barn. "You in there . . . Emma!"

But there was no sign of them. The cows weren't there

either, so she must have milked them and gotten them out to pasture all right.

I unsaddled the horse, got him some fresh oats, and left him to look around some more. I'd brush him down later.

Where could they be?

I stood in the middle of the yard between the house and barn and looked all around. It was completely quiet. Now for the first time I noticed that the dogs weren't around either. That's what made it so quiet. Then it struck me that they were probably down at the slave cabins! That must be it. She was probably setting another fire to get it ready. And maybe showing Emma what to do, or maybe fixing a place for her to hide with William if any men came looking for her.

I turned and ran down the road, then turned off to the right toward the colored town, and was there in about three minutes.

"Miss Katie!" I called. "Miss Katie . . . you in there? I'm home, Miss Katie."

But if anything it was even quieter here than back at the house. And she sure wasn't there.

I walked back up the hill to the road, then back toward the house, hoping against hope that this time when I got there I'd see Katie waiting for me. But I didn't.

Now I was downright worried.

I frantically ran everywhere all about the place, into every building, all through the house and barn. But she just wasn't anywhere.

What could have happened to her?

Suddenly I remembered Katie's secret place in the woods. That had to be where she was!

I tore off running and didn't stop till I was standing there in the little wood with the stream running past my feet.

But it was completely quiet. There wasn't any sign of Katie or the dogs.

"God," I prayed, and I was more than nervous now, I was really scared, "please help me find them."

I ran back to the house, again hoping that somehow she would have appeared while I was gone to the woods.

But Katie was still gone. There was no sign of her anywhere.

Again I walked back through the house. I stopped in the middle of the parlor and sort of half cried out, half said to myself, "Oh, Miss Katie . . . where'd you go?"

All of a sudden I heard a noise like a stick rapping against something. Then I heard a muffled voice.

It was coming from the cellar right below me!

I stepped away, pulled back the carpet, and opened the trapdoor in the floor. A flicker of light came from below. Then I heard the sound of a baby and a familiar voice.

"Dat be you, Miz Mayme? Please, God, I hope dat's you!"

"It's me, Emma . . . it's me!" I called down the hole. "But what's going on? Where's Katie?"

Emma's face now appeared in the thin, flickering light, looking up at me from down in the cellar.

"She put me an' William down here, Miz Mayme," she said. "Somebody came an' she had ter go wiff dem an' she put us down here so nuthin' would happen ter us or nobody fin' me."

"Who came, Emma . . . who was it?"

"I don' know, Miz Mayme. But look what I foun' down here." She came a few steps up the ladder and held up her hand. "What is it, Miz Mayme?"

I saw a sparkle of color in her palm and reached down and took what she was holding—three heavy coins. I expect my eyes got as big as Katie's sometimes did.

"It's gold, Emma," I said. "I think these are gold."

Now I figure I oughta tell you what had happened while I was away.

# Alone at Rosewood

# 15

THE NIGHT BEFORE I LEFT, I TOLD KATIE I'D STAY to help get the cows milked before leaving in the morning. But she said she wanted to try to do it all herself. She might have to learn sometime, she said, and she wanted to see if she could do it. At first I'd had my doubts. But then I realized she was probably right. The more she could do for herself, the better, in case someday something happened to me.

After I left the next morning, Katie had gone to the barn first thing to get started. It took her a lot longer than it did me, two hours to get them all milked. But she did it, and I think she was proud of herself.

Then she opened the gate and led the cows out onto the road and into the pasture where we were taking them for grazing. Once cows learn a routine of doing something, they keep doing it over and over. Those cows knew to follow along right behind her out to whichever of the grazing pastures she led them. When they were in the field, she closed the gate behind them and walked back to the house. I can just imagine that she had a smile on her face too. She was all alone at Rosewood—well, Emma was still back in the house, but alone without me—and she was taking care of things!

She said she was already a little tired from the milking. So she took off her milking boots and went into the kitchen to have some breakfast bread and milk. She built a fire in the cook stove, then boiled some water and made a batch of corn mush for herself and Emma, who was up with William by then.

After they had cleaned William up and Emma had fed him and eaten her own breakfast, Katie then set about the morning's chores that she and I usually did ourselves. She went back out to the barn, got oats for the horses, then brought water in a bucket to mix with the dried oats and corn to make mush in the pig trough. Stirring up the pig mush was always hard. The pigs were always so anxious, snorting and crowding around and sticking their snouts in and even stepping in the trough while you were trying to mix it up, so you couldn't get it all stirred before they were all over the place making a terrible mess of it. Sometimes you had to rap them over the head or in the nose to make them get back. They'd squeal and make such a fuss but would come right back and start all over. I can't hardly imagine how Katie managed it, but she did.

After that she brought several loads of firewood and kindling into the kitchen, collected the eggs from the chicken coop, then cleaned up her breakfast things. She wasn't going to do any butter churning or any of the bigger things we had to do regularly when I was gone. And so that was about all there was for her to do for a while in the way of morning chores.

Once all that was done she started to get a little lonely, and then a little scared. She said it wasn't the same with me gone. Even though Emma was there, it was like being alone, because she knew if anything happened she'd have to take care of it herself. And that was her main worry—what to do if someone came. But there wasn't any way to know if someone would, or how to plan for it. She'd already decided that if somebody came that she knew, like Mrs. Hammond or Mr. Thurston or the iceman or somebody like that, then she would just put Emma in the cellar and hide herself until they went away, then answer questions later. But she wanted to have a fire burning and laundry on the line so everything would look normal, just like we'd planned.

If people she didn't know came, she didn't know what she'd do.

But nobody came and the day wore on. She tried to keep herself busy, and with Emma following her about fretting and talking, it wasn't too hard. But by early afternoon she was starting to look down the road quite a bit, hoping she'd see me coming. When I still hadn't come by late afternoon, she was getting nervous. But there wasn't anything she could do about it. So she went out and led the cows back home again and took care of the evening milking.

By the time that was over, she was really tired and getting more and more worried about why I wasn't back. She washed up and fixed herself and Emma something to eat, though she said she hardly had enough energy to, then played the piano to try to cheer herself up.

She said it didn't work. Even with Emma chattering away, it just reminded her all the more that I wasn't there.

Finally it started to get dark. And I still hadn't come home. She didn't have any choice in the end but to get Emma and William settled for the night, though William wouldn't sleep all the way till morning, and then get ready for bed herself. She sat down in a chair and kept listening for sounds, hoping she'd hear the horse and me. But she didn't, and the crickets and other night sounds made the waiting all the worse.

Finally she dozed off, then woke up again.

Since I still wasn't back, she got under her blankets and went to bed for real. Since she was still sleepy from just waking up, it made it easier not to worry, though she kept the kerosene lamp burning bright all night so she wouldn't be afraid of being alone in the dark.

# ALETA
# 16

ONE THING ABOUT KATIE, SHE CAN SLEEP. SO SHE slept the rest of the night, which was a mercy. When she woke up next, it was morning. Emma had fed William when he woke up in the middle of the night and then they'd gone back to sleep and Katie had never heard a thing.

She jumped out of bed and went running into her brother's room.

"Mayme . . . Mayme, are you back?" she called.

But one look in the bed answered the question clear enough. I was still sound asleep on the grass by the stream about five miles away.

Now Katie's heart nearly sank for good. All kinds of thoughts were starting to come into her mind of what had happened to me, that I'd been hurt, or that my master had made me stay and go back to work, or even that I'd decided not to come back.

Her brain played all kinds of tricks on her, and she was

just about beside herself with worry.

But having the sun shining outside made it a lot easier than if she'd lain awake all night hounded by those kinds of thoughts. So she got dressed and got about the business of the day, like she knew she had to do whether I was there or not. And once Emma and William were up, there was plenty to do and enough noise for five or six people.

Sometime about the middle of the morning, after the cows and pigs were all taken care of and Katie was in the kitchen thinking about making something different for dinner that night, she heard a soft knock on the door.

She nearly jumped out of her skin because she knew Emma was upstairs. Now she realized the dogs had been barking for a minute or two, but she hadn't paid any attention because she hadn't heard the sound of a horse.

She'd been waiting so anxiously for me, she wanted to run and open the door and see me standing there. But she knew it couldn't be me. She knew I wouldn't just knock softly and not say anything.

She sat for a second, paralyzed on the floor. Her first impulse was to run and hide. But then whoever it was would probably hear her. She didn't have any choice but to go answer it.

Slowly she walked toward the door, reached out and took hold of the latch, then opened it. There stood a bedraggled little girl who Katie said couldn't have been more than eight or nine, dirt smeared all over and her dress torn. Katie had never seen her before.

The minute Katie appeared, the girl started crying.

At first Katie just stood and stared, then looked around

beyond her to see if there was anybody else. But the girl was alone.

"What's the matter?" Katie asked, stooping down and looking into her face.

"Something's happened to my mama," said the girl.

"What do you mean?" asked Katie.

"I don't know," said the girl, sniffling and wiping a dirty hand across her face. "We were riding and the horse stumbled and fell. I got up from where I got thrown on the grass. But I couldn't get my mama to wake up."

Katie went back into the kitchen to get a dish towel. She wiped the girl's face and nose and eyes.

"Where did this happen?" she asked.

"Over there," said the girl, pointing along the road leading west.

"How far away? I didn't hear anything."

"I don't know," said the girl.

"You walked here?"

She nodded.

"Did it take you a long time?"

"Yes, ma'am."

"Show me," said Katie, hardly noticing that she'd been called "ma'am" for the first time in her life.

Katie stepped outside, then suddenly remembered Emma back in the house.

"Wait here just a minute," she said to the girl.

She ran back inside, opened the door to the cellar, hurriedly lit one of the extra lanterns, and took it down the ladder and set it someplace safe, then went back to find Emma.

"Emma," she said, "I've got to leave for a little while."

"Leave! Where to, Miz Katie?"

"I don't know. Somebody's here who needs help. I don't know how long I'll be. I want you and William to wait for me in the cellar."

"But I'll be skeered, Miz Katie!"

"Don't worry. I lit a lantern. We'll take several blankets so you won't be cold. Now come with me, Emma."

A few minutes later, Katie walked out of the house again. The little girl was waiting patiently for her. She reached up and took Katie's hand as she approached, then led her along the road away from Rosewood, the three dogs following excitedly.

"What is your name?" Katie asked.

"Aleta," said the girl.

"I'm Katie," she said.

If she had known how far they were going to walk, Katie would have hitched a buggy. But the girl was so vague and obviously upset, she thought the accident with the horse must be somewhere close by. But they kept walking and walking, and pretty soon Katie wondered if she'd made a mistake. But the girl tugged and pulled her along as fast as they both could go, and Katie couldn't do anything but follow.

They walked for an hour or so. By the time they came to the place where the horse had apparently fallen, they were two or three miles away from Rosewood. They'd long ago passed the turnoff for Mr. Thurston's plantation, and Katie didn't recognize anything around them. Then she saw some scuff marks on the dirt and at the edge of the road and a woman's bonnet. The girl led her off the road and down a little bank.

"She's over here," she said. "We were riding on the road, but the horse stumbled down this bank. That's when we fell."

"Was the horse galloping?" asked Katie.

"Yes, we were riding real fast."

"Why were you going so fast?"

"We were trying to get away."

"Get away . . . from what?"

"From my daddy. He was drunk and my mama was afraid."

"Why was he drunk?"

"He got drunk every night," said the girl, pulling at Katie's hand. "When he came back from the war, he was mean and angry. He yelled at my mama and hit her sometimes. That's why we ran away."

"Where were you going?"

"I don't know. Somewhere Mama said we'd be safe."

They were down the embankment now. The minute Katie saw the woman lying beside the stream at the bottom of it, she knew she was dead. Her face was gray, and her neck was bent at an unnatural angle. From what Katie could tell, she must have hit her head on the rock beside her when she fell. There was no sign of the horse.

"Mama . . . Mama, please . . . get up," the little girl cried, running to her.

Katie knelt down beside her and started to cry herself. "Oh, God . . . not again," she whispered silently. "What should I do!"

"Please, ma'am," said the girl, looking up into Katie's face with the most forlorn look Katie had ever seen, "please do something to help her. Can't you make my mama wake up!"

The girl bent down to touch her mother's face. When the coldness of death met her touch, she pulled back with a start, seeming to realize something was terribly wrong. Katie took the girl in her arms and pulled her close. Now Katie was the older girl who had to comfort someone younger. They were both crying. As the girl wept in Katie's arms, the instinct that comes to people at such times told the little girl that she would never see her mother again.

For several minutes they remained just weeping. Then slowly Katie stood, took the girl by the hand, and led her back up the hill to the road.

When they were out of sight of her mother's body, Katie stopped. She stooped down to one knee, took both the girl's hands in hers and looked into her eyes while she fought back her own tears.

"Aleta," said Katie softly, "your mother can't wake up."

"Why?"

"Aleta . . . your mother is dead. We will have to let God take care of her now."

Huge new tears welled up in the girl's eyes.

Katie took her in her arms again and held her, both of them starting to cry all over again.

"Don't worry, Aleta," said Katie. "We'll take care of you until we think what is the best thing to do. We'll go back to my house and get you washed, and I'll give you something to eat, and we will decide what to do."

"But what about my mama?" wailed the despairing girl.

"We'll bring a wagon back. I'll take care of her, Aleta."

## Harsh Words

## 17

As I was still standing in the parlor holding the three gold coins in my hand that Emma had found in the basement, I suddenly realized I heard dogs barking outside. I stuffed the coins into the pocket of my dress and ran outside as Emma climbed out of the cellar with William. There was Katie in the distance walking toward the house. I was so happy to see her I didn't even notice at first that she wasn't alone. By then I had all but forgotten the coins.

I ran toward them, then all of a sudden saw the girl at Katie's side, holding her hand. I was still overjoyed to see Katie, but I slowed down as I ran.

"Who's that?" said Aleta as she saw me coming.

"That's Mayme," answered Katie. "She's a girl who lives with me at my house."

"But she's colored," said Aleta.

"Mayme's my friend. I don't even think about what color she is."

Katie let go of Aleta's hand and ran toward me. I started running again and we ran right up to each other, then slowed down, hugging and laughing as we met. I'm not sure we didn't shed a few tears mixed in with it too. It seemed like we were always crying, either happy cries or sad ones.

"I was so worried about you!" I said as I stepped back. "I got home and couldn't find you anywhere! I discovered Emma in the cellar just a minute ago."

"What about me!" laughed Katie. "I thought you'd be back yesterday, and you never came and never came, and then all night . . . I was so worried that you might not come back at all."

"I'm sorry, Miss Katie."

"What happened?" she asked.

"I'll tell you all about it. So much exciting happened, you won't believe it!"

Before we could say anything more, Katie's new little friend slowly approached and stood at Katie's side, looking over at me like I had the plague or something. It reminded me of the looks I'd gotten from the white ladies in town the day before. On top of her grief over losing her mother, the poor girl had never in her life seen anything like what she'd just witnessed—a white person and a black person hugging each other and laughing and talking like friends. Yet the expression on her face was not just one of bewilderment, but of something I've seen many times throughout my life and could never quite understand. It was a look of anger. I reckon if somebody doesn't want to like black people, or if a black person doesn't want to like white people, maybe that's their own affair. But I could never see why they'd get so *angry* if other folks saw it different. If I wanted Katie to be my friend, why should that make any other colored person mad? And if Katie wanted me for a friend, why should that make Aleta mad?

From the look on the girl's face, I'd never have suspected that she'd just lost her mama.

"Mayme," said Katie, "this is my new friend, Aleta."

"Hello, Miss Aleta," I said with a smile, holding out my hand toward her.

She pulled back with a look of disgust on her face, eyeing my hand as if it was a snake trying to bite her.

"Don't you touch me!" she snapped.

Katie looked at me apologetically, then added softly, "There's been an accident. Aleta's mother . . ."

Then she stopped.

"Aleta," she said, turning and looking back at the girl. "Why don't you run on ahead to the house," she said, not thinking at first that *another* surprise was waiting for her there just as bad as the one she'd just had! "I need to talk to Mayme for a minute," she added. "I'll be right there."

Aleta dashed off, followed by the dogs. I think she was glad to get away from me.

"I'm sorry, Mayme," said Katie. "I had no idea she would do that."

"It's all right, Miss Katie. What happened?"

Katie filled me in as we walked back to the house.

"You're sure she's dead?" I said. "You want me to go out and look?"

"Her skin was cold, Mayme," said Katie with a little shudder and a look like she was going to be sick. "She was cold and pale, with her eyes half open—ugh! When you see a face like that, you know a person's dead."

I nodded.

It was a little awkward figuring out what to do about Aleta's mother. I'd have been glad to go bury her myself, but I didn't know where she was. And Katie didn't think that'd be such a good idea with how the girl felt about me, especially since she'd told her she would take care of it. But she couldn't very well take the girl with her. But neither could she leave her with me.

"I'll go down to the colored cabins, Miss Katie, if you want to do the burying by yourself," I said. "I'll just wait there till you get back."

"Oh, Mayme, I don't want you to have to—"

"It's all right, Miss Katie," I said. "I don't mind. I'll take my reader and the journal you gave me and the pen and ink. I gotta try to write down about everything that happened yesterday."

Katie nodded.

"I'll give her something to eat," she said, "and see if I can get her to take a nap. I'll tell her to wait in the house until I get back."

"I'll go hitch up a buggy for you," I said. "Are you sure you don't want me to go along and help? I could go up the road now so she wouldn't see me."

Katie thought a minute.

"I think this is something I should do by myself," she said. "You helped me when I didn't know what to do. You buried my whole family, Mayme. Now it's my turn to try to help her. But if you would hitch the small buggy, I would appreciate it. And, Mayme, could you please put two shovels in back, the small one I usually use and a regular one."

I nodded and walked toward the barn while Katie

continued on to the house. But by then Aleta had walked through the kitchen door, then turned and ran back outside toward Katie with a scowl on her face.

"There's another nigger girl in your house!" she announced as though Katie would be as shocked as she was.

Katie stooped down, gently put her hands on Aleta's shoulders, and looked into her eyes.

"Aleta," she said, "that's Emma. And we don't call her that word. She's a nice colored girl whose skin just happens to be brown like yours is white. She came here needing my help just like you did."

"But she's in the house."

"Yes, she is, Aleta," Katie replied calmly.

"Is she your slave?"

"No, she's my friend and I let friends who need help stay here . . . like Emma, like Mayme, and now like you."

Aleta didn't change her mind about Emma and me because of what Katie said. But Katie's kindness, along with the realization that seemed to deepen within her as the afternoon progressed that her mama was really gone, enabled her at least to tolerate our presence for the rest of the day.

She avoided us, and looked at us with disgust in her eyes, but she made no more outbursts.

# Treasure Hunt
# 18

That night, after Aleta had had a bath and was asleep in Katie's bed, and Emma and William were settled in the other room, I helped Katie bathe and get cleaned up from the burying. While she was finishing up and getting ready for bed, I sat down at the writing desk and continued on with what I'd started to write earlier in the journal she had given me.

I'd never before tried to write down much of what I was thinking or feeling. I never had been able to write well enough to do that. And I still couldn't. But I wanted to try. All I'd ever done is just say what I did. Now that I was feeling so many new things—growing up inside, I'd reckon you'd say—I wanted to find a way to express it. But that's not easy. It's hard to try to put something as big as what had happened to me into just a few words.

I tried. But when I read it over, it hardly felt as big as I was feeling it inside. So much was happening all of a sudden, but when I quieted my thoughts down all I could think of was my talk with Josepha and what I'd done afterward.

*Yesterday I went bak to my ol hows agin, wifout Katie this time. I saw Josepha an the master. They wernt killd by the riders that shot the others. Josepha tol me that all slaves had been freed. I dint no what to think. It was hard to beleeve. Josepha gits pade now fer workin. She said I cud git pade to ef I wantid to stay an work wif her. But I said no. I was thinkin bout so meny things wen I lef there. She gav me leven cints. I felt lik a rich person. I rod to a town calld Oakwod en went into a store. I bot a hankechif an ribon wif ten cints an savd the las peny. I lookt at a hotel where they had a job for a colord girl like me. I wud a got ten cints a day. But then I thot bout Katie an new my home was wif her now. Wen I got back another little girl was wif Katie whos mother got throwd from her hors en killd. Shes—*

Just then Katie came into her brother's room, which she called my room now, and sat down on the bed. I turned around and smiled. I set the pen down, and after the ink was dry, closed the journal and got on the bed with her. She was exhausted from the day and had blisters on six of her fingers from two hours of shoveling.

"What are we going to do with her, Mayme?" she said.

"Have you found out where she lives or anything?" I asked.

Katie shook her head with a weary sigh.

"We oughta find out her last name," I said. "Then I reckon we could ask. Somebody's bound to know the name and where her daddy lives."

"But she seems afraid of him. What if he is really as bad as she says?"

I didn't have an answer to that.

"And who would we ask," said Katie, "without them asking about us too? We couldn't go into town and ask Mrs. Hammond or anybody else."

"I reckon we'll have to take care of her awhile," I said. "At least till we can find out more about her."

Then I started chuckling. "I guess I should say, *you'll* have to take care of her," I added. "She doesn't like me much."

Katie smiled a sad, knowing smile and reached out and put a hand on my arm. I knew she felt bad for me.

"How much should we tell her, Mayme?" she said.

I thought about that a minute. I hadn't considered it before.

"I don't know," I said. "Has she asked why nobody else is here? Why there aren't any grown-ups, only one white girl and two black girls and a baby?"

Katie shook her head. "I don't know if she's noticing much of anything. She's younger than us, Mayme, and she just lost her mother. I'm not even sure it's hit her yet. Remember how I was when you found me?"

"Do you suppose her father might come for her?"

"How would he know she's here?"

"I don't know," I answered. "Maybe he knew where they were going, or maybe he followed them and will come here asking about them."

"What would we do if he did?"

"She'd have to go with him, I reckon. She ain't an orphan like us. So we don't want to tell her too much, or she'd tell him, and we'd get found out."

"You're right," said Katie. "Maybe I shouldn't tell her

anything. But I'm too tired to think about it anymore. We'll worry about it tomorrow."

Slowly she got off the bed.

"I think I should sleep with Aleta tonight," she said, walking toward the door. "She might have a nightmare or wake up and not know where she is.—Good night, Mayme."

"Good night, Miss Katie."

Just as she left the room, I suddenly remembered. "Miss Katie, Miss Katie!" I said after her. "I almost forgot."

Katie hurried back into the room, wondering what I was talking about. I jumped off the bed and stood up. I was still wearing my work dress and hadn't gotten into my nightclothes yet. I put my hand in my pocket and pulled out the three gold coins.

"Look what Emma found in the cellar when you were gone!"

Katie looked at them lying in my hand, so exhausted from the day and bewildered at what I'd said that the bigness of it didn't sink in at first. Then slowly her eyes got real big.

"Mayme," she said, "but . . . but that's—"

"Yes, Miss Katie—it's *gold*. And it's yours! She found it in the cellar."

"But how . . . why was it there? Where did she find it?"

"I don't know. But maybe it's from that uncle of yours."

"Do you think . . . Mayme, what if there's *more*!"

We were both out of the room like a flash, trying to tiptoe so as not to wake Aleta or disturb Emma. One thing we didn't need right then was Emma yammering away and following us and asking questions!

We hurried downstairs and a minute later, hearts

pounding with anticipation, we were climbing down the steep ladder. I went first holding a lantern, Katie followed with a candle. We went down the rickety steps. It was colder than upstairs, and as the lantern lit up the place it was spooky. Katie looked around with a shudder.

"Except for getting Emma settled this morning," she said, "I haven't been here since . . . you know, since the night before you came. I've been afraid to even look down here again. I didn't want to look around this morning, but I guess I can't really help it now."

I set down the lantern and waited a bit while Katie collected herself.

The floor was hard-packed dirt, but it was dry and had a few things on it. I don't know why it should have been spookier now, in the middle of the night. The cellar looked the same in the middle of the day as in the middle of the night. But something about it was different and gave me the creeps. I know Katie felt it too. The silence was deeper, the shadows longer. I kept expecting something to jump out at us from one of the darkened corners. Just knowing that the sun was gone above us made the darkness more fearsome down here too.

There wasn't much in the place except for a few small pieces of furniture that must have been put down here to store them out of the way. How Katie's father had got them down here I couldn't imagine, unless they'd been down here since the house was built. There was a dresser, a small wardrobe, and one other big chest of some kind sitting on the ground.

"Do you know what's in those?" I asked Katie.

"No," she said. "I was only down here a time or two,

for tornados and then . . . you know."

I nodded. "Were the drawers of that one open like that," I asked, pointing to the dresser, "when you were down here before?"

"I don't remember. I don't think so."

"Emma must have been looking through them. Do you suppose that's where she found the gold pieces?"

"I don't know. It's hard to blame her—she must have been down here an hour or more."

"She was probably scared silly."

We went to look closer. Katie opened all the drawers. There were a few old clothes that smelled of mildew, some papers, but no more gold coins in the drawers. We looked in the wardrobe too, but it was empty. Then Katie walked over to the chest on the floor.

"It's locked," she said.

"Do you have any idea where the key might be?" I asked.

Katie thought a minute, then both of us seemed to remember at the same time.

"The keys in my mother's secretary!" said Katie. Again we bolted for the stairs.

I don't know how we kept from waking up the other two girls, but even in our excitement, somehow we didn't. Five minutes later we were again descending into the cellar. This time a ring of keys was jingling from Katie's hand. We hurried back to the chest, and one by one Katie fumbled with the keys to find one that would go into the padlock of the chest. When she found the one that opened it and then lifted the lid back, our hearts really started pounding. I think both of us were hoping it would be full of gold and jewels like a pirate's treasure.

But it wasn't. There were just a bunch of men's shirts and trousers, a pair of boots, and one dress-up coat that had probably been real nice once. Everything in the chest was worn and old and didn't smell so good.

Disappointed, we stared at it a minute, then Katie started rummaging through it.

"I wonder if what you said earlier's true," she said, "about those coins being my uncle's. I wonder if these are his clothes."

"Didn't you say he was here once?"

"I think so. I think that's how I got the idea into my head that he had gold. I once had a dream about it, though I imagined gold nuggets or something, not coins. But my memory of it is vague now."

She held up a second pair of trousers that was stuffed in the bottom. As she threw it back in with the rest, we heard a faint metallic sound. Katie grabbed them up again and shook them in her hand.

"There it is again!" she exclaimed.

She stuffed her hand into one of the pockets and pulled it out, holding another four coins.

"Look," she said, "they are even bigger than the others!"

"How much are they worth, do you think?" I asked.

"These all say ten dollars on them. . . . Show me one of the others."

I pulled one out of the pocket of my dress and handed it to Katie.

"This says five dollars. So that's five, ten, fifteen . . . plus these four . . . that's fifty-five dollars."

Katie now dove into what remained in the chest and threw everything out till it was completely empty. Then she searched and shook every piece of clothing. But there were no more coins.

"Fifty-five dollars is a fortune, Miss Katie," I said when she was through. "You're practically rich!"

"But it's not mine. These must belong to my uncle Ward."

"Didn't you say he was dead?"

"I don't know. I think so."

"But even if he isn't, he wouldn't mind you using it. And he ain't coming back anyway. Didn't you say he hadn't been here in years?"

Katie nodded. "It would be nice to pay off the bill at Mrs. Hammond's," she said. "I don't like her scowling at us."

"I think she'd scowl just the same," I said. "But then you could buy other things you need too."

"I wonder if it's enough to pay off my mama's loan at the bank."

"How much is it?" I asked.

"I don't know. We'll have to look at my mama's papers tomorrow. But right now, let's get some sleep."

"Where are you going to keep the gold coins, Miss Katie?"

"I don't know. Someplace safe."

"Well, you take the three little ones now too," I said. "I had them all day, but now they're making me nervous. They're yours now."

Katie took them from me and held the seven coins in

her hand a minute, just looking down at them.

"Oh, Mayme, I'm so excited!" she said. "Just when another mouth comes along to feed, we find this. God really is taking care of us, isn't He!"

# Awkward Days

# 19

Katie and Emma and I were already up and working in the kitchen when we heard Aleta's footsteps on the stairs. Katie set down the knife in her hand she'd been slicing bread with, wiped her hands, and went to meet her.

She brought Aleta into the kitchen and asked her, "Would you like some breakfast?"

"What are they doing here?" said Aleta, glancing first toward me, then with a frown toward Emma.

"I told you before, they live here."

"They live in the same house with you?"

"Yes. Mayme and Emma are my friends."

"They will never be my friends."

I turned away. I knew she was just a confused little girl who didn't know better. But the words hurt. And I knew there was nothing I could do to help. If I'd have tried to be nice to her or go over and talk to her, to show her that I was a normal person just like her, it wouldn't have done any good. If there was going to be a change in what she thought of my being black, it would have to come from inside her. Even Emma was uncharacteristically quiet. After getting used to Katie's kindness, I think the words took her by surprise and shocked her into silence.

Katie walked over and took William from Emma, cradled him gently in her arms, then returned to where Aleta stood.

"And this is William, Aleta," she said with a smile. "William is Emma's son. Isn't he a fine-looking little boy?"

Aleta stared down at him in silence.

"Would you like to hold him just for a second, Aleta?"

"No," she said.

"All right, maybe later. Are you hungry? Would you like some breakfast?"

Aleta nodded. Katie sat her down at the table, poured her a glass of milk, and began slicing some bread, talking gently and quietly to her, just like a grown-up would.

Sometimes Katie amazed me, and now was one of those times!

After a minute or two, I left the kitchen and went outside. I started walking away from the house and then heard Katie's voice.

"Mayme," she said.

I turned around. She was standing in the doorway, then took a few steps toward me.

"Mayme . . . I'm sorry," she said.

"I know, Miss Katie. It's all right," I said. "You just take care of her the best you can. She needs your help. I'll be all right."

The next couple of days were awkward and hard. Katie didn't know what to do. Aleta followed her around with the devotion of a puppy dog. But whenever she saw Emma or me, she got an angry expression on her face and tried to get as far away as she could. With William to tend to, Emma hardly seemed to notice it much. But Katie knew it hurt me, especially after how close she and I had become. She always looked at me apologetically, but we didn't know what to do.

The rest of the time Aleta had kind of a dazed look on her face. She didn't cry or talk about her mother or ask any questions about Katie's parents or why there were just three girls and a baby here. But then I remembered that I hadn't cried much at first either. Neither Katie or me knew what she was thinking. She just did what Katie told her and followed her around, or else silently stood and watched with a scowl on her face when Katie and me were talking about something or doing our work, or when Emma went into one of her fits of chattering. I tried to keep out of her way as much as I could. I figured that would be best for now.

At the end of the second day, I walked back to the house from the barn where I'd done the milking by myself. As I went in, Aleta and Katie were in the kitchen. Emma and William were napping.

Aleta glanced up and got that look on her face again.

"My daddy hates coloreds," she said. "If he saw you, he'd kill you."

"Aleta," said Katie, shocked. "How can you say such a thing!"

"He says coloreds are bad and mean and ugly."

"Then he's wrong," said Katie. "Mayme saved my life,

Aleta. She helped me just like I helped you. She's as nice a girl as you could ever meet."

Aleta didn't say any more.

"Do you want to hate people like your father does?" asked Katie. "Do you want to be like him?"

The thought seemed to sober her. She got up from her chair. "May I play with your dolls?" she asked.

"Yes," answered Katie. "Yes . . . you may."

Aleta left the kitchen and went upstairs.

# Clearing Off a Bill

# 20

In spite of the sudden change in our lives because of Aleta's coming, the seven gold coins had got right into Katie's brain. Once I'd convinced her that it would be all right to use it, she didn't waste any time trying to figure out what to do with the money. It must have been working on her all night the way things do even when you're asleep, because by morning she was ready to act like the mistress of a plantation with financial problems and do what she could about them.

Almost the minute Aleta was out of earshot, and not yet hearing anything from Emma, she spoke up about it.

"We've got to go back into town again, Mayme," she announced.

"What for?" I asked.

"I want to pay off the bill at Mrs. Hammond's store so she doesn't come calling or visiting or pestering us about the money we owe her. And we could use some things too—like flour and sugar. And we're almost out of bacon and bacon grease too."

"But if we bought bacon, she'd be liable to be suspicious, wondering why you didn't just have your own from butchering one of your hogs."

"I see what you mean. But the main thing is I don't want her fussing about the bill. She used to pester Mama something fierce, and I'd rather she wasn't asking too many questions. And I want to pay off some of Mama's loan at the bank too."

"You don't think Mrs. Hammond will ask questions about where the money came from?"

"She probably will," said Katie. "But that would be better than having her snooping around here. I hope getting her money will outweigh her curiosity."

"I see what you mean," I said, "but how can we go into town again now that Aleta's here? She would never stay with me for you to go alone—"

"I can't go alone, Mayme," interrupted Katie. "I'm not brave enough for that yet."

"Then I don't see what's to be done with Aleta."

"Couldn't we take her with us?"

"Do you think she'd stand for it, going all that way sitting beside me? And what about when we got to town and people saw her? That would make Mrs. Hammond all the more curious!"

"But maybe somebody would see her that knows her," said Katie, "and then we could find out who her father is and she would be able to go home."

"Maybe," I said, thinking about what Katie said. "But then what would they think about us? How would we explain ourselves? And Aleta would be bound to tell them there were no grown-ups at Rosewood."

"But we can't just keep her here forever. What about her father?"

"I don't know. I'm just concerned about your safety, Miss Katie."

Katie took in what I'd said and mulled it over in her mind for a while. A few minutes later Emma came in holding William, and that put an end to our conversation.

But it didn't put an end to Katie's determination to go into town and spend at least one of those gold coins. As soon as she'd poured Emma some milk and had her seated at the table eating some bread, she brought it up again.

"Emma," she said, "I've got to do something and I need for you to be real brave for me if you can."

"What dat, Miz Katie?" said Emma, getting a worried look on her face.

"Mayme and I need to go back into town again, and—"

"You's not gwine make me stay down in dat cellar agin, are you, Miz Katie?" she said, getting a scared look on her face.

"I have another idea, Emma. This time you and William can stay down in one of the cabins where our slaves used to live. How would that be?"

"Dat be right fine by me, Miz Katie," said Emma in relief.

"You'll be out of sight there, and if anyone should come, I'll show you a place to hide, just like before."

"Not in no cellar?"

"No, Emma, just out of the way. But nobody will come

and you'll be safe. We'll be home before you know we're gone."

"What about dat young'un—dat ornery white girl dat don't like me an' Miz Mayme none? You ain't gwine make me take care er her, is you, Miz Katie?"

"No, Emma—we'll take her with us."

And so it was that the following morning, Katie and Aleta and I climbed up onto the seat of the small buckboard, Katie in the middle and me and Aleta on each side of her, and headed into Greens Crossing behind a single horse, with Emma safely out of sight in Rosewood's colored town.

All the way into town Katie and I talked just like we always did, though I could tell Katie was making a special effort to show Aleta that there was nothing so unusual in a black girl and white girl being friends. Every once in a while she'd turn to Aleta and talk to her for a while, but Aleta remained mostly quiet and reserved.

"Now, you remember what I asked you before," said Katie as we began to get close to town, "whether you knew anybody in Greens Crossing, or whether they would know your papa?"

"I don't think so," replied Aleta.

"Somebody there might know your papa. Do you want us to ask the lady at the store? If you'll tell me your daddy's name, I will ask if she—"

"I don't want to go back to my papa," said Aleta firmly. "I'm afraid of him. I'm not going to tell you his name."

We jostled along a little while longer.

"All right, Aleta," said Katie, "if that's how you feel, I won't ask about him. But then you'll have to hide out of sight under those blankets we brought back there. Can you do that?"

"Why do I have to hide?" asked Aleta.

"Because," Katie began. She hesitated and glanced at me. "Because we don't want people asking us questions about you," she said after a second. "If you don't want to go back to your papa, it's best no one sees you. When people see girls like us all alone without any grown-ups with them, they get curious and wonder why. So we don't want them wondering about you. So can you hide in the back of the wagon and not make a peep?"

Aleta nodded.

Katie pulled the buckboard to a stop. "All right, then," she said. "We're almost to town. So you get back there and lie down, and I'll cover you up."

Aleta and Katie stepped down and Katie arranged her in the back of the wagon out of sight.

"You just stay there until I tell you to come out," said Katie. "We have to go into a store in town, so you might not hear anything for a while. After that we'll make one more stop. You just lie still and don't make a sound."

Ten minutes later we pulled up in front of the general store. I tried to put on my slave face as I got down from the wagon. Then we went inside.

"Hello, Mrs. Hammond," said Katie as we walked in, trying to sound confident and grown up. "My mama sent me into town to pay off our bill . . . I mean, to pay *her* bill."

Mrs. Hammond glanced up from behind the counter, looked toward me with an unpleasant expression, then at Katie.

"What is *she* doing in here with you?" she said.

"How much is the bill please, ma'am?" asked Katie, ignoring the question.

"It's something over three dollars, Kathleen."

"Good, then this will be enough," said Katie. "Here, Mrs. Hammond," she added, handing her one of the five-dollar coins.

"Gracious, child," she said, "in front of the colored girl! What does your mother teach you!"

"I thought you'd be pleased to have your bill paid, ma'am."

"Well, yes . . . of course . . . yes, I am. But . . . where on earth did your mama get this!" she said as it began to dawn on her that Katie had just handed her five dollars of pure gold.

"I don't know, ma'am. We want to buy a few more things, if you don't mind."

"Why . . . yes, I will just check your mother's account."

"Here is a list of what we would like," said Katie, handing her a small piece of paper.

Still flustered, Mrs. Hammond took it while we walked around the store trying to keep from looking at each other.

"Kathleen," said Mrs. Hammond after a few minutes, "I've put the things on your list on the counter."

"Thank you, ma'am."

"I notice this is not your mother's handwriting," she said, and I could feel that suspicious tone coming back into her voice.

"No, ma'am," said Katie. "It's mine."

"Ah . . . I see. Yes, well, Kathleen . . . in checking your mother's account, and with today's order, I find that she has one dollar and thirty-seven cents left over. Shall I just keep it and apply it as credit to her account?"

"No, ma'am," replied Katie. "I will take it home if you don't mind."

Disappointed, Mrs. Hammond fished about in her cash drawer, then handed Katie the money, in small silver coins this time.

"Put that in your pocket, Kathleen," she said quietly. "Don't let that girl see it. It's not good for them to know about money. It puts ideas in their heads."

"Yes, ma'am.—Mayme," she said to me, "get those things on the counter and take them to the wagon."

"Oh . . . and, Kathleen," said Mrs. Hammond as Katie started to follow me out, "here is the mail that has come."

She stooped down behind the counter, then handed it to Katie across the counter. I slowed my step because I was curious and wanted to hear whatever else she might say.

"Some of it looks important, Kathleen," said Mrs. Hammond. "You be sure your mama gets it. I don't want somebody blaming me if you lose it."

"Yes, ma'am."

I continued on with the sugar and flour and a few smaller things, and Katie followed me out the door.

We walked back to the buckboard, climbed up, and Katie took the reins, still holding the letters, and swatted the horse with them and we bounced away, knowing all the time that Mrs. Hammond's eyes were glued to our backs through the window of her store.

*Don't move under those blankets, Aleta!* I was thinking to myself.

A few minutes later, Katie pulled up and stopped in front of the bank.

"Why don't I just wait here, Miss Katie?" I said. "I don't think they'd like the idea of a colored girl going in there."

"I don't care what they think," she said.

"I know, but we don't want to raise too many questions."

"All right, Mayme," said Katie.

She walked inside, looked around a second, then walked over to where Mr. Taylor, the manager of the bank, was sitting at his desk.

"Hello, Kathleen," he said as she walked up. "Doing errands for your mother again?"

"Uh . . . yes, sir. I have a payment to make on her loan."

She stuffed her hand into the pocket of her dress, deposited the letters, and in their place pulled out five gold coins and set them on the banker's desk.

"Where did you get these!" he exclaimed, reaching out and taking the coins in his hand.

"From my uncle, sir," replied Katie. "He found gold in California and gave it to my mother for safekeeping. She didn't want to use the gold before this, since it wasn't hers. But now she finds she must."

"Ah, yes . . . yes, of course."

"Will this pay off my mama's loan, Mr. Taylor?"

"I'm afraid not, Kathleen," he said, still clutching the coins. "But it will make a nice dent in it. I shall apply it to the loan immediately."

Before Katie had a chance to think about whether it was a good idea to let him keep all the money or not, the banker opened a drawer, put the coins inside, then pulled out another drawer and removed a sheaf of papers and made a few notes on it.

Katie was glad she'd kept the last coin in her pocket or he might now have that too!

A few seconds later, he glanced up. "I've made the entry," he said. "This will be a good start on the loan. Is there anything else, Kathleen?"

"Yes, sir. Would it be possible to get small money for this one?"

She pulled out the last ten-dollar gold piece and set it on the desk.

"There's more?" said the banker.

"Just this one."

"Are you sure you don't want to apply it to the loan as well?"

"Yes, sir. We . . . my mama needs some coins for smaller bills."

"I see . . . right, well, I see nothing wrong with that."

Holding the coin, he rose and walked across the floor to the cashier's window. When he returned a minute or two later, he was holding a number of smaller coins in his hand.

"Here you are, Kathleen—ten dollars in coin. Tell your mother thank you for the payment. And tell her that we still need to discuss arrangements for the balance. It is really most urgent that she clear up what now remains on the first loan. Time is getting very short."

"Yes, sir. Thank you, Mr. Taylor."

Katie turned to go, but then paused and turned back toward him.

"How much is the loan, Mr. Taylor?" she asked.

"Both loans together originally totaled five hundred twenty-five dollars," he answered. "After today's payment there is a little over a hundred fifty dollars left on the first, which is the more immediately pressing. But your mother knows that."

"Yes, sir. Thank you, Mr. Taylor."

Katie walked out of the bank, her pocket jangling full of ten dollars' worth of smaller coins. I could tell from her face that she felt like the richest lady in the world.

Again she climbed up, and it was all we could do to keep from talking or smiling at each other before we got far enough away where no one could see us.

When we were about a half mile out of town, Katie reined the horse to a stop.

"You can come out now, Aleta," she said. "We're out of sight of town now. You did well."

"That was fun!" said Aleta, and she jumped up beside Katie. It was the first time either of us had seen her smile.

# The Teardrop
# 21

As much work as we'd been doing around the place, and from all the other things we had to think about, I hadn't been in the barn much in the last couple weeks, except the far end where the cows came for milking. One day I went inside and looked over and noticed the pillow and blanket and a few other things still there from when Katie'd found Emma and when she'd given birth to her baby here in the barn. None of us had ever thought to clean them up.

So I went over and picked up the blanket to take it outside to wash. Then I was going to take out the straw and dump a new bale down from the loft above, and was fixing to clean up the area a little.

All of a sudden as I swept back the straw, a little blue-and-white bit of color sparkled up at me on the hard dirt floor from the sunlight coming in through the door I'd left open. I stooped down and picked up the tiny gold piece of jewelry with its flat blue top and white gold letters in the middle of the blue.

I couldn't believe my eyes!

I recognized it. It had been my mama's! Now that I saw it again, I wondered why I hadn't found it with her things.

I held the little object for a minute, filled with reminders of my family. Mama'd had it as long as I could recollect, though I still hadn't a notion what it was. It didn't look like any kind of white woman's jewelry I'd ever seen, and was such an odd shape.

The first time I'd seen her holding it years ago and had asked her about it, she'd just smiled a sad smile and said the letters stood for a teardrop. What did that mean? I asked her. She just said, "Some memories are best left unremembered," and then she would answer no more of my questions about the thing.

Then all of a sudden I came to myself standing there in the barn, realizing that the thing hadn't got there with me.

So how had it gotten here?

I wandered outside and back to the house where I heard Katie and Emma and William in the kitchen and was going to ask Katie about it. It was a good thing Aleta was upstairs in Katie's room right then. The instant I opened my hand to show it to her, Emma burst out.

"Where'd you git dat?" she said, trying to grab it from me. "Dat's mine!"

I pulled back and closed my palm.

"What are you talking about, girl?" I said, confused at first.

"It's mine," she repeated. "I lost it. Where'd you fin' it?"

"Out in the barn. It was under the straw where you

were lying that day we found you."

"Dat's it—jes' like I tol' you. I was holdin' it an' I lost it. Gib it to me."

I saw Emma's eyes flash and took another step back, still clutching it tight. And now I was starting to get angry myself.

"What is it, Mayme?" asked Katie, confused over what we were arguing about.

I opened my hand and showed it to her.

"It's a cuff link," she said.

"What's a cuff link?" I asked.

"It's a thing a man wears to hold the cuffs of his shirt together. Where's the other one?"

"There isn't another one. I found this out in the barn just now, under the straw where Emma was laying when she had William."

"So it is Emma's, like she says?"

"No, Miss Katie," I said. "This used to belong to my mama. She had it for years."

"It's mine!" Emma said again. "I brought it wiff me when I ran away."

Katie looked back and forth between the two of us, more bewildered than ever.

"What do the letters stand for, Mayme?" she asked.

"I don't know," I answered. "All my mama would tell me is that they meant 'teardrop.' "

"Maybe this one of Emma's is the other one," she suggested. "There are always two."

"My mama only had one," I said. "How could Emma have gotten the other one.—If it's yours, Emma," I said, turning to her, still a little riled, "where'd you get it?"

"Neber min' where I got it. I got it, dat's all."

"It had to come from someplace, Emma," said Katie gently. "Won't you tell me where?"

"I foun' it."

"Found it . . . where?"

"I foun' it in a place when dere weren't nobody aroun' . . . an' it wuz dere an' it was pretty an' it din't belong to nobody, so I jes' took it."

Suddenly I remembered something Emma had said about the time she'd run away from her plantation, about going down to the colored town after everyone was dead. A chill swept through me. Why hadn't I thought of it before—*William* McSimmons was one of the McSimmons boys! And the instant the name came to my mind, with it came back the memory of the man Katie and I had seen asking about Emma in Mrs. Hammond's store.

It had been him!

"Was that before they killed the black folks, Emma?" I asked.

"Yes, dat was before den, but dey was all out workin'."

"All the slaves, you mean?"

"All da field slaves. I was a slave too, but I stayed at da house."

"But you went down to the colored village that day, when everyone was gone, and you found it then?"

"Yes'm, an' when I went inter da house, I saw it—"

All at once Emma realized I'd found her out, and she shut her mouth up tight.

"You saw it and you stole it—is that what you were about to say?"

Emma did not reply.

"You found it in one of the slave houses, didn't you?" I persisted. "The slaves were out working and you went in and saw it and took it?"

Still she remained silent.

"That was my house, Emma. And that cuff link was my mama's!"

Emma glanced away. I think her anger at me was starting to turn to embarrassment, though I think she was still mad that I'd found out her secret.

"What were their names, Emma?" I said. "When you were telling us about what happened to you—what was your master called?"

Still Emma wouldn't answer.

"Emma, answer Mayme's question," said Katie. Her voice was insistent, like she was Emma's mistress.

"Master McSimmons," Emma finally whimpered.

"So it *did* come from my mama!" I cried. "You took it from our house!"

"I still don't understand, Mayme," said Katie, now glancing toward me.

"Now we know why the baby's name is William, Miss Katie," I said. "I don't know why it didn't occur to me before."

"What do you mean?"

"Me and Emma came from the same place!" I said. "The father of her baby is William McSimmons, the son of my own master, who has about as bad a reputation as a man can have about what he does to women. I've heard talk about him and slave girls, and Emma's baby is obviously his doing. He's who was asking Mrs. Hammond about her that day."

"What dat you say?" shrieked Emma. "He been ax'ing 'bout me! Oh no . . . no!" she wailed and then started crying.

"But why didn't you know each other?" asked Katie, for the moment ignoring Emma's ruckus.

"I don't know, Miss Katie," I said. "I can't figure that out either. I don't know why I didn't see her at the plantation. I'd figured the McSimmons were all dead till just a few days ago."

Again I turned to Emma.

"How long had you been at the McSimmons place?" I asked.

"I don' know," whimpered Emma, "maybe a year. I wuz always gettin' bought an' sold. Da master hadn't bought me too much before dat, I reckon. I'm sorry, Miz Mayme. I din't know it wuz yer mama's. I din't mean ter steal it. It wuz jes' so pretty an' I neber had something so pretty, but I din't mean ter steal it."

She was so sad and pitiful when she cried and blubbered like that, how could I stay mad at her?

"It's all right, Emma," I said. "What's done is done and it's over now."

"Thank you, Miz Mayme. Yer so good ter me too, jes' like Miz Katie."

Her words didn't go down too easily in light of how angry I'd gotten at her. I was angry with myself for getting so upset. With Aleta here now, and five of us to take care of instead of just me and Katie ourselves, I couldn't let myself be angry and selfish over something so little as a cuff link. Katie was acting like a grown-up, and I had to too. I had some serious growing up to do, that was for sure.

Even though we'd temporarily solved the riddle of the cuff link's origin, the incident still raised a lot of questions in my mind that I didn't have answers for. Along with the gold from the cellar and where Aleta had come from, there were sure a lot of mysteries to think about all of a sudden.

# Respect
# 22

I STILL HADN'T HAD A CHANCE TO TELL KATIE everything that had happened when I'd been gone. It was such a private and personal thing, I couldn't just blurt it all out with Aleta around glaring at me, or when we were milking the cows and doing our chores, or when Emma was likely to start yammering away or asking me a lot of questions about if she was free too. It had to be the right time. I wanted to tell her when we didn't have to worry about getting interrupted by something.

Aleta had been with us a few days, and we were doing our best to get back to our normal routine, even though nothing had been normal since Emma got there. Having other people around made everything so different than it had been before.

One night Katie came into my room and got under the blankets with me.

"Is Aleta asleep?" I asked.

"I think so," answered Katie.

We both lay there a minute or two just enjoying the silence of being together under the covers, warm and safe and content.

"It's nice with William sleeping through the night," said Katie.

"Emma's starting to get the hang of mothering a little, isn't she?" I said. "That little boy's mighty special to her."

"I walked in on her today and she was babbling away in his face—I couldn't understand a word she was saying!"

"Black folks have a baby talk all their own," I said.

"It's nice, isn't it, Mayme, having other people to take care of? It makes me feel like I'm doing something important."

"It's helps us forget our own problems for a while, that's for sure," I said.

We lay quietly for a while.

"What happened when you went back home?" Katie asked after a bit. "You said it was something really exciting."

I'd been wanting to tell Katie about it ever since getting back. But it took me a little while to settle my thoughts and know what to say. Sometimes the most important things are hardest to talk about, and you wind up spending all your time talking about little things that don't really matter. But I waited till I was ready because I really wanted to tell her about what I'd found out and everything I'd been thinking and feeling.

"I saw the housekeeper at the big house," I said finally. "Nobody there had been hurt, only the slaves at the cabins. I wish I'd have known about Emma then so I could ask about her. I still can't figure why I never saw her. But Josepha—that's the housekeeper's name—told me that the war was over and all the slaves had been set free."

I looked over at Katie. The news didn't seem to shock her when she heard it like it had me.

"Like Henry's son?" she asked.

"*All* the slaves, Miss Katie," I said. "Everywhere. It's against the law for anyone to own slaves now."

It still seemed like the idea wasn't altogether getting through. Maybe it was, but it wasn't affecting her like it had me. How could it? She hadn't been a slave all her life, so maybe the news didn't seem so huge to her.

"But she was still there," said Katie, "the housekeeper, I mean. Wasn't she still your master's slave?"

"No, Miss Katie. She didn't *have* to stay no more. She wasn't a slave anymore. She was free to go."

"Then why was she there?"

"She wanted to stay. She was getting *paid* now to be the master's housekeeper. And if I'd have stayed, I'd have gotten paid too. She tried to get me to stay and work for Master McSimmons for pay like she was doing. If a black person works for a white now, he's gotta get paid just like a white person would."

"So that must mean . . . that means *you're* free too, Mayme."

"Yes, that's what I said was exciting," I said. "I'm not a runaway, Miss Katie. I'm *free*!"

Katie took in my words with a puzzled expression that gradually changed to worry. At first I didn't understand it. I thought she'd be happy and excited too. She was starting to see a little more of what it meant, but in a different way than I was seeing it.

There was a long silence. When she next spoke, her

voice was soft and I could tell she was nearly in tears.

"Do you want to leave Rosewood, Mayme?" she said.

Now I realized why she had reacted so strange.

"Oh . . . no, Miss Katie. That's not why I was saying it. I just wanted you to know, that's all."

"But . . . you're free. Don't you want to go somewhere else?"

"No, Miss Katie," I said. "Where else would I go?"

"You could go back there."

"This is my home now, with you. I *want* to be here."

It was quiet a few seconds.

Then suddenly a new thought struck her and Katie's face brightened.

"Then we don't need to pretend you're my slave anymore," she said. "You can be just like me."

"Except that this is your plantation," I said. "I don't have anything but . . ."

I remembered the handkerchief. I jumped out of bed and went and got it where I'd set it on the dresser, and brought it and showed it to her. Then I told her about the eleven cents and all about my ride into Oakwood.

"I bought this," I said. "It's the first time I've ever bought something in my life."

"It's pretty, Mayme," said Katie.

"I'm sorry I didn't come right back," I said.

"It's all right. I'm glad you could buy it. It makes me happy to know that you're free. I was just worried at first that you wanted to leave."

"No, I don't want to leave, Miss Katie."

"Maybe I should pay you too. I should have given you one of the gold coins.

"No, Miss Katie!" I laughed. "I don't work for you. We're just friends trying to make out the best we can together."

"Well, if we're equals now," Katie went on, "don't you think it's best if you called me just plain Katie instead of *Miss* Katie."

"We're not equals, Miss Katie," I said. "The slaves have been set free, that's all. But you're still white and I'm black."

"What's being white or black got to do with it?" she said.

"I don't know, Miss Katie. But it'd seem funny just to call you by your name. I still gotta show you respect."

"Why should you show me any more respect than I show you?"

" 'Cause we ain't the same. And 'cause this is your house."

"No, we're not the same. But neither of us is any better than the other."

"It just sounds respectful to say *Miss Katie,*" I said.

"But we should show each other the same respect. You don't want me calling you *Miss Mayme,* do you?"

I couldn't help laughing as she said it.

"No," I said. "That would sound wrong."

"If you don't call me just *Katie,* then," said Katie, "I'm going to call you *Miss Mayme* . . . or maybe even *Miss Mary Ann* or *Miss Jukes.*"

We laughed some more.

Neither of us had any idea that in the next room Aleta hadn't quite gone all the way to sleep after all and was lying awake listening to us.

I don't know what she thought about all Katie had just

said. Katie couldn't see it as clearly as I could, but she had almost become like a mama to the poor little girl. Aleta hung on her every word and followed her around and did what she said, almost as if she was her mama.

And I think seeing that Katie and I loved each other was maybe starting to get inside her skin.

# Bedtime Stories
# 23

As Katie and I lay there in my bed, it got quiet for a while.

"I miss our reading and story times, Mayme," said Katie after a bit.

"Me too," I said.

"I'm glad we can help Aleta, because this is horrible for her," said Katie. "But we hardly get to talk anymore. And I know we've got to help her, until we find out about her daddy. But I don't like how she treats you."

Again it was quiet.

"Tell me a story, Mayme," said Katie after a minute.

"Now?" I said, looking over at her.

"Yes, please. We haven't done stories for more than a week. Tell me a story about Mr. Rabbit."

"All right . . . let me try to remember a good one."

I thought a minute and then started a story as Katie snuggled down into the pillow and sighed contentedly.

When I finished it a few minutes later, I looked over and Katie was fast asleep.

I got up, turned down the kerosene lantern, and got back into bed next to her, happier than I had even been a few days ago after finding out that I was free.

The next evening after supper when we were starting to think about bedtime, Katie suddenly said, "Aleta, Emma . . . as soon as you're both ready for bed, we're going to have a surprise."

I saw Aleta's face light up for an instant, which was just what Katie was hoping for.

"What about me?" I said laughing. "Don't I get a surprise too?"

"You *are* the surprise!" said Katie. "So, Aleta—go out to the outhouse if you need to and then go upstairs and get your nightclothes on. Then come back and we'll sit in the parlor."

I still wasn't sure what Katie was up to, but she had a smile on her face, and Aleta seemed to be catching a little of her excitement and scurried off to do like she'd said.

Ten minutes later we were all seated together, Aleta cozied up to Katie, who had her arm around her, Emma in another chair with little William at her breast, and me in a wooden rocking chair.

"Aleta and Emma," said Katie, "how would you like a story before bed?"

"Oh, yes'm, Miz Katie," said Emma, "dat be right fine. I habn't herd a story in eber so long."

"What about you, Aleta—would you like a bedtime story?"

Yes," said Aleta softly.

"Tell us the story you were telling me last night, Mayme," she said, turning toward me. "I went to sleep before it was over."

Now I saw what Katie had been up to!

"All right," I said. "It's a story about Mr. Rabbit and Mr. Fox when Mr. Fox was going hunting for something to eat."

I looked at Aleta.

"Would you like me to tell it in a funny old black man's voice, Aleta?"

I think she was surprised that I'd spoken to her. At first she didn't say anything, but then slowly nodded.

"All right, then," I said, "it goes like this . . . it seems Mr. Rabbit was out walkin' one day when he ran into ole Mr. Fox, who was going huntin'. Mr. Fox, he ax Mr. Rabbit fer ter go huntin' wid 'im, but Mr. Rabbit, he sorter feel lazy, en he tell Mr. Fox dat he got some udder fish to fry in da way er huntin'. Mr. Fox was mighty sorry et havin' t' go huntin' alone, but he say he b'leeve he try his han' at it enny how, en off he went.

"He wuz gone all day, en he had a monstus streak er luck at huntin', Mr. Fox did, en he bagged a big sight er game."

By now Aleta was snuggling down into the sofa beside Katie, and I thought I could see the faintest little smile on her lips as she listened. How much she understood I don't know.

"Bime-by, on to'rds evenin'," I was saying, "Mr. Rabbit sorter stretch hisse'f, he did, en think hit's mos' time fer Mr. Fox fer ter git 'long home. Den Mr. Rabbit, he went en mounted a stump fer ter see ef he could hear Mr. Fox comin'. He ain't bin dar long when sho' nuff, here come ole Mr. Fox thoo de woods, singin' like a black man at a frolic. Mr. Rabbit, he lipt down off'n de stump, he did, en lay down in de road en make like he dead."

"Why he do dat?" asked Emma in a dreamy voice. William was already asleep, and I don't think Emma was far behind.

"Just wait and see, Emma," I said. "So Mr. Fox come 'long, he did," I went on, "en see Mr. Rabbit layin' dar. He look at 'im, en he think dat rabbit'd make a mighty fine supper. So he look closer, en he tu'n im over, he did, en 'zamine 'im, en say, sezee, 'Dish yer rabbit's dead. He look like he bin dead a long time layin' in de hot sun. He dead, but he mighty fat. He de fattes' rabbit what I ever see, but I reckon he bin dead too long ter eat. I feard ter take 'im home,' sezee.

"Mr. Rabbit ain't sayin' nuthin.' Mr. Fox sorter lick his chops, but he went on walkin' en lef' Mr. Rabbit layin' in de road.

"But dreckly he wuz outer sight, Mr. Rabbit, he jump up, he did, en he run thoo de woods en git ahead er Mr. Fox agin. Mr. Fox, he come up on da road, en dar lay Mr. Rabbit, 'parently all col' en stiff jes' like befo'. En Mr. Fox, he look at Mr. Rabbit, en he sorter study da situation a mite more, en he thinks 'bout all deze dead rabbits all roun' all er sudden.

"After while, he onslung his game bag en say ter hisse'f, sezee, 'Deze yer rabbits gwine ter was'e. Dat don' seem right ter me. I'll jes' leave my game bag yer, en I'll go back'n git dat udder rabbit, en I'll come back yer en git this yer rabbit, en I'll make folks b'leeve dat I'm ole man Hunter from Huntsville baggin' all deze yer rabbits,' sezee.

"En wid dat he drapt his game en loped back up de road atter de udder rabbit. En when he got outer sight, ole Mr. Rabbit, he jump up en snatch up Mr. Fox game bag en head off fer home.

"Nex' time he see Mr. Fox, he holler out, 'What you kill de udder day, Mr. Fox?' sezee.

"Den Mr. Fox, he sorter comb his flank wid his tongue, en holler back, 'I kotch a han'ful er hard sense, Mr. Rabbit,' sezee.

"Den old Mr. Rabbit, he laff, he did, en up en answer 'im, sezee, 'Ef I'da know'd you wuz atter dat, Mr. Fox, I'da loant you some er mine.' "

I looked over at Katie. Aleta was asleep and Katie had a smile on her face. It almost felt like having a family again.

After that, we started having stories together almost every night. Either I would tell one myself, or Katie would read us all something out of one of her storybooks.

# WASHDAY
# 24

BECAUSE OF ALETA BEING THERE, KATIE'D BEEN occupied with her all day. I could see that it was tiring Katie out having a little girl dog her steps every minute. Some of our chores were falling behind too.

"I reckon we oughta be doing a wash soon, Miss Katie," I said one day. It was a hot day early in June. "The aprons and drying cloths are getting a mite greasy."

"I was thinking just last night," said Katie, "how nice it would be to have clean sheets on the bed again. Shall we wash today?"

I saw Aleta look back and forth between Katie and me at the idea of Katie asking *me* what to do. But she didn't say anything.

"An' William's diapers," put in Emma. "I'm about out ob da ones I washed afore, an' dey's getting too ripe even fo his own mama's nose!"

I couldn't help laughing. "Then I think we oughta get

everything ready today," I said, "and do the wash tomorrow. It'll take a good long while to get the water hot enough. We'll have to start in the morning."

"Aleta," said Katie, "you and I will go through the house today and gather up everything, our clothes and the bedcoverings, and the kitchen things."

"And I'll bring wood and set the fire outside," I said. "But I'll need the rest of you to help lift the tub over the fire pit."

"I kin help, Miz Mayme," said Emma eagerly.

"We'll all lift it together," I said, though when the time came Aleta didn't do much. The three of us managed to get it onto the iron stand, though how much weight Emma lifted was doubtful too.

By the end of that day we had everything all ready and a nice big fire set in the pit with the washing tub in place on the rack over it. There was a wooden washing platform to keep the washing area from getting muddy, with the fire pit on one side of it and a metal frame where the tub sat. So the fire burned under part of the tub without setting the platform on fire, and we stood on the other side to do the wash. A second tub—the rinse tub—had its own pump and sat on another wooden platform near the clotheslines.

We filled the main washtub with water that we carried in buckets from the pump. Then all that was needed was to light the fire and wait till the water got hot enough to get the clothes clean.

I was the first one up the next morning, like I usually was. I got up and went downstairs, thinking that I'd get the fire lit so the water could be warming. It looked like it was gonna be another hot day, and the sooner we got the wash done, the better we'd feel. I walked outside and looked around. The air was still and cool, and all the birds and other creatures were starting in on their day's noises—the pigs and the cows, and of course the roosters had already been at it for an hour. And then here came the dogs to greet me and make a fuss like they'd never seen me before.

I walked around a little bit, thinking about how things were. Just when Katie and me had been starting to get used to having Emma around, now we had Aleta to think about. Were things ever going to be normal again? I wondered. Of course, in our lives what was normal anyway? Not that I didn't want Aleta here, but it changed things, that was for sure. And yesterday I'd noticed a funny little change in Katie too. I think it might have been because of what I told her about the slaves being freed. I never would have expected it, but she almost seemed to be treating me different, occasionally looking at me and not saying anything, and hesitating before she spoke, almost *more* respectful or something. You wouldn't think that'd be something I'd mind. But it made it a little awkward a couple of times to have her look at me that way. I'd been comfortable knowing how to act before. And now it was a little confusing. I reckon it was a change we would both have to get used to. I didn't feel any different inside. I was still the same person I'd always been. But being free rather than a runaway slave was a big change, whether I felt any different or not.

I went back inside the kitchen and scooped out some coals from the stove and carried them outside in a bucket. I emptied them carefully beneath the fire pile, keeping the coals together so they'd stay hot. I put a few bits of straw on top of them, then kindling, and blew on it. The straw jumped up into flame right away and pretty soon the whole fire was going.

I went back in and stoked up the fire in the kitchen stove with some fresh wood. By the time it was going, the other girls were getting up. When we'd milked the cows and fed the pigs and chickens and horses and dogs, we took the cows out to pasture. Aleta went with Katie and me for the first time while Emma saw to William, and though she walked back next to Katie, it seemed like she might be gradually getting used to me. As we got back to the house, I could see steam starting to rise from the washtub.

"Let's check the water," I said. "I think it's ready."

Aleta scampered ahead and stuck her hand in it.

"Ouch!" she cried. "It's too hot!"

Katie and I laughed, and by now Emma was trudging out with a basketload of her things and she laughed too.

"Get a bucket of water from the pump," I said to Aleta, "and douse the fire."

While she was doing that, Katie and I went inside to help Emma lug out the piles of laundry. Our first load was the sheets and aprons and our underclothes. We took them out and dumped them into the tub, then added soap and bluing.

"Grab your pile, Emma," I said, "and dump it in."

She did, and then we swished it all around with two laundry sticks, working from the wood platform on the opposite side of the tub from where the fire in the pit underneath was still smoking and smoldering and sizzling from Aleta's dousing. We'd wash the white things first, and when they were done, do the work dresses and quilts and heavier things, and at the very last, do our dirty work dresses that had manure on them from milking and cleaning the stalls.

"Shall we get the rinse tub ready, Miss Katie," I suggested, "and leave these to soak a spell?"

"Aleta," called Katie, "why don't you keep stirring the clothes with Emma while Mayme and I fill the other pot."

Aleta came round and took hold of the stick from Katie and started stirring energetically.

"Stir and bounce and swish the clothes all around," said Katie. "Watch what Emma's doing—that's right . . . good, Aleta."

We walked over to the rinse tub and first cleaned it out, which we hadn't done since our last wash. We wanted to make sure the rinse water was nice and clean. After dumping it upside down, we set it back on the platform and pumped in new water.

"I reckon it's time to start scrubbing," I said as we returned to Aleta and Emma.

"I'll go get the two washboards," said Katie.

"I don't mind doing the scrubbing, Miss Katie," I said.

"That's silly, Mayme. I'll help too."

As we went Katie glanced at me with an unspoken look of hopeful question as we slowly left Emma and Aleta alone, stirring and swishing in the washtub while we walked away. I heard them talking a little but couldn't make out too clearly what they were saying. But I know it warmed Katie's heart just to hear them talking at all.

"Dat real good, Miz Aleta," Emma was saying as we returned. "She's washin' dese here clothes, right good, Miz Mayme," she said to me.

"I can see that, Emma," I said. "It looks like the two of

you have them ready for the washboards. You know how to use a washboard, Emma?"

"Dat I do, Miz Mayme. I done washed like dis a hunner times."

"Good. Then let's you and me scrub these clothes and get them the rest of the way clean."

When Katie came back with the two washboards, we set them in the tub leaning against the rim. Aleta kept stirring—though she was already starting to run out of energy and was slowing down—and Katie joined her. Then Emma and I leaned over and scrubbed each thing one at a time. Once we started getting them done, we wrung them out, and Katie took them over and dumped them into the rinse tub.

It went a lot faster with four of us than the last time we'd washed and I'd done all the scrubbing myself. Katie was really learning how to work hard! Every once in a while I'd glance over and think to myself, *Is this the same Katie?* I hadn't ever known her mother, but I doubted she could have been a harder worker than Katie when Katie got going.

We did three loads of different wash, and scrubbed and wrung out and rinsed and wrung out again all morning. By noon there were clothes and sheets and towels and linens and stockings and quilts and aprons and dresses all hanging from the line, and we were almost finished. Our arms were so tired from the scrubbing that they were about ready to fall off! The last of the quilts were so heavy when they got wet, we didn't scrub them as hard as the rest—we mostly just stirred them around and let them soak in the water, though the wash water was pretty dirty by then too. But we were just getting too tired to scrub them any harder.

"I'm tired," said Aleta.

"Me too, Miz Aleta," said Emma.

"And me," I said, "but we're almost done."

The day was hot by then too, and we were sweating like horses out for a hard ride.

Katie was just wringing out one of the last work dresses when it fell back into the rinse tub. The water from the splash came up and hit her in the face.

"Oh, that cold water felt good!" she said.

Instead of picking it back out, she just stood there for a minute, as if she was too tired to do anything. Then she started to laugh.

All of a sudden she slammed her hand into the water toward where I was standing on the other side of the tub, sending a big spray of water all over the front of my dress.

"Katie, what are you doing!" I cried.

She was laughing all the harder by now. She swatted the water again. I jumped away. Then she picked up a bucket and scooped it half full of water and ran toward me. I saw what she was about to do and tried to run. But it was too late. I felt a flood of water all over my back, followed by a shriek of laughter.

"Katie," I yelled, "I can run faster than you!"

I dashed for the nearest bucket and then back. But as I was dipping it into the rinsing tub, Katie was pouring another bucketful over my head.

"Ohh!" I exclaimed. "Just you wait!"

It was cold, but after the first shock it felt good!

I spun around and there was Katie running across the grass. I went after her with my own bucket of water. I tried to throw it as I ran but only got one of her shoulders wet.

By now Aleta had a bucket and was chasing us both. I didn't see her coming, and the next thing I knew water was dripping from my head again.

"I got you, Mayme!" she cried.

"Yes, and now I'm gonna get you!" I said, turning and chasing after her.

She howled in a frenzy of terror and fun and ran away from me. Katie was running to one of the water pumps to fill up her bucket again, and within another minute, an all-out water war had begun.

At first Emma just stood watching, too bewildered at the sight to enter in. Sometimes I wondered if her brain just went a little slower than other folks'. But finally, after laughing at the rest of us, it seemed to dawn on her that she could join us in the fun herself. But I think she was still a little intimidated at the thought of being too free with white folks, so when she finally started splashing water about, it was always toward me. Before long she was running and laughing and shrieking too.

All four of us were running around back and forth between the clotheslines, the barn, and the house. Within ten minutes we were soaked to the skin from head to foot. But after all the work and the heat of the day, it felt as good as swimming in a creek.

Pretty soon we were laughing too hard to keep running and were just taking turns pouring buckets of water on each other. Aleta and Emma were laughing as hard as me and Katie.

Right in the middle of it, as we were standing there

dripping and starting to think about going back to finish hanging up the last few things, Aleta interrupted our laughter.

"There's somebody coming," she said.

# New Windows

## 25

ALETA'S WORDS QUIETED US ALL IN A BIG HURRY! We looked where Aleta was pointing to see a wagon coming from the road into the yard. It was too late to do anything about it. The man rode up in front of us as we stood there soaking wet, watching him approach.

He looked down at us with a curious expression. All of our dresses were dripping water down onto the ground. I can't imagine what he must have thought to see two white girls and two black girls in such a mess. He stared at me a second, then turned back toward Katie.

"Your mama home, Kathleen?"

"Uh, no . . . no, she isn't," answered Katie, wiping at her hair, which was dripping down all over her face.

"I heard you had some broken windows you wanted me to fix."

"Oh yes—that's right. I'll show you."

He got down off the wagon and Katie led him toward

the house, her feet squishing in her boots, still trying to wipe her hair back out of her face as she went.

"You girls look a mess," the man said.

"Yes, sir. We were doing the wash and started throwing water at each other."

"I can see that," said the man.

"Who's the tall colored girl? Ain't seen her before. She's got an uppity look in her face."

"She, uh . . . works for us now," said Katie. "She used to be a slave."

"Yeah, well I reckon a lot of things is changing now for everybody. I didn't recollect you having a younger sister, Kathleen."

"Uh . . . no, sir," said Katie and kept walking.

Aleta and Emma and I gradually started moving back in the direction of the rinse tub, but I was trying to listen to Katie and the window man at the same time.

"There are the windows, Mr. Krebs," said Katie, pointing to the four broken ones. "My mama's not going to be home till later. Can you fix them and she pay you later?"

"Yeah. Just take me about an hour. I'll cut the glass and get 'em glazed. I'll send her a bill."

"Thank you, Mr. Krebs," said Katie. "Well, I guess I should see about the washing."

Katie walked back to where we were standing watching.

"He's going to fix the windows," she said, as if it was nothing out of the ordinary.

We continued with the last of the wash, not saying much now, both Katie and me glancing kinda nervously toward the house every now and then.

"Emma," said Katie after a minute, "you'd better go

back in and change your clothes and tend to William so he doesn't start crying."

"Yes, Miz Katie."

"She can't go in like that," I said. "Miss Katie, why don't you take her around and through the front door so he won't see her. Aleta and me will finish up here. We can do that, can't we, Aleta?"

"Yes," said Aleta.

Katie and Emma left, and the man didn't seem to be paying any attention to us anyway. Katie came back a few minutes later, and it took us about an hour to finish getting the rest of the things hung up on the lines. We were still wearing the wet things we had on. And it felt good in the hot sun. Before we knew it, the man was walking back out toward us.

"The new windows are in, Kathleen," he said. "Tell your mama they're fifty cents apiece. I'll write it down and leave it with Mrs. Hammond."

"Yes, sir," said Katie. "Thank you, Mr. Krebs."

He went back to his wagon and a few minutes later was clattering back down the road toward town. As we watched him leave, Katie turned to me.

"That wasn't so hard," she said with a kind of pleased expression on her face.

"He didn't seem to mind that it was just us," I said. "But we still gotta be careful."

Suddenly we heard a splash. We turned, and there was Aleta sitting in the middle of the rinse tub with her clothes all still on.

We ran over to her laughing.

"What are you doing?" laughed Katie.

"Taking a cold bath," she said. "It's so hot, it's like going swimming."

As we watched I had to admit it looked like a pretty good idea at that! Katie was obviously thinking the same thing.

"I'll go get the soap from the house," said Katie. "I want to take a bath too! I'll wash your hair under the pump, Aleta.—Would you wash mine, Mayme?"

"If you'll wash mine!"

While Aleta was playing and splashing in the water, Katie and I went back inside and got some clean towels and soap and a scrubbing sponge.

We came back outside, then took off our dresses and took turns getting each other all clean.

Even with my underclothes still on, that was about the best bath I'd ever had! We got Emma back out, and she and William cleaned up real nice too, though she howled a little at the cold water from the pump on her head and back.

When we were done, we pulled the stopper from the bottom of the tub and let the water drain, where it ran in a little trough that had been dug from under it out to the field. Since most of our clothes we'd been wearing were hanging on the lines, we put on robes of Katie's mama's till the things on the line had started to dry, which didn't take too long in the heat.

After that, for most of the rest of the summer, we took cold baths outside almost every day.

As we were walking back to the house, I realized that Aleta had been listening carefully before when Katie had been talking to the glass man.

"Where is your mama?" she asked.

The question took Katie by surprise as much as it did me. She glanced over at me, but all I could do was shrug. I didn't know what to say.

"She's not here," answered Katie after a bit. "She's gone for a while."

"Where's she gone?" said Aleta. "Why haven't I seen her?"

"She's gone for a long time, Aleta," said Katie. "That's why Mayme and I are here together, and why we have to work so hard."

# A Request
# 26

I WAS OUT AT THE WOODPILE THE NEXT DAY GETting ready to chop some firewood when I heard a soft step behind me. I turned, surprised to see Aleta standing there. For an instant I stiffened inside, getting ready for whatever hurtful thing I was about to hear. But then I realized that there was a different, almost timid expression on her face.

"Mayme," she said, and her voice was as different as the look on her face. "Would you please tell me another story about Mr. Rabbit and Mr. Fox, like that one you told us a few days ago?"

"Did you like it?" I asked.

She nodded. "But I couldn't understand it very well," she said. "And I fell asleep before it was done. Why did you talk in such a funny voice when you were telling it?"

I smiled and put down the ax, then sat down on the chopping block.

"You want to sit down?" I said.

Aleta sat down on another piece of wood opposite me.

"That voice is the way my uncle tells the old stories," I said. "Miss Katie likes to hear them that way so she'll know how the stories sounded to me when I was a little girl."

"You heard it from your uncle?"

"Not my real uncle. When I was a slave, we called all old black men uncles. They're the ones who told the old stories that they'd heard when they were young from the uncles before them."

"Were you really a slave, Mayme?"

"Yes I was, Aleta."

"Was it hard?"

"Real hard."

"Why aren't you a slave now?"

" 'Cause some bad men killed my family, and I ran away and came here. Miss Katie . . . Miss Katie's family," I added, feeling a twinge of guilt as I said it, "they took me in and let me stay here and work for them. After that, I found out all the slaves had been set free."

"What kind of men were the bad men?" she asked. "Were they white or colored?"

"They were white men."

"My daddy says whites are better than coloreds."

"He'll find out someday that's not true, Aleta," I said. "All white folks have to find that out sometime. Where does your daddy live?"

She shrugged and didn't answer.

"Is it far away from here?"

"Pretty far."

"How long had you and your mama ridden before you fell?"

"I don't know—maybe an hour."

"Was your daddy chasing you?"

"I think so. Mama kept looking back."

"Well, Aleta," I said, "whites can be just as bad as coloreds. And coloreds can be just as bad as whites—if there's not love in their heart. That's what makes folks different, not the color of their skin. Some folks have love in their hearts, others don't."

She was still young, but I think she understood what I'd said. She seemed to be thinking about it anyhow.

"My daddy doesn't have love in his heart," she said.

I didn't think I'd ever heard anything so sad for a girl to say about her father. It almost made me cry. I waited a minute, then spoke again.

"Do you want to hear about Mr. Rabbit now?" I asked.

"Yes . . . please!" said Aleta, her eyes gleaming with anticipation.

"How much did you hear before you fell asleep?"

"I don't know, but tell it all, tell it to me from the beginning."

From the kitchen porch, Katie had come outside, then paused as she saw us together. She was now watching us sitting at the woodpile talking. She didn't know what we were talking about, but the softened expression on Aleta's face brought tears to her eyes.

# Questions in Town
# 27

KATIE," I SAID ONE DAY, "NOW THAT THERE'S FIVE of us to feed, I think we oughta start doing something to save the milk. And with summer coming and it getting hot, if there's a drought, the cows could dry up. So we gotta make sure we've got plenty of cheese."

"Do you know how to make cheese, Mayme?" she asked.

"Not really," I said. "You just boil the milk, I think. I watched my mama and Josepha do it once, but I forget what they did."

"I think you've got to put something in it to make the milk turn to cheese," Katie said, then added, "I think my mama's got a book about it."

We went to the pantry and looked around.

"Here's the book my mama was always using," said Katie. She laid it open on the counter and started flipping through it. The book was called *The American Frugal*

*Housewife's Guide to Food Preparation and Preservation.*

"Does it tell about cheese?" I asked.

"I'm looking . . . here it is," said Katie, turning the pages.

She bent down to read for a minute.

"It says, 'Take the inner membrane of the fourth, or digestive stomach of a young mammal living on milk, preferably a young calf—' "

"Ugh!" I said. "How are we going to get a calf's stomach!"

Katie kept reading. " 'Dry the stomach lining in salt, then, when needed, soak in water. The resultant liquid will contain the fermented enzyme, rennet, which has the property of curdling milk. For basic cheese preparation, heat three gallons of fresh milk to approximately 140 degrees . . .' "

She stopped and looked over at me. "How can we make cheese if we don't have this rennet thing and the calf's stomach?" she asked.

"Now that I think about it," I said, "I think I remember something about using thistles or nettles too."

"We could find plenty of those!" said Katie.

"But maybe your mama has a dried stomach skin around here someplace."

"I don't even like to think about it! And I haven't seen anything like that."

"I wonder if we could get anything to use at Mrs. Hammond's store."

"I don't know," said Katie, looking at the book again and reading to herself. "It also says you need salt and cheesecloth. We forgot to get salt last time we went to town."

"Do you have any cheesecloth?"

"I don't think so. Maybe we should go to town and see if we can get what we need at the store."

Thinking of going into town reminded me of seeing Henry in Oakwood. I told Katie what had happened. "I don't know if I should go with you," I said.

"I could go alone," said Katie. "I think after last time I could do it alone if I had to."

"Or we could go to Oakwood instead."

"Then we'd have to pay for it," said Katie, "and I'd rather put it on my mama's bill at Mrs. Hammond's so we don't use up our money."

"But what about Aleta?" I asked.

"Let me talk to her," said Katie. "I'll see what she says to the idea of staying with you."

The next morning after the cows were out to pasture, Katie and I got the small buggy hitched up and ready for a trip into town.

We walked into the house.

"Aleta," said Katie. "I need to talk to you for a minute. I have to go into town today. I'll be gone two or three hours."

Aleta stared back at her with a blank expression.

"Would you mind staying here with Mayme and Emma while I'm gone?" Katie asked.

Aleta glanced over at me.

"Would you tell me a story, Mayme?" she said.

"If you're nice," I answered with a smile, "I might even tell you *two*."

"Then I don't mind staying," said Aleta.

"Good," Katie said, smiling. "I'll get back as fast as I can."

Katie got up and she and I walked outside. Aleta followed us.

"Is there anything else we need, Mayme?" Katie asked as we went.

"I was just noticing that we are getting a little low on oats for the horses."

"I'll go to the feed store, then, after Mrs. Hammond's."

Katie climbed up onto the buckboard and looked down at me and Aleta.

"I'll try to hurry," she said, then flicked the reins, leaving Aleta and me and Emma together for the first time. I think Emma was more nervous at the prospect of it than any of the rest of us.

We went back into the house and heated up the irons on the kitchen stove. When they were ready I started ironing some of the laundry. As I worked I told Aleta stories. She sat at the table and listened with great big eyes, not saying a word. Pretty soon Emma was sitting there listening too. It was almost like when I used to tell my own brothers and sisters stories, except that now one of them was white. The time went so fast that before we knew it Katie was back, telling us all about what had happened in town.

She'd gone to the general store first. Mrs. Hammond, as always, had been full of questions.

"Where's that ugly slave girl of yours?" she asked when Katie walked in.

"Haven't you heard, Mrs. Hammond?" said Katie. "There are no more slaves. They're free now."

"What's the girl doing, then?"

"She helps us at Rosewood and lives with us."

"Well, I never," mumbled Mrs. Hammond.

Katie was getting up her gumption more and more, I thought as she told us about it.

"I was sent into town for cheese-making supplies," Katie went on. "But I forgot the list. But if you will tell me what I need, I'll remember it."

The shopkeeper humphed a little, which it seemed she liked to do every minute or two.

"Well, all you need is your cheesecloth," she said, "and something to clabber the milk."

"Yes, that's what we need," said Katie.

"What were you planning to use, then? I've got dried nettle in my herb supplies."

"Is that the best thing to use, Mrs. Hammond?"

"Of course it's not the best. The best thing is to use rennet. But your mama knows that. Does she have a dried calf's stomach?"

"I don't think so."

"You mean tell she wanted store-bought, with all those cows you've got out there?"

"Yes, ma'am, I think she wanted me to get one."

"A whole skin! How much cheese is your mama fixing to make?"

"I don't know, ma'am. Maybe just a part of a skin, then?"

"What did your mama tell you to get, for heaven sakes?"

"I'm sorry, I don't know, ma'am. Just whatever we need to make cheese."

"Gracious, but you are a dense one! I'll cut you off a

quarter piece of dried lining. It's got to be kept in salt until you're ready to soak it and remove the extract."

"How much do you soak at a time, Mrs. Hammond?"

"Well, I swan! Next thing, you'll be wanting me to make the cheese for you! Just cut off a little piece and soak it overnight. Heavens, child—your mama knows all that. Why are you asking so many questions!"

Mrs. Hammond turned and disappeared into another room. When she came back a minute later, she was carrying a little brown paper package.

"Tell your mama to get this in salt as soon as you get home."

"We need some salt too, Mrs. Hammond."

"How much—five pounds, ten pounds, twenty pounds?"

"Uh . . . twenty pounds, I think," said Katie. "And the cheesecloth, please."

Mrs. Hammond muttered something else about Katie's intelligence, then went to get the other two items. As she did Katie looked around the store. First she noticed the newspapers and remembered that her mama always bought one every time she came into town. Maybe she ought to get one too. After that the stick candy particularly caught her eye.

"All right then, Kathleen," said Mrs. Hammond, setting the salt on the floor and a roll of cheesecloth on the counter, "is there anything else?"

"I want to get a newspaper, and would you please give me four of these peppermints," she said, pointing to the glass jar on the counter.

Mrs. Hammond glanced at her with a curious expression.

"Four?" she said.

"Yes, ma'am. And four of the molasses drops."

"Does your mama eat candy, Kathleen?"

"No, ma'am."

"Are you going to eat these all yourself, then?"

"No, ma'am."

"And you want . . . *four* of each?"

"Yes, ma'am."

Deciding it was best not to wait for any more questions, Katie bent down to pick up the bag of salt to carry it outside.

"Oh, I think it's too heavy for me," she said. "I won't be able to lift it up."

"Here is your candy, Kathleen," said Mrs. Hammond, handing her a bag, "and the rennet skin . . . and the cheesecloth and the paper. You take those. I'll put the salt in the wagon for you."

"Thank you, Mrs. Hammond," Katie said and followed her to the door.

Ten minutes later, as Katie was sitting in the buggy waiting for Mr. Watson to load in the second bag of oats, Katie saw Henry walking slowly toward her from the direction of the livery stable.

"Mo'nin, Miz Kathleen," he said as he ambled up. "Where dat little black frien' er yers?"

"Uh . . . she's back at the plantation," answered Katie.

"What she doin'?"

"Working."

" 'Peers ter me you been a workin' mighty hard too,

Miz Kathleen," said Henry, glancing toward Katie's hands as they sat holding the reins in her lap. " 'Specially seein' all dem blisters on yo han's."

Unconsciously Katie pulled back her hands and stuffed them into the folds of her dress.

"Uh, yes . . . it's hard work for Mama and me."

"Why, ain't yo daddy back? I hear'd folks sayin' dey ain't seen hide or hair o' him since da war ended."

"I don't know. He just isn't back."

"Effen you say so, Miz Kathleen," said Henry, looking out of the corner of his eye with a bit of a suspicious expression. "But sounds ter me like sumfin a mite peeculiar's goin' on."

Mr. Watson came with the oats and dumped the bag off his shoulder into the back of the buggy, bouncing it up and down a few times.

"There you are, Miss Clairborne," he said.

"Thank you, Mr. Watson," said Katie. "Well, good-bye . . . good-bye, Henry."

"Now jes' you hol' on er minute, Miz Kathleen," said Henry before Katie could start up, while Mr. Watson walked back inside. He laid a hand on one of the reins to hold the horses back. "Is you sho' dere ain't nuthin' you want ter tell yo frien' Henry?"

As he said it he looked straight into Katie's eyes.

Katie glanced away nervously. Back in the direction of the livery stable, she saw Henry's son standing watching.

"You sho' dere ain't nuthin' I kin do fer you, Miz Kathleen?" Henry added.

"Thank you, Henry," said Katie. "I'll tell Mama—"

"I ain't talkin' 'bout yo mama, Miz Kathleen," he said

even more insistently. "I'm ax'in' effen dere ain't sumfin I kin do fer *you*."

"No . . . no, nothing," said Katie.

"I see you's still hitched up wiff dis frayed bridle, an' I don' know why you won' let yer frien' Henry—"

"Thank you, Henry. I'll take care of it another time."

Katie took the rein and yelled to the horses. Henry let go, and the buggy jumped into motion.

As she bounced along down the street, Katie knew the tall, lanky black man was staring at her as she rode away. But she was afraid to look back.

That night after Aleta was in bed and she was telling me about it, Katie looked at me seriously.

"I didn't like the look in his face, Mayme," she said. "It was almost like . . . he knows."

# Making Cheese
# 28

The next day we looked in Katie's mama's book again to learn all we could about making cheese. Katie read the directions again and we both gradually remembered seeing it done. I wasn't sure whether we'd be able to do it by ourselves. But most of the milk was going to waste anyway, what we couldn't drink and what we didn't churn into butter and buttermilk. And we were about out of the cheese that was stored in the pantry. So we had to figure it out pretty soon.

That day we sliced off a few inches from the dried stomach lining Katie had bought and soaked it overnight. We weren't sure how much to use or how much water to put in. We just put in what looked like the right amount and hoped it would work. We saved up all the milk from both milkings that day and brought it into the kitchen.

The next morning we were getting excited about trying it to see if we could do it. The book said to heat up three gallons of milk to one hundred forty degrees. We didn't know how hot that was. Katie said she thought it was hot enough that you could put your finger in it for a second without it burning. So when it seemed about right we set it off to the side of the stove, then poured in the rennet water and stirred it all around. Then we were supposed to let it sit for half an hour till the milk started to get harder.

We tried to wait patiently, but all we could do was watch it and wait for the time to go by, with Emma and Aleta asking questions we didn't know the answers to.

"It's hardening up," said Katie, looking down into the pot. "I'm pretty sure at least."

"What are we supposed to do next?" I asked.

" 'Stick your finger in and see if the curd breaks apart cleanly,' it says."

"Should I do it?"

"Go ahead," said Katie.

Timidly I put my finger into the warm white liquid. It had hardened a little but was still mushy.

"I don't think it's ready," I said.

We waited another ten minutes. This time Katie tried it, and instead of mush, the curd split apart and the watery whey filled in the crack.

"I think it's ready," she said.

"Now what?" I asked.

Katie went and read in the book again.

"It says to cut it into long cubes with a knife and then cook it again and keep stirring it real gently so the cubes don't stick together."

I went and got a long, sharp knife.

"You cut it," I said, handing the knife to Katie, "then we'll scoot the pan back over the fire."

It looked funny, all soft and jiggly, when Katie sliced down into the hardening milk, but the curds held together. As we heated it we stirred it real slow and gentle with wooden spoons. The curds broke apart into big chunks that swam in the clear whey that had filled the pan from the cutting. Gradually the curd chunks got harder. We were supposed to keep it at one hundred five degrees for an hour. Katie said that wasn't very hot at all, just warm.

This time we tried to busy ourselves with something else for the hour. When we came back, it looked about the same.

"Take a piece out and eat it," said Katie.

"Why . . . you mean now?"

"We've got to see if it's ready."

"How will we know?"

"The book says it will feel squeaky."

"All right," I said. "I'll try it."

I took a little piece that was floating on top and ate it.

"It *is* squeaky," I said laughing. "It feels funny."

"What does it taste like?" asked Katie.

"I don't know . . . like warm milk," I said. "Warm milk that's a little sour."

Katie took a piece and ate it too, then giggled at the feel of it.

"Do you want a piece, Aleta?" she asked.

Aleta glanced slowly into the pot, then shook her head.

"How about you, Emma?" said Katie. "It's good. Come on—try it. Here, I'll break you off a piece."

She did, then handed it to Emma. She chewed it slowly, then kind of grimaced, and both girls smiled together.

"I want to try it too," now said Aleta.

Katie handed her one of the curds and she ate it, with the same kind of reaction as Emma's.

"It's hard enough to pour it into the cheesecloth now," said Katie. "We'll need another pan."

She went to the pantry, where most of the kitchen things were kept, and came back with another deep pot and set it on the floor. "We need to line it with cheesecloth," she said.

She brought the roll and rolled out enough to cover the top of the empty pot, draping it down about halfway into it, then cut it off the rest of the roll with a pair of scissors.

"Emma," she said, "can you hold the cheesecloth so that its edges don't fall into the pot?—Here, hold it like this."

When Emma had the cheesecloth in place, Katie and I lifted the cooking pot off the stove and carefully poured the mixture into the new pot. At first the whey came pouring out easily. Then gradually the lumps of curds plopped onto the cheesecloth. When it was empty we set the warm pot aside, then slowly lifted the cheesecloth up with the dripping curds in the center.

"Is that cheese?" asked Aleta as she watched. She sounded impressed that Katie and I would be so smart to know how to make cheese.

"Not quite yet," I said. "But it's halfway there."

"Now the book says to wrap the cheesecloth around it and put a press on top of it," said Katie. "Oh yes, now I remember—there's a cheese press. Why didn't I think of it before! I'll get it."

She ran into the pantry. I could hear her lugging the ladder out of the corner and climbing up to one of the shelves above her head. She came back a few minutes later with a small wood box contraption that I recognized from Josepha's kitchen.

"There was a cheesecloth bag up there on the shelf with it that I'd forgotten about," she said. "I guess we didn't need to buy the cheesecloth after all."

"What do you do with that?" asked Aleta, pointing at the box.

"We put the cheesecloth in the bottom of it," said Katie. "I remember seeing my mama do it. Then fold it over the top and put the slab of wood over it with weights on top. It will press down on the curds and slowly push all the rest of the whey out of those little holes on the sides of the box until the curds get hard."

"Won't it make a mess?" said Aleta, following Katie outside.

"We'll put it outside, on the worktable next to the kitchen," said Katie. "The whey will drain out through the cloth."

"I remember now too," I said. "That's exactly how Josepha did it."

"I saw her do dat once afore I left too," said Emma. "Why din't I eber see you dere, Miz Mayme?"

"I don't know, Emma," I answered. "But I don't reckon I was up at the big house more than once a year. You must have come after the last time I was there. Where'd you come from before Master McSimmons bought you?"

"I don' know, someplace ober yonder. I got bought an' sold all da time. I reckon dey din't think I was too full a wits fer a house slave."

"Do you know how long you have to leave it?" I asked Katie as Emma and I watched.

"Let me look," said Katie, going back to the book.

"It says to press it for ten hours, then cover it for four days, then turn it over and rub it all down with salt, and then let it sit for six months."

"Six months!" I said. "We'll be out of cheese way before that."

"You can eat it anytime, it says, but it gets better as it gets older."

"You take the press out to the table and I'll carry the cloth outside," I said.

Twenty minutes later our first slab of cheese was sitting under the press, with clear whitish liquid slowly oozing out the sides of the box onto the table.

"Now it's time to clean up the mess we made!" I said as we all walked back inside.

"We should make cheese every day, or at least every two days," said Katie. "Now that we know how to do it, there's no reason to waste the milk."

"And we need it to eat!" I said.

"Why do you talk about your mama like she's never coming back?" Aleta asked abruptly. The question took Katie off guard. Neither of us had noticed that we'd been talking more freely than we realized. We also realized that Aleta had more natural curiosity than Emma, and that we'd likely have to answer her questions eventually.

Katie glanced at me with a concerned look. Then she looked back at Aleta.

"I'll tell you all about it," she said. "Just not today. Can you be patient and let me tell you another—"

# INTERRUPTION 29

SUDDENLY WE HEARD A KNOCK ON THE DOOR.

We all stopped right where we were. Katie and I glanced at each other with wide eyes. The kitchen was silent as a tomb. We'd been so involved in the cheese making that we hadn't heard any horse or buggy approaching. And we'd been outside just a minute earlier.

Katie looked at me again, then slowly began moving toward the door. I didn't know whether we should all scatter and hide or stay where we were and pretend that nothing was wrong. But it was too late to hide anyway—there we were, all messy and with our sleeves rolled up, and there was the figure of whoever it was standing at the window of the kitchen door.

Slowly Katie opened the door. Standing in front of her was the last person we'd expected to see . . . Henry's Jeremiah.

"Afternoon t' you, Miz Clairborne," he said. "My pa

thought dat you might be needin' dat bridle ob yers fixed so it don' break on you."

Still taken by surprise, Katie just stood there for a second or two. From where I was standing on the other side of the room, I saw that he was holding some leather and tools.

"Is . . . uh, Miz Mayme here?" he asked.

I heard the question in his deep voice. I don't know if he saw me or not, but my heart started beating faster the minute he said my name. I didn't know why. In the middle of my thoughts, I heard my name again. But this time it was Katie.

"Mayme . . . Mayme," she was saying. "Henry's son . . . uh, Jeremiah brought a piece of leather to mend that broken bridle—would you show him where it is . . . in the barn?"

I could tell from her voice that she was nervous—especially after what she'd told me after her last trip into town, that she'd had the feeling that Henry knew all about us. I knew she didn't want anyone, least of all someone who was curious, looking too closely at what was going on inside the kitchen—though he was standing right there at the open door. In Katie's mind I was the logical one to get him away from the house.

I walked toward the door and outside. The instant I was on the porch Katie shut the door behind me. I was left alone with Jeremiah.

I didn't look at him but walked down the steps and toward the barn. He followed. I glanced back and saw Katie's face in the window.

"Where's your horse?" I asked.

"Don' have one, Miz Mayme," he said. "I walked."

"All the way from town?"

"Yes'm."

"That's a long way."

"My pa thought Miz Clairborne might be needin' dat bridle. He's been worried it would break."

I thought to myself that I wished Henry showed a little less concern about us.

"An' I been wantin' a chance t' try ter see Miz Clairborne an' yerse'f agin," he added, speaking slowly. Heat rose up the back of my neck. I didn't say anything and didn't dare glance over at him.

"Ain't too many young folks my age 'bout town," he said. "Leastways, no coloreds. Now dat we're free, dey all lef', I reckon.—Is you free too, Miz Mayme?"

"I reckon so," I said. "I heard about that proclamation, whatever it's called."

"Why you still here, den?"

"Where else would I be?"

"Why ain't you lef'?"

"I've got no place to go. This is my home."

"Your ma an' pa here too?"

"No."

"Where are dey?"

"I don't know."

"Don' you want ter fin' dem, now dat yer free?"

"I can't find them," I said. I was getting uncomfortable with so many questions, especially about my kin. "I told you—this is my home. I don't have anyplace else to go. I don't want to go someplace else."

"Mister an' Mistress Clairborne pay you?" he asked.

The question took me off guard. I didn't know what to say.

"I've got all I need," I said. "I've got food and a bed, and . . ." I paused briefly, ". . . and folks who care about me."

"Yep . . . I reckon dat's mighty important."

"And I feel like I'm needed," I added. "And Katie . . . I mean, Miss Clairborne needs me."

I don't know why I was talking so much, but I realized it was easy to talk to him. We'd already reached the barn but had unconsciously stopped while we kept talking. I'd been around plenty of boys of my own color. But this was so different from any situation I'd ever been in before in my life . . . just *talking* to a black boy my own age. Back at the colored town where I'd lived, if I'd been standing together with a black boy like Jeremiah, we wouldn't have been talking. We'd have been standing there keeping our mouths shut, while some white man looked us over wondering what kind of babies we'd make together.

But now we were just two people . . . two *free* people. Nobody was watching us. Nobody was thinking anything. And we could just talk. It felt strange, but good.

"Dey really *need* you?" asked Jeremiah. His voice sounded like he'd never considered such a thing—that a white person could need a black person. "And you think Miz Clairborne cares 'bout you? You make it soun' like yer frien's."

"We are," I said with a little laugh. "What's so strange about that?"

"I jes' neber considered dat afore, I reckon."

"Miss Katie couldn't get by without me . . . or me without her either. I don't know what would become of us if we hadn't—"

I stopped myself, realizing I'd gone too far. Feeling comfortable talking to Jeremiah was one thing, but what was I thinking!

"I mean . . . *they* . . ." I said, fumbling to correct myself, "—*they* took me in and helped me, and . . . well, that's all."

Again I stopped. He was looking at me funny.

"What do you mean . . . took you in?" he said. "Din't you used ter be one ob dere slaves?"

"Uh . . . yes . . . that's what I meant to say. I mean, they let me stay after I was free."

"Where's Mister and Mistress Clairborne?" he asked. "My pa wanted me t' ask dem somethin' fer him."

"Katie's pa ain't back—"

"What about Mistress Clairborne—she in da house? I din't see nobody but jes' two other girls, an' one ob dem was colored."

"She's . . . she's somewhere and it ain't . . . well, it ain't none of your business where she is," I said. Then I turned and led the way into the barn. "Here's that bridle," I went on. "Just fix it and mind your own business."

He set about his work with the straps of leather and few tools he had. I saw him looking around the barn. I knew he was noticing things—maybe we'd done a few things wrong, but at least it was pretty clean.

I walked outside, more mad at myself than at him. I hoped I hadn't got us into a worse fix than we were already in.

I went back to the kitchen where Katie and the others were waiting for me. Katie sent me a look of question and I just shrugged.

"I don't think he'll be too long," I said. "We can finish the cheese when he's gone."

Then I went back outside and waited on the porch. I didn't figure it'd do anybody any good for him to come snooping around looking inside again.

Five or ten minutes later I saw him coming out of the barn. I got up and walked over to meet him.

"Got it mended," he said. "Reckon I'll jes' tell Miz Clairborne."

I didn't like the idea of him looking into the kitchen again, but after what had happened I figured I'd better not protest too much.

We walked in silence back to the house. He climbed the steps and knocked on the door again. Katie had been watching and immediately opened it.

"Bridle's fixed, Miz Clairborne," he said.

"Thank you."

"Anything else you'd like done aroun' da place?"

"Uh, no . . . but thank you," said Katie. Then without waiting for anything further, she closed the door, leaving me to get rid of Jeremiah by myself.

Slowly he came back down the three or four steps.

"Well . . . reckon I'll be headin' back t' town," he said slowly. "You, uh . . . you min' if I come out agin?"

"I don't think Miss Katie, I mean Miss Clairborne—" I started to say.

"No, Miz Mayme . . . I mean, does *you* min' if I comes fer a visit?"

"What would you want to visit for?"

"I thought maybe I'd come t' visit you, dat's all. An' my pa, he said dat if I asked 'bout Mistress Clairborne an' got no answer 'bout where she was an' din't see her wiff my own eyes—an' I wasn't sure what he meant, but dat's what he said, an' he was serious when he said it—dat he wanted me ter make sure you young ladies was all right."

"What did he mean by that?" I said.

"Nuthin', miss . . . just what I said. Dat's why he wanted me t' come out an' men' dat bridle, 'cause he wanted t' know if you an' Miz Clairborne was all right."

"Well. you can tell him that we're fine," I said. "And that he ought to mind his own business too."

I shouldn't have said it. But it was clear enough that Henry was thinking more than either he or Jeremiah was saying.

Jeremiah looked at me real funny, then nodded and shrugged and turned and started walking along the road back toward town. I watched him a minute, then suddenly ran after him.

"Jeremiah!" I called out.

He stopped and turned back toward me.

"Please . . . don't tell," I said.

"Tell what?"

"What you saw here—who you saw in the kitchen . . . what you said before about only seeing us girls."

He looked at me seriously, and it was the first time we'd both looked in each other's eyes.

"What you really want me not t' say," he said after a few seconds, "is what I *ain't* seen, an' dat's Mistress Clairborne—ain't dat right, Miz Mayme?"

"Please," I said without really answering him, "you *can't* tell. Please promise you won't tell anyone."

"Dat's a hard one, Miz Mayme," he said finally. "Reckon I'll have t' think on dat some on my way home."

# The Rest of the World
# 30

I went back inside and was a little sober as we cleaned up the mess from the cheese making. Aleta and Emma didn't think any more about it, but Katie and I knew that Jeremiah's visit could change everything, and we talked about it later when we were alone. We were pretty sure that someone from town now knew how it was at Rosewood, someone we'd just barely met. I was especially worried, since it was my fault for blabbing out what I had. I was afraid he'd tell his pa, and I didn't know what Henry might do.

But the days went by, and then a week, and no one else came to call, and I gradually began to think that Jeremiah might not tell after all.

It was a good thing Katie had bought the newspaper when she'd been in Mrs. Hammond's store that day. From it we found out a lot about what was going on that we might never have known.

The newspaper sat where Katie put it on the sideboard

in the parlor for several days, along with various farm magazines and almanacs. I'd seen her come home with it. I don't know what made me notice it one day and pick it up. Maybe I just got curious. I sat down to see if I could read any of it. I could make out a lot of the words, but I couldn't understand much of what they were talking about.

Katie came and sat down beside me and started looking it over.

"Tell me what it says," I said. "Read something to me. I've never heard what a newspaper sounds like."

She looked it over, then started to read.

"It says here that a lot of black people are moving about," she said. " 'Now that the war is over,' " she read, " 'the flow of former slaves into the Northern states has slowed, though many freedmen are still migrating in search of work. With the South in shambles from the fighting, and with resentment of whites high, jobs for free blacks are scarce. Opportunities in the cities of the North, however, remain plentiful.' "

She stopped and looked over at me.

"Keep reading," I said. "That's interesting."

" 'The economy of the South has been dealt a serious blow,' " she continued. " 'Many plantation owners are having difficulty harvesting their cotton, tobacco, and sugar cane crops from lack of slave labor. Some are predicting an entire collapse of the former Confederacy. Confederate paper money is now worthless, and Congress is considering the best course of action for the reconstruction of the ravaged South.

" 'At the same time, there is evidence of an increased incidence of racial violence of whites, not only toward

Negroes but toward whites and plantation owners who are seen as sympathetic to the Negro cause. Lynchings of Negroes and burning of white homes have been widespread. The violence of marauding bands of former deserters and renegades which spread during the closing stages of the war is reportedly on the decline.' "

She looked up from the paper again and we glanced at each other, both reminded that we were part of all this, whether we'd known much about the war or not.

As we sat with Katie reading the paper out loud, Aleta came into the room and listened for a while. Pretty soon she started asking questions. I'd never realized how much Katie knew about things until she started answering Aleta's questions. It was like all the schooling and teaching she'd had when she was little all of a sudden started coming out, and now *she* was teaching *us*.

"Where did slaves come from?" Aleta had just asked.

"They are—were—the workers on the farms and plantations," Katie answered. "It takes a lot of workers to grow things."

"Why was there a war?"

"Because the South had slaves and the North didn't. When Mr. Lincoln started talking about setting the slaves free, the South didn't like it and decided to start its own country. Then war started."

"Who's Mr. Lincoln?" said Aleta. "I heard my father say he hated him."

As we sat on the couch, now Emma wandered into the room and stood listening.

"He's the president," answered Katie.

"What's a president?"

"He's the leader of our country. Our first president was George Washington. That was way back in the last century when the United States was a brand-new country. But we've had lots of presidents since then, and Mr. Lincoln is president now."

"But what's this, Katie?" I asked, pointing to some big black letters on the page. "Doesn't that say President *Johnson*?"

"Yes . . . yes, it does," Katie replied, looking at it. "I don't know why."

She looked over the paper for a bit. All of a sudden she gave a little gasp, then started reading more intently.

" 'With the death of John Wilkes Booth, murderer of President Lincoln at Ford's Theatre on April fourteenth,' " she read aloud, " 'and last month's trial and hangings of the other conspirators in the assassination, the administration of President Johnson is at last able to focus all its attention on putting the nation back together.' "

"What does all that mean?" asked Aleta.

"It must mean that President Lincoln was killed," said Katie.

We all sat for a minute in somber silence. Just when I'd found out I was free, and that this was the man responsible for freeing me, now I found out that he was dead. It didn't seem right. So many people were dead because of this war!

All of a sudden the paper wasn't so interesting. Katie set it aside and we all sat there for a minute, then gradually got up and went back to our work. The rest of the day was kind of quiet. We hadn't known much about President Lincoln. But if he was the president, and he had set the slaves free, then he must have been a great man. It wasn't right that he'd been killed.

After that we thought we oughta read a newspaper once a month. Doing what we were doing, we needed to know what was going on in the country around us. Of course, when I say that we oughta read it, I meant that *Katie* read it. I was learning, and tried a little, but newspapers were still too hard for me. But I was still reading in the readers and simpler books Katie gave me to read.

As the summer progressed it got hotter. It rained enough to keep the grass growing for the cows. We went and looked at the planted fields every few days and everything was growing fast by now, though we didn't know what we would do with it later. The cotton was full of weeds and I knew that was bad. But I didn't see what just two of us could do about it.

I found myself thinking every once in a while about Jeremiah. But every time I did, it made me confused. I was glad we hadn't seen any more of him. The more time that passed, the more sure I became that he hadn't told Henry anything to make him more suspicious than he already seemed to be.

So I didn't want to see him for fear of him raising awkward questions we couldn't answer. But every once in a while I'd find myself glancing along the road, or listening to see if someone was coming, halfway hoping it might be him. And more than once I found his face and voice coming to my mind.

Gradually we kept working more and more parts of the plantation. Now that it was summer and there was so much to do, we worked sunup to sundown. Katie was showing

Aleta and Emma how to tend the vegetable garden, and we were starting to have lots of fresh vegetables. We canned as much as we could for next winter, and dried some of it. Fruit was coming on too, peaches and strawberries first, though apples and the wild berries weren't ripe yet. The iceman came regularly now as we were going through the ice faster. So far he hadn't seemed to mind that he hadn't seen Katie's mother. Since Katie was paying him now, he didn't seem to ask too many questions. William was growing like a weed, and Emma was looking a lot healthier herself.

We continued to make cheese every few days and started to get a good supply built up. Most of the things in the root cellar from last year were either gone or spoiled, but now we started collecting a new supply from this year's onions, potatoes, turnips, sweet potatoes, carrots, cabbages, and squash, though we wouldn't be able to harvest most things till a little later. We were about out of honey too, so we smoked the bees out of a couple of nests and collected what we could. Emma was scared to go with us and stayed back at the house, and Aleta ran around as terrified and excited as one of the bees herself. We continued to churn butter, which we stored in the root cellar in a big barrel of well water. We still had some corned meat in the brine barrel left over from Katie's mama. What we would do when we ran out, I didn't know. The only animals we'd had to kill so far were a few chickens. But we didn't eat that much meat, except for the poultry.

The cows kept milking, though with the heat they weren't giving as much milk. We ate a lot of johnnycakes, though I knew we would have to resupply the corn bin before next winter or we'd run out of corn too.

All the hard work was showing in Katie. She was getting stronger and was becoming tan and hardy. I could see her changing in so many ways. Though every once in a while, out of the corner of my eye, I'd see her stop for a few seconds and wipe her hair back out of her face and let out a sigh that almost seemed to say, *It never used to be this hard around here!* But she didn't lose her composure anymore.

Then she'd always go right back to work without complaining. I think she knew she had to stay strong for the sake of Aleta and Emma. Even though Emma was a mama, in so many ways it was like having two young'uns to take care of. Without Katie telling her what to do, Emma was just about as helpless a creature as I'd ever seen.

# Alone With My Thoughts

THE SUMMER WENT BY AND SOMEHOW WE MANaged to survive and no one bothered us. Though the work was hard sometimes, it wasn't anything like it used to be for me, and we had enough of a routine by then that the days seemed almost normal. Working hard as a free person was a lot different than working as a slave.

"Katie," I asked one morning, "what day is today?"

"Uh, Tuesday, I think," she said.

"I mean the number of the day."

"You mean the date," she said and went and looked at the calendar.

We hadn't paid that much attention to the days and weeks, and I hardly knew how to read a calendar. Mostly we'd been keeping some track of the time by getting newspapers once in a while, but Katie had only been into town twice more.

"It's August twenty-second, Mayme," said Katie. "That is, if it's Tuesday."

I smiled.

"Tomorrow's my birthday," I said.

"Mayme, why didn't you tell me? How old are you going to be?"

"Sixteen."

"That's old, Mayme. You're practically a grown-up!"

I laughed.

"You're a year older than me again," she said.

"Not a whole year."

"Well, it sounds like a year.—We will make you a cake."

"You don't have to do that."

"I want to! We'll have a party and dance and sing again. Let's teach Aleta the slave songs!"

I laughed to hear Katie getting all excited.

"Do you think she'll sing them?" I asked.

"She likes you now, Mayme. She just had a daddy that didn't understand about black people. But she's getting over it."

"She's still a mite distant from Emma."

"That's true, but Emma's different from you, Mayme. It's funny to think that she was a house slave, but you weren't, when you seem to know a lot more than she does. I thought house slaves were usually the smartest."

"Not necessarily," I said. "Sometimes it was all because of looks or manners—they'd put slaves in houses that were lighter in skin color or were the prettiest. I know my skin ain't so dark as some, but I sure ain't pretty."

"I think you are, Mayme."

"That's nice of you to say, Katie, but most white folks aren't of the same mind when they look at me."

Telling Katie I had a birthday coming was all she

needed. She ran off to tell Emma and Aleta what she'd found out and what she wanted to do. For the rest of that day, she and the other two had all kinds of secrets. Katie would tell me to stay out of the kitchen, and then I'd see her running upstairs and she'd glance at me and giggle and tell me to mind my own business.

I began to wish I'd never said anything about my birthday!

When I woke up the next morning, I heard Katie already downstairs. I got dressed and went down. Aleta was still asleep, and Emma sat in a chair nursing William and watching Katie.

"Good morning, Katie," I said as I walked into the kitchen.

"Happy birthday, Mayme!" she said, glancing toward me from the counter, where her hands were full of flour. "I'm starting on your cake. I hope it won't be a flop."

"Happy birf'day, Miz Mayme."

"Thank you, Emma."

"Are you sure you don't want any help?" I asked.

"But it's your birthday cake!" she laughed.

"I can still help."

Then Katie got a serious expression on her face and looked at me, still stirring the batter.

"You've done so much for me, Mayme," she said. "I want to see if I can do this for you all by myself. I know it's only a cake, but there aren't many ways to show you how grateful I am. So maybe this is something I can do that will mean more than just being a cake."

Her words warmed my heart so much!

"I understand, Katie," I nodded. "That's real nice of you

to say. I'll look forward to it. But you won't make me eat it all by myself, will you? You're going to share it with me?"

"Oh yes! I'll make it, but we will all eat it!"

I went outside. It was still early. The sun was up and it was already warm, but it was that early morning kind of quiet. I took in a deep lungful of the warm air and looked around.

I thought I'd like to go on a walk, a birthday walk, just to be alone for a while. I went back inside.

"Katie," I said, "would you mind if I went to your special place in the woods?"

"Oh no, Mayme. I would like you to go there."

"Thank you," I said.

"That will be my birthday present to you," said Katie. "From now on it will be your special place too."

I went back outside and walked slowly to the woods.

Everything felt so fresh early in the morning like this. Even the woods felt different. There was still dew on the grass. Some of the pine trees were so wet that drops of water dangled from their needle tips, waiting to fall. Birds were everywhere in the trees, chirping and singing. I saw one little rabbit scamper by in the distance. Then I remembered how Katie said animals came to her secret place more at night and in the early morning than any other time. So as I crept through the trees, I tried to be real quiet.

I got to the opening into the little meadow, tiptoeing as softly as I could.

There was a deer standing drinking from the stream!

And the raccoon Katie had told me about was a little ways behind it, walking slowly across the grass!

I stood there watching, not making a sound.

Black folks loved to catch raccoons to eat. But I couldn't imagine eating either of those two beautiful creatures.

As I watched, the raccoon ambled off and into the woods with his hind end up in the air and wobbling back and forth.

After another minute the deer raised his head. I don't know how, but he seemed to sense that I was there. He looked toward me and just stood. For a minute it almost felt as if our eyes were seeing into each other. He didn't make a sound or twitch a muscle for the longest time. Then all of a sudden he bounded away and was gone.

I sat down on one of the big rocks and started thinking. This was my first birthday without my family. Maybe Katie was right in what she said about me growing up. Of course, no one grows up on one day more than any other. Just because this day was August twenty-third didn't mean I would do more growing than I had yesterday. But birthdays help you look at yourself every year and kinda take stock of where you've come from.

More important, I reckon, they give you a chance to ask yourself where you're going.

So many changes had come in my life in the last few months—both bad and good, I reckon—that I couldn't help getting confused every now and then about just who I was . . . who I was supposed to be. Just a few months ago I'd been a black slave girl worried about getting sold or whipped or bedded down by some boy a few years older than me. All of a sudden my whole family was dead, I wasn't a slave anymore, and I was living with a white girl, trying to pretend we were running a white man's plantation.

That's a lot of changes in a big hurry!

But deep down inside, was I still the same person? I felt the same in some ways . . . but different in others.

Who was I anyway? What did the words *Mary Ann Jukes* really mean? If sometime after I was dead and gone, somebody heard that name, what would they think? What kind of person would they say Mayme Jukes had been?

For the first time in my life, I had to try to figure out who I was apart from my parents and my brothers and sisters, apart from Master McSimmons, even apart from Katie . . . who was I just for *myself*? I guess Katie and I had to think about that more than most folks. I figure it's something everybody's gotta face sometime in their life—who they are. But me and Katie got put in a situation where we had to think about it sooner than most. I don't know if Katie was thinking of such things yet. But then I was a little older, so I figured I oughta be thinking about them sooner.

Then it occurred to me that maybe when you're trying to figure out who you are and what your life means, it's not enough to ask it just for yourself. There was one person who would always be with you no matter what happened. Even if everybody else in the world deserted you, or even died, He'd still be with you.

That person was God.

So maybe when a body was trying to figure out who they were and what their life meant, He was the one to ask to help figure it out.

"God," I said quietly. "What is going to become of me? What kind of person do you want me to be? Who do you want me to be down inside?"

I drew in a deep breath in the quiet morning and kept staring into the stream as it gurgled and trickled past me.

Then the thought came to me, and I don't know if it was an answer to the question I had just asked or not. But what came into my mind were the words, *I want you to be my daughter. That's the kind of person I want you to be. And I want to share your life with you.*

I remembered hearing some of the excitable colored preachers talking about the voice of the Lord calling out from heaven. Whenever I heard them talk that way it always made me a little afraid. I thought it would be like thunder or lightning or something.

But if God had just spoken to me as I sat there in the woods, it wasn't anything like that. It had been soft and still, the kind of voice I probably wouldn't have heard unless I was being real quiet myself. It reminded me of the early morning when I felt God telling me to stay at Rosewood.

And it felt good inside.

# A Special Birthday

# 32

When I got back to the house, I'd probably been gone an hour. Katie was still in the kitchen and was just pouring the cake into the pan to bake.

"I'll go get started on the cows," I said.

"I'll be out to help in a few minutes," said Katie.

Most of the rest of the morning went pretty normal. Katie had made a stew and was roasting sweet potatoes from the root cellar to go with the cake. She wouldn't let me help with any of it, though she asked me a few questions about what to do now and then.

We ate early in the afternoon and then had the cake. Katie had made sugar icing to spread all over the top of it, and had written the words *Mary Ann Jukes* in a thin line of brown molasses over the top of it. It was real good too! I ate so much I thought I would pop. Besides the cake, Katie had made candy.

"They're called molasses chews," she said as I ate one

and got it stuck in my teeth. "It's heated molasses and butter. Emma and I made them yesterday. That's why we had to keep you out of the kitchen."

"You helped make these, Emma?" I asked.

"Dat I did, Miz Mayme," replied Emma proudly.

"Well, thank you—they're really good."

"Now, stay right here," said Katie. "I'll go get your present!"

She jumped up from the table and ran upstairs and came back a minute later.

She handed me a little box. I shook it and heard a jingling sound. I opened it, and it was full of coins.

"But . . . this looks like a lot of money!"

"It's only a dollar," said Katie. "You enjoyed buying that handkerchief so much, I wanted you to have enough that you could buy yourself a really special birthday gift, either at Mrs. Hammond's or that same store where you got your handkerchief."

"But . . . a dollar!" I said. "You only had a dollar and thirty-seven cents left over from Mrs. Hammond's. You can't give me this much."

"And the ten dollars from the bank, Mayme. We've got lots of that left."

"I found some more money in the cigar box in the pantry," she said. "I don't know why I didn't think to look there sooner. There was a little over two dollars in it."

"That's still not enough to pay back what you owe that man at the bank."

"I want you to have this," Katie insisted. "I want you to get something nice with it. You are free now, and so you deserve to have some money of your very own."

I sat staring down at the little pile of coins in my hand.

"Do you think . . ." I began, then hesitated.

"Do you know what I'd like more than anything?" I said again. "I'd like to put this money in the bank. Do you think they'd let me open a bank account of my own?"

"I don't see why not," said Katie.

"That would make me feel real proud, like a real person, not a slave."

"I think it's a good idea, Mayme.—I have something else for you too," said Katie.

She got up again and went to the bookcase. She pulled a sheet of paper out of a book where she'd hidden it. She came back with a serious look on her face.

"I wrote a poem for you," said Katie. Her voice was quiet now as she handed me the paper.

This is what I read:

*"To My Friend.*
*May I tell you of something that is better than gold?*
*It will still be with you long after you're old.*
*It's a treasure that increases the more of it you spend.*
*I'm speaking, of course, of love for a friend.*
*When you discover that treasure, what will you find?*
*If you're seeking true friendship, look for this kind:*
*A friend is someone who knows about you what you yourself don't know.*
*A friend sees your faults and still likes you, and helps you grow.*
*A friend is someone you can talk to about things you wouldn't tell another soul.*
*A friend is someone you like to be with because they make you feel whole.*

*A friend is someone you can laugh with, cry with, and is always true.*
*A friend is someone you know who loves you, and that you love too.*
*Now let me tell you about my special friend,*
*Who came and helped my heart's grief to mend.*
*She lifted my spirits, though our past lives were dead,*
*Now we're trying, like sisters, to look ahead.*
*When He sent this wonderful person to me,*
*God gave me a gift that turned I into we.*
*If I had the riches of the whole world to spend,*
*It wouldn't compare with having you for my friend."*

I was crying long before I finished reading it.

"Thank you, Katie," I said. "That's the most beautiful thing anybody's ever said to me in my life. I won't ever forget this."

It was quiet a minute. I sniffed a few times and wiped my eyes. The next voice I heard took me by surprise.

"I don't have anything that nice to give you, Mayme," said Aleta softly. "But I made you this."

She now handed me a paper too, with a pencil picture on it. It was of four girls walking along, two white, two black. They were all holding hands. On the bottom it said, *Four Sisters.*

"Did you draw this, Aleta?" I asked.

"Yes. I made it for you, Mayme."

"Oh, Aleta—thank you," I said. "It's wonderful. It is just as special to me as Katie's poem. In fact, I think they should always stay together, don't you? You have made a picture of what the poem says."

"I'm sorry I was mean to you before," said Aleta,

looking into my eyes and then starting to cry. "Katie was right," she said. "You are nice."

I opened my arms and she came to me and we held each other for a minute.

Katie looked away, tears filling her eyes.

"I din't make you nuthin', Miz Mayme," said Emma. "I'm sorry. I don' know how ter make nuthin' wiff my hands like Miz Katie an' Miz Aleta does."

"What are you talking about, Emma?" I said. "You made me that delicious candy. That was a wonderful present."

"Dat's right, I guess I did at dat."

"And maybe I'll just ask you to make me some more when it's gone!"

"Oh, I kin do dat!" said Emma with a big smile of pride. "I's make you mo as soon as dat's all gone."

Slowly Katie got up and went to the piano and began playing quietly. Pretty soon she was softly singing.

*"How dear to my heart are the scenes of my childhood,*
*when fond recollection presents them to view."*

Aleta and I smiled at each other, wiped our eyes, and walked over and stood by the piano as Katie continued to sing. Pretty soon Emma was humming softly and rocking William gently in her arms where she stood.

*"The orchard, the meadow, the deep tangled wildwood,*
*and every love spot which my infancy knew.*
*The wide spreading pond, and the mill that stood by it.*
*The bridge and the rock where the cataract fell.*
*The cot of my father, the dairy house nigh it,*

*and e'en the rude bucket that hung in the well.*
*The old oaken bucket, the ironbound bucket.*
*The moss covered bucket that hung in the well."*

The nostalgic tune made us all quiet for a few seconds as the music and Katie's voice faded away. But Aleta was full of energy and immediately clamored for another song.

This time Katie started playing fast and lively.

*"I come from Alabama with my banjo on my knee,*
*I'm g'wan to Lousiana, my true love for to see."*

"Sing with me, Aleta!" she said.

*"Oh, Susanna, oh, don't you cry for me.*
*I've come from Alabama with my banjo on my knee.*
*It rained all night the day I left, the weather it was dry.*
*The sun so hot I froze to death, Susanna, don't you cry."*

Now Aleta and I joined in.

*"Oh, Susanna, oh, don't you cry for me.*
*I've come from Alabama with my banjo on my knee."*

"That's silly!" laughed Aleta when the song ended.

"It's not supposed to make sense," said Katie. "You teach us one now, Mayme."

I thought a minute, then I started singing. My song was slower and more sad-sounding than Katie's had been, especially without the piano. My voice was lower than Katie's too.

"Sing with me, Emma," I said, "if you know it."

*"We planted this cotton in April,"* I began, *"on the full of the moon.*

*We've had a hot, dry summer. That's why it opened so soon.*
*Cotton needs a-pickin' so bad, cotton needs a-pickin' so bad,*
*Cotton needs a-pickin' so bad, gonna pick all over this field."*

By now Emma was joining in and I was amazed. Her voice was beautiful. Before we were done, she was already wandering all around with harmonies I never even knew the song had.

*"Boy, stop goosin' that cotton, and take better care.*
*Make haste, you lazy rascal, and bring that row from there.*
*Cotton needs a-pickin' so bad, cotton needs a-pickin' so bad,*
*Cotton needs a-pickin' so bad, gonna pick all over this field.*

*"Hurry up, hurry up, children, we ought to have been gone.*
*The weather looks so cloudy, and I think it's goin' to storm.*
*Cotton needs a-pickin' so bad, cotton needs a-pickin' so bad,*
*Cotton needs a-pickin' so bad, gonna pick all over this field."*

"That was so beautiful!" said Katie. "How did you learn to sing like that, Emma?"

"I din't learn it no place, Miz Katie. It jes' comes outta me, dat's all."

"Well, it's just about the prettiest music I ever heard.

The two of you sounded like a choir, didn't they, Aleta? It makes me feel almost like I was out in the fields picking cotton myself."

"Be glad you're not," I said. "It ain't fun at all."

"Can we sing another one?" Aleta asked.

Katie turned the pages of her songbook. Here's a good one—do you know it?"

*"She'll be coming round the mountain when she comes.*
*She'll be coming round the mountain when she comes.*
*She'll be coming round the mountain, she'll be coming round the mountain, she'll be coming round the mountain when she comes."*

"Let's do it again," said Katie. "This time you both sing with me."

She started playing and we repeated it twice more.

"Now it's our turn again, Mayme," said Katie.

I stopped to think a minute.

"All right, here's one," I said.

*"Oh, Lord, I want . . . two wings to veil my face.*
*Oh, Lord, I want . . . two wings to fly away.*
*Oh, Lord, I want . . . two wings to veil my face.*
*So the devil can't do me no harm."*

"That part's the chorus," I said.

"I know it . . . I know it, Miz Mayme!" exclaimed Emma.

"Good, then you help me teach Miss Katie and Aleta.—Now here comes the verse, so everyone's gotta help."

*"My Lord, did he come at the break of day?"*

I sang and Emma joined in with me.

"Now you shout, 'No!'—I'll sing my part again—"

*"My Lord, did he come at the break of day?"*

Katie and Aleta shouted, *"No!"*

*"My Lord, did he come in the heat of noon?—No!*
*My Lord, did he come in the cool of the evening?"*

"Now the answer's yes!" I said.

We all shouted *"Yes!"*

And as we came to the last line, I quieted way down so that Emma could sing it herself.

*"And he washed my sins away!"*

"Let's do it again!" said Aleta, laughing. "Please . . . can we do it again!"

"Wait . . . sing a little again, Mayme, Emma," said Katie. "Let me see if I can find the tune on the piano."

After a few minutes of experimenting, Katie was playing the whole song, but in what she called a different key, which made it so that I had to sing it a little higher than before. I had a pretty low voice compared to either Emma's or Katie's, so when I sang the words "two wings," it was about as high as my voice would reach. But with Emma's voice along with me, it was just right. Then we all sang it together.

*"Oh, Lord, I want . . . two wings to veil my face.*
*Oh, Lord, I want . . . two wings to fly away.*

*Oh, Lord, I want . . . two wings to veil my face.*
*So the devil can't do me no harm.*

*My Lord, did He come at the break of day?—No!*
*My Lord, did He come in the heat of noon?—No!*
*My Lord, did He come in the cool of the evening?—Yes!*
*And He washed my sins away!"*

With Katie playing along on the piano and with two white voices and my low black girl's voice and Emma again singing harmony, it was just as pretty-sounding as you could imagine!

"Can we do the minuet again?" I asked Katie when we finished. "I really liked that last time."

"Yes, and we'll teach it to you, Aleta."

"What's a minuet?" she asked.

"A French dance," said Katie.

She played it through once, then got up from the piano.

"Now watch, Aleta, Emma," she said. "We will show you how it goes.—Do you remember it, Mayme?"

"Not all of it."

"Emma, why don't you set William down on the couch where he'll be safe? Then you join us."

"Yes'm, Miz Katie."

We all took hands and Katie led like before. Pretty soon I was remembering how it went, and we danced all around the room like we were a French prince and princess or something, though I don't know which one of us was which!

"Come, Aleta," said Katie, taking Aleta's two hands in hers. "I'll show you.—Emma, you and Mayme sing the tune while we dance."

We did, while Katie went through it once with Aleta, then went back to the piano.

While she played, now Emma and I took each other's hands. I couldn't remember it perfectly, but we tried it with Katie playing and calling out to us what to do, and gradually we got better.

Pretty soon we were all four laughing and dancing and taking turns dancing with Katie at the piano, or Katie dancing while we sang, and having more fun than we'd had since being together.

# Suspicious Caller
# 33

We were right in the middle of singing and dancing and had been making so much noise that we hadn't known anyone else was within miles.

All of a sudden we heard a knock on the front door.

We all froze. Katie's hands looked like they were stuck to the piano. The sounds of the music died away. I glanced over at her, wondering if I had just heard what I thought I'd heard, or if she'd kicked the piano or something. But the look on Katie's face told me instantly she'd heard it too.

Then the metal knocker sounded again on the wooden door.

*Bang! Bang! Bang!* it echoed through the house.

"There's somebody at the door," said Aleta. "Aren't you going to see who it is?"

Whoever it was had come to the front door rather than the back at the kitchen, where most folks came. So it must not be someone who came regularly.

"Quick, Aleta," said Katie, jumping up from the piano stool, "run upstairs to my room and be as quiet as you can."

"Why?"

"Never mind why. I'll tell you later."

Luckily Aleta didn't argue about it and ran for the stairs.

Katie glanced at me, and I knew we were both thinking the same thing—what to do with Emma!

"Emma," I whispered, "pick up William and come with me as fast as you can.—But," I added, quickly putting my finger to my lips because I saw that she was about to start talking, "—don't say a word. We can't make a sound."

I think she saw the danger from Katie's and my reaction to the knock on the door, and by now a terrified look came to her face and she did what I said. A few seconds later me and Emma, with William in her arms, hurried from the parlor into the kitchen and out the back door to go light the fire in the slave cabin, hoping we'd be good and out of sight from the front of the house.

When we were both gone, Katie tried to calm herself and walked to the door. There stood a man she had never seen before.

"Good day, miss," he said. "I'd like to see the mistress of the house."

"Yes, sir . . . my mother's not here."

"Will she be back soon?"

"Uh . . . probably not, sir."

"Well, I need to inform her of a serious disease that has infected the colored folk of this region," the man said. "With all the changes after the war and all, and with the coloreds moving about looking for work and going up North, we're trying to get word to everyone, especially plantation owners, to be on the lookout for any coloreds with newborns."

Katie tried to stay calm, but at the word "newborn" her eyes shot open wide.

"Why is that, sir?" she said, hoping her voice wasn't trembling.

"Because the disease affects only babies. You ain't got any blacks with infants here, do you?"

"Uh . . . no, sir. But how do you know what to look for?"

"We'd have to see it for ourselves. But what do you care . . . you sure you ain't seen no colored babies? Nobody's come by asking for help, nothing like that?"

"No, sir. I was just curious."

The man eyed her carefully.

"Well, just the same," he said. "I'll be back in a day or two to talk to your ma. We're trying to spread the word roundabout to be on the lookout for girls with babies so we can help them and put a stop to this thing."

"What happens if you don't?" asked Katie.

"The disease is fatal, miss. If they don't get to us for help, the babies will die."

Katie drew in a sharp breath of shock at the words. The man turned to go.

"I'll be back to see your ma," he said. "You tell her I'm coming and I'll explain to her all about it."

"But I told you," said Katie, trying to recover her composure, "we've got no baby here."

"I'm under orders to tell everyone, miss. So tell your ma I'll be back."

By the time I was walking up from the slave cabin, the

man was coming around back on his horse on the road north. I kept my head down and shuffled slowly by, but I don't think he even noticed. I'm not sure he saw the smoke from the fire either. As soon as he was past me I picked up my pace and hurried back to the house. Katie was hurrying out toward me at the same time.

"What did he want?" I asked.

"Where are Emma and William?" she asked excitedly, answering my question with a question of her own.

"Back there in the cabin," I said. "They're hiding. He won't see them."

Finally Katie started to calm down. Then she told me everything the man had said.

I thought about it for a minute. "I don't know," I said. "It sounds a mite suspicious to me."

"Why?" asked Katie.

"Because of everything Emma said about those men chasing her and trying to kill her. It sounds to me like somebody's trying to find her baby."

"But what if there really is a disease? Should we tell Emma what the man said? What if William is in danger?"

I thought for a minute more.

"I don't know," I said. "I don't like the thought of her getting all upset. I wish we could find out more about it first." As I said it, I glanced along the road to see which way the man had gone.

"We could go ask the doctor in town," suggested Katie.

"And call more attention to ourselves at the same time," I said. "I'd rather know more about this thing before we did that. If William really is in danger, why didn't that fellow say anything about a doctor?"

"That's right," said Katie, "he didn't."

"And if they're just after Emma, then we have to be careful because anything we do could put her in danger."

I glanced down the road again. The man was just disappearing from sight.

"Miss Katie," I said suddenly, "I'm going to go saddle two horses. We've got to follow him!"

"Why . . . you mean you and me?"

"Yep," I said, then I turned and ran for the barn.

"What about Emma and Aleta?" called Katie after me.

"They'll have to take care of themselves. You talk to them. We've got to know what's going on. But don't tell Emma why. She'd come orful streaked if she knew. Just tell them we'll be gone for a few hours."

# On the Heels of Danger

# 34

WE KNEW WE WERE TAKING A BIG RISK TO LEAVE Aleta and Emma alone. I'd gotten the horses ready in less than five minutes. Katie told Aleta and Emma just to be careful and on the lookout if anyone came, and to hide down in the cellar if they did. With Aleta there with her, even though she was just a girl, Emma didn't seem to be as afraid to be left alone as before.

We rode off quickly in the direction the man had gone until, about ten minutes later, we saw him in the distance. Then we slowed. He stopped at several other places along the way while we waited out of sight.

After his third stop, Katie had an idea.

"You wait here, Mayme," she said once he was out of sight again. "I'm going to go ask Mrs. Travis what he said."

"You know her?" I asked.

Katie nodded and rode off in the direction of the farmhouse. She dismounted and walked up to the door.

"Hello, Mrs. Travis," she said when the woman answered, "I don't know if you remember me—I'm Kathleen Clairborne, from over at Rosewood."

"Yes, hello, Kathleen," she said. "You've certainly grown since the last time I saw you. How is your mother?"

"Uh . . . not too well, ma'am," said Katie. "She wanted me to ask you if there has been a strange man about recently asking you questions."

"Why, yes, there has . . . he just left. He was asking if we had seen any coloreds with infants about."

"Did he say anything more?"

"Only that there was some disease going about and that they had to find all the colored babies in the area.—Why, Kathleen?"

"She just thought it seemed a little strange, that's all," said Katie, "and she wanted me to see if he had told you the same thing. Good-bye, Mrs. Travis."

"Just a minute, Kathleen," the lady called after her as Katie turned to go. "I have a question for you.—That strange fellow asking about colored babies isn't the only man who has been asking questions. Has the reverend been out to your place?"

"Reverend Hall . . . why, no, ma'am," said Katie, "—what about?"

"He was here just two days ago asking about some lady and her little girl. And you say he wasn't out to Rosewood?"

Katie shook her head.

"I don't know what it's all about. He wouldn't tell me who it was or why he was interested in them, but he had a serious expression on his face. Just seems like a strange coincidence, that's all."

Katie turned and walked back to her horse, leaving the bewildered woman staring after her, not sure what to make of Katie's visit after the other two she had had recently.

Katie rode back to where I was waiting for her out of sight and told me what she had heard.

"Do you think the minister's looking for Aleta?" I asked.

"I don't know. We'll have to worry about that later," said Katie. "What should we do now?"

"I guess there's nothing else for us to do," I said, "but to keep following him, that is if we want to know what he was doing."

After a few more stops, the man rode off in a direction that at first seemed to be toward Greens Crossing. As he got closer, Katie began wondering what we would do when he got into town. We couldn't follow him up close, or let people see us.

But then at the fork in the road, he turned off in the direction of Oakwood.

By now we had been gone more than an hour. We looked at each other, wondering what to do. But we had come this far without finding anything out. If we turned around now, we would know nothing. So we continued to follow.

But then suddenly everything changed when he turned off the road at the sign leading to the McSimmons plantation and my old home—and Emma's too, as we now realized.

Again we stopped. But by now our curiosity was so

high it didn't take us long to decide to keep going. After all Emma had said and what I knew myself, I was beginning to have even stronger suspicions than before. As we drew closer, we let the man get out of sight, and I began to get nervous all over again. I tried to tell myself that I had nothing to worry about and that I was free now and just like anyone else—white or black. But it didn't help. Because I knew there was still a difference, and I was on the bottom end of it.

"What are we going to do when we get there?" asked Katie as we rode. "We can't just go in and say we were following that man."

"First we have to find out if he's just coming here to ask about black babies like everywhere else," I said. "If so, then I reckon the McSimmons haven't got anything to do with him and then we ought to go up to him and tell him about Emma. But we have to find that out first."

"What will we say when we get there?"

"I thought we would just pretend to be paying Josepha a visit," I said.

"But what if they do something to you, Mayme?" Katie said in a worried tone.

"What can they do? I'm not their slave anymore, remember?"

"I know . . . but I just don't want anything to happen to you."

As we rode into the plantation and toward the big house, there was a lot more activity than the last time I was there. People and men and animals and wagons were all moving about. It reminded me of how it used to be, though I didn't see too many coloreds around.

We stopped and tied up our horses in front of the house. A few people looked at us, but no one said anything. I could tell Katie was nervous. I whispered to her that she didn't need to be, since no one knew her. But I guess I was nervous too. Having a secret, I suppose, always makes you nervous.

I led her around to the back of the house to the kitchen door, where I figured to find Josepha. I didn't see any sign of the man we'd been following.

The door was a little way open. I peeked in. Josepha stood with her back to me on the other side of the room. I walked in and Katie followed.

"Hello, Josepha!" I said, walking up to her.

Startled, she turned around. But when she saw me, the look on her face was completely different than the last time when she had been so happy to see me. I could see anxiety in her eyes.

"Mayme, chil'," she exclaimed, "wha'chu doin' here?"

"I came . . . for a visit, Josepha," I answered. "I wanted you to meet the mistress of the place where I'm staying now . . . I mean it's her mother and father's plantation.—This is Miss Katie Clairborne."

"I'm pleased ter mee'chu, Miz Clairborne," said Josepha, "—but chil'," she added, turning to me again, "you shouldna come."

"Why not?"

"Things is a heap different now wiff der old master gone."

"Where is he?" I asked.

"He be dead, chil'. Da poor old master, he died. An' now der young master William, he be married an' da new mistress, she don' like coloreds none, an' she an' he's different dan his daddy. An' effen she fin' me jabberin' wiff you, I's git a whuppin' fo' sho'."

"But you said you're not a slave anymore. How can they whip you?"

"Dey whips who's dey likes," she answered, shaking her head. "I may not be no slave, but dey act like dey neber heard ob no Lincoln or no 'mancipation proklimation or nuthin'. So you two's better skedaddle afore she sees you here."

"We wanted to know if a man's come around here asking about colored babies," I said.

Josepha's eyes narrowed. "What's all dis talk 'bout colored babies?"

"He says there's some disease only colored babies have."

"Who's dis man yo's talkin 'bout?"

"He came to Miss Katie's asking if we'd seen any black babies around."

"An' what did you tell him?" she said, her eyes squinting all the more.

"Uh, nothing," I answered. "But it just struck me as a mite curious that he'd be asking, that's all."

"Well, dere's black babies an' den dere's black babies," said Josepha cryptically, "an' some ob 'em ain't as black as dey seem, dat's all I be sayin'. An' dere ain' nuthin' I can tell you 'bout it, 'cause I ain't seen no sech man askin' no sech questions," she added.

"Do you mean—" I began, but she interrupted me with a wave of her big fleshy hand.

"I don' mean nuthin' mo dan da speculations ob some ole black folks what used ter be slaves dat oughta learn ter keep dere moufs shut. Ain't no black baby roun' here gwine come ter no good no how."

Suddenly a voice startled us all into silence. "Josepha!"

We turned to see a tall white lady walking into the room. How much of Josepha's previous speech she had heard, I don't know, but her eyes were on fire. She had a long thin face and wasn't pretty to my eyes. But Josepha was obviously cowed by the sight of her. Seeing Katie, she turned temporarily from the tongue-lashing she had apparently been about to deliver.

"Who are you?" she said abruptly.

"Uh, Kathleen, ma'am," mumbled Katie.

"What do you want . . . what are you doing in my home?"

"I, uh . . . we just came for a visit, ma'am," said Katie hesitantly.

"A visit—who are you visiting? I have never seen you before."

"No, ma'am. We were visiting Josepha."

"Josepha? What could you possibly want with her? She works for me, and it's precious little work I get out of her too, especially as long as she is standing here wagging her fat tongue to the likes of you. Well, speak up, girl—I asked you a question. What do you want with Josepha?"

"I don't . . . I mean, Mayme used to live here, ma'am . . . and she wanted to visit."

For the first time the woman now seemed to notice me. She turned and glared at me, sending her eyes up and down my front as if I was an object of scorn.

"*You* . . . used to live here?" she said, her voice suddenly very much changed.

"Yes'm," I said. "My family was all killed in the colored town yonder."

"Yes, the massacre—I'm aware of that. Why weren't you killed?"

"I escaped, ma'am."

"How?"

"I hid."

"And then what did you do?"

"I ran away."

She seemed to be thinking for a second, and after the way she'd been eyeing me as she drilled me with questions, I probably should have contemplated a little more directly what she might have been thinking about.

"Wait here!" she said, speaking like she was used to ordering people around, which from what Josepha had said, I guess she was.

If I'd have had my wits about me, I'd have run right then. But I didn't think about it, and I was afraid to do anything to get Josepha in trouble. As different as my outlook on life was by then, it didn't take much to intimidate me and make me start thinking like a slave again. And this lady was downright intimidating! So Katie and I just stood there like a couple of statues while the lady turned and walked out of the room. I could tell from the look Josepha gave me that she was worried for us. Maybe she and I weren't slaves anymore, but we were still afraid of what white folks could do to us.

None of us suspected what was coming. If she had known, Josepha would have run us out of that kitchen and made us get on our horses that instant no matter how many whippings it cost her. But she didn't know any more than I did, and so we all just stood there while William McSimmons' new wife disappeared into the next room.

# CAPTURED
# 35

I HAD NO IDEA THAT THE FATHER OF EMMA'S BABY was anywhere nearby until we heard the voices of the two McSimmons raised in argument from some other room of the house a minute or two later.

The doors must have been wide open between here and there, because their voices carried as if they were in the next room. I don't suppose they figured an old fat black woman and a young black former slave were human enough to worry about what they thought. And as for Katie, they had no idea who she was. For all they knew, she might have been what folks later called poor white trash. And from the way the lady spoke to us, I had already seen Katie start to retreat into what I call the old Katie, the way she was before she started to change and get more confident in herself. So the lady might have thought her an idiot too, for all I know. But as the couple argued it was clear they didn't care what any of us thought and whether we heard what they said.

All of a sudden I realized that they were talking about *me*!

"I'm just asking if there's any chance it could be her," said Mrs. McSimmons in a demanding voice.

Then I heard William's voice, though deeper and softer, so that it sounded a little muffled.

". . . don't see how . . . why would she . . . look like?"

"Ugly . . . ugly as sin," said the lady.

"Not likely, then."

". . . want you to make sure . . . if there's a chance . . ."

Then some conversation followed that I couldn't make out. Even now I don't know why we didn't scoot out of there while the two of them were arguing. Telling it like this stretches it out longer than it actually was, and it was happening fast. It's hard to describe how much a white person could make a black person go weak in the knees way back then. It was such a different world than we know now. So we just kept standing there as the danger crept closer and closer without us knowing it.

Now the lady's voice again came into hearing.

". . . were no illusions. You and I both . . . purely a marriage of social and political convenience. I know what went on at some plantations, but I would never have agreed had I suspected . . . heard the rumors . . . you should have told me . . . too late now . . . so you had better take care of it."

". . . no danger of . . ." said William McSimmons, but I couldn't hear the last of what he said as the lady's voice interrupted him.

". . . always danger . . . brat running around with white blood . . . different world now . . . times changing . . . I want no surprises . . . don't want my children competing with some bastard coming back making claims . . . you take care of it . . . I'll divorce you and take my money if . . . just take care of it!"

Their voices stopped. It was clear enough that the lady was furious.

"Josepha, what's—" I began.

But now Josepha seemed to come to herself.

"Mayme, chil'," she said urgently, "you gots ter git away from here!"

"But what were they—"

"*Now,* chil'—else sumfin bad's gwine happen! Dere's been talk among da black folk. At first the lady din't know, but now she do. She muster been listen'n somewheres an' now dere ain't no tellin' what da master might do . . . an' she thinks it's *you* dat's caused all her trouble!"

"Thinks *who's* me?"

"No one—jes' some fool nigger girl who din't hab sense ter keep her dress down, an' ran away afore da young master could git rid ob what could come back ter haunt him, an' when the mistress foun' out, by den dey was dun married an' she dun threaten fer ter leab him, dat's what dey's sayin roun' 'bout . . . so go, chil'.—Miss Kathleen," she said, now turning to Katie, "effen Mayme won' listen, you gotter go, you's gotter git outta here. I don' know where you's from, but git back dere and take Mayme wiff you. Go, chil'!"

But already heavy boots were descending the stairs. Finally the look in Josepha's eyes told Katie and me how serious she was, and we made for the door.

William McSimmons ran into the kitchen just as we ran through the opposite door across the room and made for our horses.

Behind us we heard the whack of his hand across Josepha's face and a cry of pain.

"You meddlesome old fool!" yelled McSimmons. "Who told you to interfere in my affairs?"

"Run, chil'!" Josepha's voice called out after us.

We sprinted to our horses as fast as we could go, untied them, and quickly mounted. By now we were really frightened. But just the fact that we were running away, I suppose, made us look guilty. And just like a dog will chase you the minute you're trying to run away from him, when William McSimmons ran out of the kitchen and saw us galloping away, it threw him into an even wilder rage than before.

"Stop them!" he cried to some of his men. "Go after them and get the nigger girl. Don't let her get away!"

We were hardly out of sight from the house when I looked back and saw three of his men digging their heels into their horses and galloping after us. We tried to outrun them, but it was no use. They caught up with us in less than a minute.

One of them rode alongside me, shouting terrible things at me, then reached over and grabbed my reins to stop me.

"Ride, Katie!" I screamed as I felt my horse slow. "Go home . . . I'll meet you there!"

She glanced back with a look of terror on her face to see the men yanking me off my horse.

"Mayme!" she screamed.

"Ride, Katie . . . ride!" I cried before a vicious slap across my face silenced me.

Tears flooded Katie's eyes. But there was nothing she could do to help me now.

Once they had me, the men ignored her. In a few more

seconds, sobbing and terrified, she galloped out of sight.

Katie rode hard all the way back to Rosewood. She kept looking back, half hoping to see me riding after her, but fearing she would see McSimmons' men chasing her instead.

By the time she got back to Rosewood, her tears had dried up for a while, but she was worried sick about me. She went inside and started calling out to Aleta and Emma that she was back. She found them in the cellar, where they had gone the minute they heard the sound of her horse riding toward the house.

"Where's Mayme?" asked Aleta as she climbed up and back into the parlor.

"She's not here," said Katie in a trembling voice. She helped Emma and William up from the cellar, then told them what had happened.

"But where was it, Miz Katie?" said Emma. "Why'd dey take her? What was you doin' someplace where dey'd do dat?"

"It was at the McSimmons plantation, Emma," Katie replied. "That's where we went after that man came."

"Why'd you go dere!"

"We wanted to find out if you and William were safe."

"Dey don' know where I am."

"But we had to find out. That man said . . ." Katie hesitated, realizing what she had been about to say. "Mayme was afraid that man might have been looking for you."

"You mean . . . Mayme did dat for me?"

"Yes, Emma. She cares about you and doesn't want anything to happen to you. She was worried that William McSimmons might have sent that man to try to find you."

Emma's eyes opened wide in fear.

"But don't worry," said Katie. "They don't know you're with us. And they don't know where we live anyway. You and William are safe."

"But then why did they take Mayme?" asked Aleta.

"I don't know," answered Katie. "I think there are some bad men there, Aleta, who are looking for Emma. They might think Mayme knows where Emma is since they both ran away from the same plantation."

"But she won't tell, will she, Katie?" asked Aleta.

"No, of course not. Mayme would never tell."

By then it was late in the day, and after sitting for a little while in silence, the three of them seemed to remember all at once that it was my birthday. That made them all the sadder, and finally Aleta started to cry.

Katie took her hand, and pretty soon the three of them were sitting together on the floor of the parlor, holding hands and crying and thinking how alone they all felt without me there with them.

Gradually Katie began to realize that she had to try to be strong for the sake of the other two.

"God," she said, "please take care of Mayme."

Then she wiped her tears and stood up.

"Let's have something to eat," she said. "It will make us feel better, and if Mayme was here that's what she would want us to do. Let's have some more of Mayme's birthday cake."

They tried to keep their spirits up, but every five minutes one of them would look out the window to see if I was coming yet and then sigh. But I didn't come, and evening came and the shadows lengthened and pretty soon night was falling. By then Katie was getting really scared, but she tried not to show it to the other two.

She helped them get ready for bed and then they prayed together.

"What do you think Mayme is doing right now, Katie?" asked Aleta as Katie settled her into her bed.

The question stung Katie to the heart because she was so worried about me.

"I don't know, Aleta," she said, trying to smile. "But two things I'm surc of, that she is safe and that she is thinking about us."

# INTERROGATION
# 36

KATIE WAS RIGHT ABOUT ONE THING—I WAS thinking about them and missing them and wishing I was with them. Whether or not I was safe . . . I wasn't so sure about. I didn't feel too safe.

Once they'd gotten me off my horse, as I heard the hooves of Katie's horse fading into the distance, one of the men dragged me back to where William McSimmons stood. He was probably more angry at his wife for her threats than he was at me, 'cause he hardly knew me, but as they pulled me up toward him I saw that his face was red and his fists were clenched. The man shoved me toward him, then backed away while he looked me over.

"I want to know what you're doing trespassing on my property," he said in an angry voice.

"I'm sorry, sir," I said. "I used to be one of your slaves. I came back to visit Josepha. I didn't mean to trespass."

"All right," he said to his men, who had gathered

around hoping to see a beating, "you can go. I want to talk to her alone."

The horse I'd been riding wandered away out of sight, which worried me some 'cause I was still hoping to get out of here and follow Katie home. The men dispersed and gradually wandered off toward the barn, the corral, and the bunkhouses, where some of the new men were staying who had been brought on to replace the slaves who had left. The dozen or so blacks who had decided to remain as hired hands were all out working in the fields. I still had only seen two colored men about the place, and no women except for Josepha. One of the men who had joined the group was the same one Katie and I had followed here, the one who'd been asking about black babies. He hadn't come around until Katie was gone, and as I glanced at him out of the corner of my eye, I don't think he recognized me. If he was one of William McSimmons' hired men, we must have been right—there was no disease, he had just been trying to get on the trail of any black newborns in the area so that they could find out where Emma had disappeared to. I couldn't tell, but I don't think McSimmons recognized me either from that day he'd come into Mrs. Hammond's store. And why would he? Right now the only colored girl he was thinking of was Emma . . . how to find her and get rid of her.

By now Mistress McSimmons had come out the door to see what the ruckus was about. Slowly she approached, and the closest thing I can think to call the look in her eye was hatred. Ever since the slaves had been set free, it seemed like some white people's feelings toward blacks had turned to hatred. They may have looked down on us when we were slaves, but in another sense there was a part of them that respected us for what we did for them. They looked down on us, but they didn't hate us. But now that we were free, they did.

McSimmons turned. "It's not her," he said. "Though I think she was one of my father's slaves."

"Where's she been till now?"

"I don't know. I don't remember her."

"Where have you been, girl?" Mistress McSimmons asked me.

"I told you, ma'am," I said. "I ran away when everyone else was killed."

"Don't be impertinent with me—I asked you where you've been!"

"With some other people, ma'am—they took care of me."

"*Where,* you fool!"

"Over yonder, ma'am," I said, pointing in the opposite direction from Rosewood. "I ain't sure exactly."

"With that white girl's family who was with you?"

"Yes'm."

"Do her people have a name?"

"Uh . . . I forgot, ma'am."

"You're as stupid as you are ugly! I don't believe you. —She knows, William," the lady said, turning to her husband. "I can see in her eyes that she's lying. I'm telling you again what I told you before—you take care of it, or else you won't like the result."

She turned and walked back into the house, leaving me alone with William McSimmons. It was all I could do to keep from quivering from head to toe, because even if he didn't remember me, I sure remembered him. He was the meanest of the McSimmons boys, besides being the oldest, and I'd felt the lash of the whip from his hand more times than I wanted to remember. And he was different than his pa when he whipped us—William McSimmons seemed to enjoy it, which I don't see how anyone could, no matter what color anyone was.

He grabbed my dress by the back of the neck and half dragged me alongside him toward the barn.

"I'll teach you to lie to your betters, girl," he said. "You'll tell me where the other girl is if you know what's good for you."

"But I don't know what other girl you mean, sir," I said.

"Shut up, you! We'll see what you know when you taste the end of my whip."

I winced in pain, trying not to cry out. One thing I knew about men like William McSimmons is that crying out made them all the angrier. He hauled me into the barn and half threw me to the dirt floor while he grabbed a whip from where it hung on the wall. Then he walked toward me again where I was struggling to get back to my feet, and ripped at my dress two or three times till my back was bare, then started lashing me with his whip.

I'd almost forgotten how much it hurt to be whipped with those tiny little leather straps. I screamed in agony at the first lash, but after four or five, the shock from the horrible pain silenced me until I just waited, trembling in terror, for each new lash.

"I see from your back that you're an ornery one," he yelled. "Did me or my pa do that to you?"

"Yes, sir," I whimpered.

"Are you ready to tell me what you know?" he asked. "She—curse the fool girl, I can't even remember her name!—disappeared not long after you did. You must have helped her. She could never have survived on her own, she was such a half-wit."

"I don't know who you mean, sir. All the rest of the slaves but me was killed when—"

"She wasn't a field slave. She didn't live with the rest of you. She was a house slave and was fat as a cow when she disappeared. Now where is she!"

Three more sudden lashes whipped across my back, and again I screamed out. I could feel that my back was starting to bleed. I couldn't help thinking of Emma and little William and what would happen to them if this terrible man found them. How could anyone be so evil that he'd want to kill his own son? But I had no doubt that's what was on his mind.

I fell to the floor, feeling like I was going to faint from the pain.

"I'm sorry, sir," I whimpered. "I don't know who you mean."

"Then you are an imbecile! Maybe you'd rather die yourself."

He turned and strode angrily out of the barn. I took a deep breath and just lay there sobbing, wondering what was going to happen to me. Before I had the chance to think about getting up and making a run for it, two men came in, grabbed me without even letting me cover myself up with my torn dress, and dragged me out of the barn.

Two or three minutes later I found myself sitting in a corner of the ice house listening to the sound of a lock as the door closed above me, leaving me in near total darkness.

And that's the way it stayed all night, though I could hardly tell when darkness came outside. Nobody came back to give me anything to eat or even a drink of water. But I was in so much agony I couldn't have eaten anyway and would only have thrown up. And if I got thirsty enough, I suppose I could have licked at the ice. But the exhaustion of the pain left me so weak I became sleepy and somehow managed to sleep on and off through the night. I had nightmares that everything with Katie had been a dream and that William McSimmons had killed my family, and then he'd found me and brought me here and after whipping me some more was going to rape me and then kill me with all the rest.

Never had the idea of freedom seemed further away. I'd completely forgotten that it was my birthday.

# Katie and Aleta

# 37

Katie probably got less sleep that night than I did, listening to every noise, both afraid of what they might be and yet straining to hear at the same time, hoping she would hear me coming back. She dozed off now and then and finally awoke just about the same time I was waking up where I lay.

With the coming of morning, all the fears that had assaulted her throughout the night retreated a bit. She began to feel better just because she had to take care of Emma and Aleta all by herself, and doing your duty is about the best thing you can do when sad thoughts are trying to conquer you. Though seeing the horse that had found its way home when she got up, standing outside waiting for someone to feed it, reminded her of the fix I was in.

With me gone and obviously in danger, all three of them, Katie and Emma and Aleta, found themselves quieter and more thoughtful. They didn't feel like doing the chores. There was no laughter. A deep sadness hovered over Rosewood, Katie said, like a thick, depressing fog.

Sometime late in the morning, when Emma had gone upstairs for a few minutes and left William on the couch in the parlor with pillows stuffed around him so he wouldn't fall, Aleta came in and saw him there alone.

She paused, then timidly approached at just the time William began to whimper. She stood above him as his crying grew louder, then gently sat down on the edge of the couch beside him.

"It's all right, William," she said softly. "Your mama will be back soon."

She reached out and took one of his hands and felt the tiny black fingers immediately close around one of her own.

"It's all right," she whispered, "I'll take care of you till your mama gets back."

Gently she extended her index finger toward the tiny mouth. Instantly William stopped crying and began sucking on the end of it. Aleta giggled at how it felt.

Just then Katie walked into the room. Embarrassed, Aleta quickly pulled her hand away as Katie approached.

"I was just . . ." she began. "I was trying to make him stop crying."

"I think William liked it," said Katie. "He's just a helpless little baby. He needs people to care for him just like your mother once held you and cared for you. That's why Emma needs all of our help."

The sadness of the day and worrying about me had opened up some places in Aleta's heart that she'd kept closed all this time, ever since the day Katie found her on the doorstep. Now those doors were opening and emotions were pouring out that she'd kept hidden all that time.

All of a sudden Katie noticed her lips beginning to quiver. Her eyes filled with tears as the saddest and most forlorn look she had ever seen came over her face.

"I won't ever see my mother again," whimpered Aleta.

Katie sat down on the other side of the couch from where William lay and took Aleta in her arms. For the first time since her mother's death, Aleta broke down and sobbed. Katie held her close, stroking her hair and whispering words of love and comfort in her ear.

"I don't have a mama anymore either, Aleta." Katie said softly. "Neither does Mayme. I don't know about Emma. I don't know why this happened, Aleta, but God brought us together to help each other and take care of each other and to be a family to each other, just like you were helping to take care of William just now. That's why we've got to be sisters to each other, because we don't have mamas and sisters and brothers of our own."

"But I want my mama back!" wailed Aleta.

"I know, I know . . . me too," said Katie. "But we'll see them again in heaven someday. But until then we've got to be the kind of girls our mamas would want us to be. We've got to be strong, and you can be strong, because you know that there are four people who love you."

"Four?" said Aleta, sniffing and wiping at her nose.

"Mayme and Emma and I, and someday this little baby will grow up to love you too. I know that your daddy loved you once, and we will pray that he will love you again."

It was silent a minute as Aleta's tears slowly subsided. Unconsciously her hand again began to stroke William's arm beside her, and a moment later his tiny fingers were again clutching her finger as if his very life depended on it.

"I miss Mayme," said Aleta after a few seconds. "I hope nothing bad happens to her."

"Nothing bad will happen, Aleta," Katie said. "God will take care of her."

"But why did He let this happen to her and let that bad man take her?"

"I don't know, Aleta," answered Katie. "God doesn't keep bad things from happening, or make bad things happen himself. But when they do, He takes care of us through them. And I know He is taking care of Mayme right now."

"But why do they want to hurt her?"

"Some people hate other people just because their skin is a different color," said Katie.

Aleta was quiet. She was still too young to realize how much she herself had changed.

"But someday," Katie went on, "babies like William will be born, and they won't know if they are black or white until somebody is unkind to them. Someday maybe babies will be born and it won't matter what color their skin is."

# Nightmare Upon Nightmare
# 38

Meanwhile, when I woke up in the McSimmons' icehouse, cold and cramped and hungry and thirsty, it was like waking up in the middle of a nightmare and discovering that the nightmare was still going on. My back was in such pain I could hardly move.

I thought about Katie and Emma and Aleta and whether they were safe, wondering what they were doing. It's funny how you worry more about other people than yourself when you're in danger. It seems you can be stronger for yourself, but you don't want others to have to endure the same suffering.

I was suffering all right. My back hurt so bad I could hardly stand it. I couldn't move a muscle in my whole body without wincing in pain. But I had been whipped before and I knew the pain would eventually go away. But I was so worried that somehow they'd know where to find Emma, that maybe they'd followed Katie home and were doing awful things to the rest of them too. My mind made up all kinds of terrible things I was afraid might be happening. And the worst of it was I couldn't do anything to help. I had no idea they were all back at Rosewood waiting and worrying about me, and hoping every minute that I'd come riding in.

Sometime in the morning I heard voices above me, followed by the sound of someone fumbling with the lock. Then bright sunlight exploded around me as the icehouse door opened. A little white girl about ten or eleven climbed down the stairs and brought me a pitcher of water and a hunk of bread. She looked at me crumpled in a heap in the corner with that same expression I'd seen on white faces lately but had never noticed before—hatred.

Why would a little girl who had never seen me before hate me? I suppose I might have hated her back, but I couldn't. The look she gave me hurt, but I couldn't help feeling sorry for her, 'cause I knew what that hatred was going to do to her inside—it was going to spoil all the good things that might have grown in her heart instead.

"Thank you," I tried to say, but my throat was so dry my voice sounded like the croaking of a frog.

She just looked at me without replying, then turned and walked back up the stairs, then the door closed behind her.

A few hours later it opened again. This time I knew it was no little girl coming down the stairs 'cause I heard heavy footsteps and his voice. I glanced up and shuddered to see that he held a whip in his hand.

"On your feet!" said William McSimmons. He grabbed me and dragged me up out of the icehouse. I cried out because he'd twisted my arm and it felt like he'd almost broken it.

He pulled what remained of my torn dress off my shoulders again.

"I'll give you one more chance to tell me where she is," he said.

"Please, master," I said, "I'm telling you God's truth—I left here that day those men on horses killed everyone at the slave village. I had gone for water and they didn't see me. I ran and ran. I didn't know what direction I was going. I didn't see anybody else. I thought everyone was dead. I thought you and the master were dead. That's why I didn't come back. That's the honest truth—I saw no one."

"You're lying!" he shouted. "Maybe you ran away like you say. But you've got to know where she is now! So tell me!"

"I'm sorry, sir . . . please, I don't know."

He erupted with even more fury than the day before, and a minute later I fell senseless in a faint on the dirt, blood covering my back. The last thing I remember was the sound of his boots kicking me back down the steps and then tramping back up. Then my brain went black.

How long I was out, I don't know. It might have been midafternoon when I gradually began to come to myself in an agony of throbbing and burning torment. I don't know what hell is going to be like, but if it's anything like what I felt that day, I pity the folks who wind up there. I heard voices above me outside again. Men's voices mixed with evil laughter.

"He said I could have her first."

". . . make it fast, then . . . I'm next and . . . got to get back to work . . ."

There was more low laughter, then the door opened

and again light flooded the icehouse. As I came more fully back to myself I saw that a man was coming down. I struggled to pull the top of my dress and underclothes back up around my shoulders and breasts.

"Don't mind all that, missy," said the man with a lecherous grin, "you won't be needing it."

He knelt down beside me and began pulling my clothes off, fondling me and moving his hands all over me as he forced me onto my back. I winced in pain when my whipped back scraped against the hard dirt floor.

Then he started to take his trousers off, and I knew he was about to rape me.

Suddenly I heard an angry voice from above us.

"Get up and come out of there!" cried a woman's voice.

The man turned around. Beyond him I saw the silhouette of a tall form in the light from the opening of the door. It was the mistress.

"Get out!" she repeated. "I don't care if she's trash, I'll have none of your evil, disgusting games at my home. Get out, and the rest of you," she said to some others who must have been standing nearby, "leave her alone. If she's going to meet her end, let it be in the way we deal with coloreds. If I see any more of this, I'll kill you myself."

Somehow the men seemed to know that she meant it. The man stood, pulled up his trousers, and left the icehouse. Again the door closed. I pulled my clothes back over myself and started to cry.

This time I couldn't stop.

I didn't see or hear from anyone else the whole rest of the day or night.

# Resolve
## 39

Aleta was young and wasn't really aware of the implications of what was happening, but as the day wore on Katie grew more and more worried about me. She knew that the more time that passed, the worse the outcome was likely to be.

Emma sensed it too. Katie said she was quieter and more thoughtful all that day. She knew they were looking for her and that whatever was happening to me was on account of her.

Slowly the day passed, then the evening, and finally they went to bed again, more worried than ever about me.

The next morning after they'd eaten breakfast, Emma said she was going to go outside and take a bath.

"Can I hold William?" asked Aleta.

Emma looked at her in surprise.

"I reckon so, Miz Aleta. He probably be 'bout ready fer sleep. His tummy's full er milk."

"Can I take him into the parlor and rock him in the rocking chair?"

"Yes'm, Miz Aleta. Dat be fine. Jes' put a towel under him in case he make a mess from one end or da other."

Katie went out with Emma to help her get the water to bathe in the washtub. When she was finished and drying up, Katie went back into the house. As she entered the kitchen she heard the soft sound of singing coming from the parlor. Slowly she stole across the kitchen floor to the door.

There sat Aleta slowly rocking William and quietly singing.

*"Day is dying in the west, angels watching over me, my Lord.*
*Sleep my child and take your rest, angels watching over me.*
*All night, all day . . . angels watching over me, my Lord.*
*All night, all day . . . angels watching over me.*

*Now I lay me down to sleep, angels watching over me, my Lord.*
*Pray the Lord my soul to keep, angels watching over me.*
*All night, all day . . . angels watching over me, my Lord.*
*All night, all day . . . angels watching over me."*

Slowly Katie walked into the room.

"Where did you learn that?" she asked.

"Mayme taught it to me."

"It was beautiful, Aleta. William must like it too—he's sound asleep."

Katie sat down and began humming the tune again, and in another minute they were both quietly singing it together.

A few minutes later they heard the sound of Emma's footsteps. Before she was even into the room, she was humming along in high harmony. When she saw her little son sleeping in Aleta's lap, she said a surge of motherly affection went through her heart like she'd never felt before.

She sat down and slowly the song came to an end and the room grew quiet. It was Emma who first broke the silence.

"We got ter do sumfin 'bout poor Mayme, Miz Katie," she said.

"I don't know what to do, Emma."

"But we *got* to, Miz Katie. I don' think we can do dis alone, 'cause I ain't like Mayme. I can't do things like she can. You an' she's always havin' ter take care er me, an' I ain't smart like the two er you an' I'm feared sumfin sick ob what's ter become ob us if Mayme don' come back. Yer real smart, Miz Katie, an' yer so good ter me, but I ain't gwine be much help like you need."

"You've been a big help, Emma," said Katie. "And you're learning to do more things all the time. And you're taking fine care of William."

"Oh, Miz Katie, yer jes' always so nice, but I knows dat I ain't got da brains in my head dat you gots in one hand. So I'm jes' sayin dat we gots ter do sumfin'. Cause dis is all my fault, an' poor Miz Mayme wouldn't be in dis fix 'cept fer me bein' such a cocked loon wiff dat bad egg."

"It's not your fault, Emma. Sometimes bad things just happen."

"Miz Mayme wouldn't be in dis fix 'cept fer me, an' if I know what she's doin' right now, it's dat she's not tellin 'em where I's at. She's in danger on account er me. So it's my fault, Miz Katie, an' we gotter do sumfin 'cause if dey git riled enough dey's bound ter string her up. I seen what whites kin do when dey git riled. I member where I was at afore when dey strung up an ole uncle jes' 'cause a chicken was missin'. An' dat William McSimmons, he's a mean one when he wants ter be. So we gotter go help her. I's gotter try ter do sumfin."

Katie thought a minute.

"All right, then, Emma," she said. "I'll go back to the McSimmons place. I don't know what I will do, but you're right, I have to try to do something."

"Dat ain't what I said, Miz Katie. I said *I's* gotter try ter do sumfin. So if you's goin, den I'm goin' wiff you."

"What about William?" asked Katie.

"I'll take care of him, Katie," Aleta now said eagerly.

"Can you stay here alone, Aleta?" Katie asked. "Without getting scared?"

"Yes, I promise. I've seen you feed him out of the bottle sometimes, and I know how to clean him if he makes a mess. And if someone comes, we'll hide in the cellar."

Katie turned again to Emma. "Aren't you afraid of being seen, Emma?" she asked.

"I reckon I am. But if dat's what's gotter be done fer Miz Mayme, den I reckon dat's what's gotter be done."

Katie drew in a deep breath of resolve, then stood up.

"Then I guess we'd better get ready," she said. "Why don't you fix a bottle or two of milk for Aleta and anything else she needs, and I'll go saddle two horses."

When Katie came back into the house ten minutes later, she was both scared and determined. She had been thinking about all Emma had said and realized she was right—they had to try to do something. If hard times took courage, then now was the time when she had to find out how much she had.

She walked into the house and saw a determined look on Emma's face too. She said it was like watching Emma grow up three years in just a few minutes. They looked at each other, and both knew it was time to do what they had to do.

"Will you be all right, Aleta?" said Katie.

"Yes, Katie."

"You know everything to do?"

Aleta nodded.

"Good girl," said Katie. She gave her a hug, kissed her on the cheek, then turned back to Emma.

"Well, are you ready?"

"I's ready, Miz Katie."

Then Emma picked up her little son. "You be good fo Miz Aleta," she said, then kissed him and handed him back to Aleta.

Katie glanced around the kitchen, then walked across the floor and picked up a small carving knife from the counter.

"What dat for, Miz Katie?" said Emma in alarm.

"I hope nothing, Emma—but if Mayme is tied up somewhere, I don't want to have to go ask Mrs. McSimmons if we can borrow a knife."

Then another thought seemed to strike Katie. She turned and hurried toward the parlor. Emma followed, and when she came into the room she saw Katie standing in front of the open gun cabinet, removing one of her father's rifles.

Emma's eyes widened.

"What you doin', Miz Katie!"

"We don't know what we're going to find, Emma," she said. "But if that man is hurting Mayme . . . well, I don't know what. But I'm going to take this with me. Mayme showed me how to use these guns once before, and maybe I'm going to have to use one again to rescue her."

She closed the cabinet and turned to go, then stopped. She turned back, took out another rifle, grabbed another handful of shells and put them in her dress pocket, then led Emma from the room, back through the kitchen, and outside to the two waiting horses.

# RESCUE PARTY
# 40

KATIE AND EMMA RODE AS QUICKLY AS THEY could back toward the McSimmons plantation without galloping their horses. Emma'd only been on a horse a time or two in her life, and Katie almost had to teach her how to ride as they went and was afraid she might fall off if they went too fast. As they drew closer Katie realized that she still had no plan of what they would do once they got there. The two rifles sticking out of their saddles behind them wouldn't do much good against a whole plantation of men.

As they reached the fork where the road to the McSimmons plantation split off, suddenly Katie had an idea. I reckon you could say it was an idea that would change our fortunes in a lot of ways. But right now she wasn't thinking that far ahead.

"Emma," she said, "I'm going to ride into town as fast as I can. You need to hide here till I get back."

"What you doin' dat for, Miz Katie? I don' want you

ter leab me alone. What about Mayme?"

"That's why I'm going to town—I'm going to try to get some help."

Katie led Emma down off the road and amongst the trees, quickly dismounted and tied Emma's horse so it wouldn't wander off, then helped Emma down.

"You stay right here, Emma, until I come back. I won't be more than fifteen or twenty minutes, I promise."

Without waiting for Emma to protest further, she mounted again, urged her horse back onto the road, and galloped away toward town as fast as she could. By now she wasn't worried if anyone saw her. She was desperate and didn't care. She wasn't even thinking about being found out or what Mrs. Hammond or Henry or anyone else might think.

Six or seven minutes later she was galloping past the church and into town, past Mrs. Hammond's store and down the street, still as fast as she could go. The sound of the hooves pounding down the middle of the street past the bank made everyone stop and stare as she flew by, wondering what was going on. But Katie wasn't paying them any attention and didn't slow down until she came to the livery stable, where she reined her horse to a dusty stop. Even Henry's looks and questions weren't enough to make her lose her determination now.

"Where's Jeremiah?" she asked as she ran toward him, out of breath.

"Back dere cleanin' out da livery," began Henry. "But what's you in sech an all-fired—"

Already Katie was past him and running inside the

building. She would have to figure out how to answer the questions later.

"Jeremiah . . . Jeremiah!" she called out as she hurried into the dim light. "Jeremiah—it's Katie Clairborne . . . please, I need your help. Mayme's in trouble."

Jeremiah dropped the pitchfork in his hand and strode toward her.

"Some men have got Mayme," said Katie frantically. "White men . . . and I'm worried and afraid and we're going to go try to help her, but I'd feel a lot better if you were with us."

"Jes' lead da way, Miz Clairborne," said Jeremiah, "an I'll do what I can—"

Katie turned and ran back outside as Jeremiah, still more than a little confused, hurried to catch up.

"—but I ain't got no horse er my own."

"You can ride with me!" said Katie, running to her horse and jumping up onto its back. "Just climb up and sit behind the saddle," she called down, not even thinking of the impropriety of such a thing.

Less than a minute later, Katie was flapping the reins and galloping back through town the way she had come, leaving a bewildered Henry watching them go, along with a wake of townspeople, shocked, no doubt, to see a white girl and a colored boy flying down the street on the back of the same horse.

Katie caught a glimpse of Mrs. Hammond standing in front of her store, watching the scandalous scene with her mouth half open. "Well, I never—" she began, but the drumming hooves drowned out whatever else she was about to utter.

Jeremiah asked no questions, and Katie did not even try to explain until they slowed down and she led the way off the road.

"I'm going to say the same thing to you," she said, glancing behind her, "that Mayme said to you before. Please . . . don't tell what you see or who you see or anything. I can't make you promise because there's no time to worry about it, and we've got to try to rescue Mayme. But I hope you'll keep quiet, as I'm sure you've been doing, since nobody's come around asking us questions—well, except for one man, which is why Mayme's in trouble."

Before Jeremiah could reply, Katie had stopped the horse and was dismounting.

"Who dat?" asked Emma, looking up at the young man who was just as surprised to see her as she was him.

"Never mind who it is," said Katie. "He's the boy who came out to the house one time and he's going to help us.—Jeremiah," she said, turning back to him, "would you ride behind her on the other horse? She's not too secure in the saddle."

Jeremiah jumped down and obeyed.

"Get up," Katie said to Emma. "It will be all right—he won't let you fall."

In another minute they were on their way again, more slowly now the closer they approached the McSimmons place. As they went, the horses side by side, Katie briefly tried to explain the situation to Jeremiah.

"These are mean people, Jeremiah," she said, "and if they see too many more black faces, there is no telling what they might do. For reasons I can't tell you about, if they catch so much as a glimpse of Em—I mean, if they see her," she added, still not sure how much it was safe to divulge and nodding toward Emma as she said it, "they're likely to kill her. So we've got to stay out of sight. And I don't want you to be in danger either. So if anything bad happens, you get away and take her with you. Get as far away as you can and take her back to my house until I get back."

"What about you, Miz Katie?"

"If anything happens, I just want the two of you to get away as fast as you can. They won't hurt me—I'm white."

"What you plannin' ter do?" asked Jeremiah. "If dey's got Mayme, how you gwine fin' her?"

"I don't know. We need to sneak up to the house somehow," she said. "There's a black servant lady named Josepha that we've got to find without anyone seeing us."

"I kin git in da house, Miz Katie," now said Emma. "I know where dere's a way in wiffout bein' seen. I snuck in an' out lots er times. I'm sorry, Miz Katie, but I was a crack-brained coon an' I done things I shouldna done."

"We won't worry about that now," said Katie. "You can talk to God about it if you want to, but right now we've got to try to get Mayme away from there. So how do you get into the house without anybody seeing you?"

"Dere's a cellar dat don't nobody go in much where dey keep wood an' coal fer da winter. An' it's got stairs down to it from under da pantry window, an' if dere ain't nobody at dat window, dey can't see nuthin' ob you from all da way to behind the chicken shed. Dat's how I sometimes went out, up from dat cellar, den I'd run across to da chicken shed."

"Can we get to the chicken shed without being seen?" asked Katie.

"I reckon we can try, Miz Katie, hidin' dese horses in

da trees nearby an' den creeping to da shed when dere ain't nobody lookin'."

"Then we will have to be very careful to make sure no one sees us on the road, and then ride off into the woods when we get close to the place."

They continued on their way and did just as Katie had said. But once they were off the main road and getting closer to the plantation, Emma wasn't much good with directions, and it took them quite a while to find it. But at last they saw the house in the distance through the trees. They tied their horses and dismounted.

"Maybe you ought to stay with the horses, Jeremiah," said Katie. "Just in case somebody sees them or something. I don't suppose there's any sense in all three of us getting caught in the house. Remember what I said, if anything bad happens, you two get away and don't worry about me."

Katie and Emma continued on foot until they were at the edge of the trees.

"See, Miz Katie," said Emma softly, "dere's the chicken shed. We gotter run dat far in da open."

They looked about. Most of the activity was on the other side of the house where the barn and storage buildings were located. Katie looked all about until it seemed like the way was clear.

"All right," she said, "let's go."

"I'm gettin' skeered, Miz Katie."

"Me too. But we've got to do it for Mayme, remember? It's time for you to be brave."

"All right, Miz Katie, I'll try."

They ran out from behind the trees, hurried across about fifty yards of open field, quickly climbed a short wood fence, and dashed for the shed. A flurry of squawking came from inside as they crouched down behind it, but it soon died back down.

"I hope nobody seen us!" said Emma.

"I hope so too," said Katie. "What do we do now, Emma?"

"Stick yo head aroun' da corner, Miz Katie."

Katie did so.

"You see dat slanty cellar door under dat part ob da house dat sticks out from da rest—dat's da pantry and dat's da cellar beneath it."

"What if it's locked?"

"It ain't neber locked dat I recollect."

"Then let's run for it."

"Wait, Miz Katie! You gotter make sure nobody's in dat window dat can see us."

Katie looked around the corner of the shed. "There *is* somebody there," she said. "A black lady."

Emma stretched her neck around the corner to look. "Dat's Josepha! I don't reckon it matters if she see us."

"That's who we're trying to see anyway," said Katie. "Let's go."

They inched out from behind the shed and in a few seconds were dashing for the house. Inside the pantry the movement caught Josepha's eye. She looked down to see a white girl and a black girl just disappearing from sight under the ridge of the house.

"Land sakes!" she exclaimed under her breath. "Effen it ain' dat fool Emma an Mayme's white frien'!"

She turned and waddled hurriedly back into the kitchen and kept going straight through.

"Where are you going, Josepha?" a voice said after her as she went by.

"To da cellar, Mistress McSimmons," answered Josepha without slowing down.

"What for?"

"I . . . got ter git sumfin I lef' down dere da other day. I's be back up in er jiffy."

As fast as she dared Josepha opened the door. The cool dank air of the cellar met her face. Closing the door behind her, she inched down the narrow stairway into the darkness, each step groaning beneath her weight. When she reached the earthen floor, she took a match from her pocket, struck it on a stone, and held it in front of her, looking for a candle. But before she could find one, two figures suddenly approached through the thin light at the far end from the outside door by which they had entered.

"Tarnashun!" she exclaimed in a loud whisper. "Where'd you two come from!—Emma, you guttersnipe, whatchu doin' here? Da master's like ter kill you effen he finds you! He been lookin' high en' low fer you, an da mistress, she be as mad as a cornered coon on account er you."

"Please, Josepha," said Katie, "we came back to find out what they've done with Mayme. Where is she?"

Josepha looked away. But Katie had seen the fear in her eyes at the question.

"Where is she, Josepha?" she repeated.

"Dey had her in da icehouse all day yesterday," she said. "But den dis mo'nin' I hear'd dem sayin' dat da whuppin's wasn't doin' no good an' dat dere wuz only one way ter make a stubborn nigger loosen up his tongue."

"And what was that, Josepha?"

Again Josepha looked away.

"Josepha," said Katie, reaching out and forcing the large black woman's face back in front of her, "I want you to tell me what they meant."

"I'm feared, Miz Kathleen," she said as tears filled her eyes, "I'm mighty feared dey wuz fixin' ter take her out to da big oak."

Emma gasped. "Da big oak!" she whispered.

Katie glanced around and saw Emma's eyes as big as plates and filled with terror.

"What is it?" said Katie.

"Come wiff me, Miz Katie. We gotter git outer here!"

"If Mayme's at something called the big oak, then that's where we're going too. Do you know where it is, Emma?"

"Yes'm, but—"

"Emma!" said Katie. "Remember—we came here to help Mayme."

"If dey've taken her to the big oak, chil'," said Josepha, breaking into tears, "dere ain't nuthin' you can do fer poor Mayme now."

Suddenly light flooded the stairway up to the house behind where Josepha stood.

"Josepha, what's taking you so long? Get back up here!"

Katie and Emma crouched down out of sight, hoping no sound of feet on the stairs would follow the mistress's voice.

"Yes'm," said Josepha. She wiped quickly at her eyes, then turned and trudged back up the stairs, moving as slowly as she could, it seemed, to give the two girls time to make their escape.

Katie and Emma crept out of the cellar and dashed back

across the yard. They reached the safety of the chicken house and then continued straight on past it, over the wooden fence, and to the safety of the trees. There stood Jeremiah watching for them, crouching low behind a tree, holding one of the rifles.

"What are you doing with that!" exclaimed Katie softly as she ran past him.

"Listenin' t' you talk about how dangerous dese people is, I figured I'd best be ready ter shoot if dey was comin' after you an' tryin' ter hurt da two er you."

"Nobody saw us . . . come on!"

Two minutes later they were back in their saddles, and Emma was leading the way as best she could remember to the fateful tree.

# THE BIG OAK
## 41

IT TOOK THEM TEN OR TWELVE MINUTES TO reach the place.

The big oak stood in a clearing in the middle of a large field of pastureland. The nearest shelter where they could stay out of sight was two hundred or more feet away.

"Dere it is—dat's da big oak!" whispered Emma.

Katie could feel the fear in her voice.

"An' see—dere's six or eight men on horses all dere together! Oh, Miz Katie, I'm mighty feared 'bout what dey's doin', an' I'm feared we be too late!"

They dismounted as carefully as they could, tied their horses, and crept to the edge of the trees.

"No—look, there's Mayme in the middle of them," said Katie. "We're not too late. She's on one of the horses and—"

Suddenly Katie gasped in horror.

"She's blindfolded . . . and they've got a rope around her

neck!" she exclaimed. "It's tied over that limb up above!"

"Dat's what I feared, Miz Katie! Dat's what I been tellin' you."

"Dey's fixin' ter string her up, all right," whispered Jeremiah, his voice suddenly sober and a look of determination on his face. "I heard 'bout dis eber since da war. I almost got in some trouble like it myse'f wiff some white men dat had been drinkin'."

"Oh, Miz Katie—Mayme's so good," Emma was babbling. "She must not hab told 'em about me. She gwine git herself strung up fer me. How can a body be so good dat dey'd do dat fer a nuthin' like me, an—"

"Emma!" whispered Katie as loudly as she dared, not worrying any longer if Jeremiah knew her name. "Get hold of yourself. We've got to do something!"

"Dere's a whole parcel ob dem, Miz Katie. Dey kill us too if we—"

"Shush, Emma! We're *not* going to let them kill Mayme."

"Yes'm."

"No, we ain't," added Jeremiah, anger rising in his voice at what he saw. "I'll kill 'em all if I have to! I'm goin' t' git one ob dose guns!"

"Just a minute, Jeremiah!" said Katie. "We've got to think first.—I wonder why some of them are wearing white hoods over their heads."

"I heard ob it," said Jeremiah. "Some kind er white man's religion, I think."

"It looks like one of the other men's talking to her."

"Dat's William McSimmons," said Emma. "I can see him from here. He shoutin' at her—he plenty riled."

"Then we've got to hurry!"

"Jes' tell me what ter do, 'cause I'm feared outer my wits."

"What should we do, Jeremiah?" she asked.

"I'd like t' kill 'em all," he said. "But dere's too many. I hate 'em. To tell you da truf, I neber shot a gun in my life, an' I don' know if I could kill a man, eben effen he's white."

"We don't have to kill anybody. We can just try to make them think we are. It's a trick Mayme showed me.—Let's get the guns."

They ran to the horses and pulled out the rifles.

Quickly she explained as she and Jeremiah loaded the rifle and each took a handful of shells.

"I'll go ober dere," said Jeremiah, "ober in dat clump er trees. I think I can git a little closer dere. Den we'll start shootin'."

"You've got to hold real tight because it knocks back on your shoulder," said Katie.

"Jes' 'cause I ain't shot a rifle don' mean I don' know how dey is," he said with the hint of a grin. "I'd be mo worried 'bout you, Miz Clairborne, dan I is fer mysel'."

"Just be careful. I don't want you really shooting someone . . . or hitting Mayme."

"Don' you worry, Miz Clairborne, I'll jes' aim up in da air ober dere heads."

Jeremiah moved off, leaving Katie holding her rifle and Emma trembling beside her.

They tried to watch and listen. Katie could just barely make out William McSimmons yelling things like, ". . . know where she is . . . know what's good for you . . . not worth losing your life . . . some bastard baby . . ."

She wasn't inclined to wait around to see what might happen next. She glanced through the trees. Jeremiah was already out of sight.

They were far enough away from each other, Katie said to herself. She knelt down behind a tree, put the rifle to her shoulder, then aimed out toward the gathering of men at the tree.

*Please, God, don't let me hit anyone,* she whispered, *especially Mayme.*

Then she set her finger to the trigger and fired a shot over the heads of the men.

In spite of her warnings to Jeremiah, she'd forgotten what a kick the gun had. She nearly got knocked on her rump. Emma cried out from the sound as Katie steadied herself and fired again. Then came the sound of Jeremiah's first shot.

As the echo died away, Katie fired again. Then a few seconds later three or four more shots came from Jeremiah's gun in rapid succession.

*Watch out, Jeremiah,* she thought to herself, *I don't want to hear any bullets coming toward me!*

Taken by surprise, the men turned toward the shots, yelling and swearing in confusion.

Katie fired again. A loud curse roared as William McSimmons grabbed his leg in pain where she'd accidentally hit him in the thigh.

"Let's get out of here!" he cried. "We've done what we came to do. She's practically dead now anyway—we'll let the tree finish the job!"

A few more shots sounded. Katie saw him give the horse I was sitting on a great swat on the hind end with his whip. The horse lurched forward as McSimmons galloped away after the others.

Katie's first thought was elation. Then she saw a horrifying sight—there I was dangling helplessly from the tree with the rope cinched tight up around my neck.

"Mayme!" she screamed, dropping the rifle on the ground and running toward me while Emma stood paralyzed in fear.

Katie was about halfway to the oak when Jeremiah came out of the woods and broke into a run after her. She heard him and turned.

"Jeremiah!" she cried. "Go back and bring the horses! Hurry, Jeremiah!"

Where she stood watching from the trees, in the midst of her panic and confusion and fear, Emma understood the urgency in Katie's voice. She turned and ran for the horses. Before Jeremiah reached her, she had untied them and was running back toward him. He grabbed one set of reins and leapt into the saddle.

Katie ran on toward the oak.

"Mayme . . . Mayme!" she called, tears filling her eyes. "Mayme, we're here now—we're going to help you."

But when she reached the tree, she realized there was nothing she could do. I was nearly ready to faint and was barely conscious that she was there at all. My hands were tied behind my back and my windpipe was nearly crushed from the pressure of the rope and I couldn't make a sound.

"Mayme . . . Mayme . . . oh, Mayme—God, help me!" Katie cried frantically, grabbing my feet where they dangled up in the air almost as high as her shoulders. She tried to lift my legs to take the pressure off my neck. But I was so close to unconsciousness, I just hung limp and couldn't help her.

"Oh, God!" cried Katie. "What should I do?"

By then Jeremiah was flying toward her at a full gallop, followed by Emma, pulling the second horse by the reins.

Jeremiah reined in and walked the horse forward to get it under me. At the same time he was fumbling with his hands, trying to grab hold of me.

"Mayme . . . Mayme, sit up on the horse!" cried Katie from the ground.

While Jeremiah tried to steady the horse, Katie tried to push my legs over its back. But in the noise and confusion, the horse kept moving about and Jeremiah couldn't get it to stay still. And all the while I was just hanging there like dead weight, with my neck stretching farther and farther. I could feel the horse and someone trying to grab me, though I had no idea it was Jeremiah.

"Emma," cried Katie, "the knife! Get the knife. It's in the saddlebag."

They kept struggling with the horse and my legs.

"Here it is, Miz Katie," said Emma as she ran forward.

"Can you climb the tree, Emma?" said Katie.

"Dat I can, Miz Katie. I's real good at climbin' an' I—"

"Then climb up and cut the rope, Emma! Climb faster than you've ever climbed before!"

Emma scurried up the trunk with the help of a few low limbs while Katie kept lifting my legs and Jeremiah was trying to hold me up around my waist to take the weight off my neck. In a few seconds Emma was scrambling with the agility of a cat out onto the thick branch with the rope tied around it.

"Be careful, Emma . . . don't fall—but hurry!"

Ten or fifteen seconds later the rope gave way. I dropped into Jeremiah's arms. But the sudden weight of my body made him lose his balance and we both fell off the horse's back and into a heap on the ground. Frantically Katie struggled with trembling fingers to loosen the noose around my neck as Jeremiah pulled himself out from under me. As she did, Katie saw the ugly, burning gash where the rope had dug into my skin.

Finally she got it loose and the rope off my neck as Emma scampered back to the ground.

"Mayme . . . oh, Mayme!" said Katie, smothering my face with kisses and trying to wake me up. "Please God . . . oh, Mayme, don't be dead!"

She saw Emma running toward her.

"Emma, is there any water anywhere?"

"I don' know, Miz Katie. I think dere's a stream ober yonder."

"Go, Emma—get some water! Get it in anything. Soak the bottom of your dress—anything!"

Again Emma was off like a flash while Katie continued trying to revive me. Jeremiah knelt beside me too, though there was nothing he could do that Katie wasn't already doing. My eyes were closed, my lips were parched and bleeding, and I had a cut above one eye and a big welt across one cheek. I looked so bad she thought I was dead. And I suppose I nearly was.

Katie was sobbing and calling my name and stroking my hand and face, and it seemed like forever before Emma got back. She knelt down beside my head, the bottom half of her dress wet from the stream. Katie took hold of the hem of it and gently began to dab at my face and eyes. The cool wetness seemed to get through to my brain and finally I was able to open my eyes a crack.

Katie saw my eyelids flutter and went wild with joy.

"Oh, Mayme!" she cried.

I felt her kissing my face and eyes and cheeks and forehead. She was weeping, and her hot tears mingling with the cold dampness of Emma's dress revived me a little more.

I opened my eyes a bit wider and tried to force a feeble smile to my lips, then lifted my hands and pulled the two faces down to mine. For a minute we just lay there embracing each other—Emma and Katie crying like a couple of babies. I didn't have the strength to cry. I just lay there relieved. Vaguely out of the corner of one eye I saw Jeremiah's face where he was kneeling behind them. I was too weak even to wonder how he came to be there, but I tried to smile.

The next voice I heard was his.

"Dose men be boun' ter come back before long," he said. "If dey fin' dat we spoiled dere lynchin', dey's like ter string up all three ob us next time."

"You're right," said Katie, "we've got to get out of here."

With some difficulty they got me to my feet. Jeremiah lifted me onto one of the horses. Now that I was coming awake, all the pain from every part of my body was coming awake too. But I tried not to show it because I didn't want Katie to worry about that right then.

"Jeremiah," said Katie. "You're stronger than me. You ride with her and keep her in the saddle."

He climbed up behind me, and it felt good when he put

his arms around me to grab on to the saddle horn. It hurt and it was all I could do to stay in the saddle, even with Jeremiah holding me to keep me from falling over.

Katie mounted the other horse, then reached down and pulled Emma up behind her.

"Hold on to me, Emma," she said.

Katie and Jeremiah led the two horses back to the woods where they had hidden. There we stopped. My brain was still faint from pain and hunger and thirst. But I was awake enough to help Emma figure where we were and how to get back toward the road without running into anyone from the McSimmons plantation. We went slow. Katie was listening hard for any sound of voices or horses. She knew what Jeremiah had said was true and we were still in a lot of danger.

We didn't go back on the McSimmons road at all but eventually made it to the main road to Oakwood. Katie got off while the rest of us waited on the horses out of sight. She walked out of the woods on to the road to make sure it was safe. When she saw no one, she came back and we continued on. We still had to pass the place where the McSimmons road turned off. When we saw it in the distance we again went off the road into the woods and underbrush till we were well past it.

We were hardly on the road again when we heard thundering hooves coming.

"Off the road!" cried Katie.

She and Jeremiah led the horses back into the trees. We were barely out of sight when five or six riders galloped past on the way from Greens Crossing to Oakwood.

"Dat's dem," said Emma. "Dey's huntin' fer us!"

"Well, if they're going back in the opposite direction from where we're going," said Katie, "they're not going to find us."

As soon as they were out of sight, they led us back onto the road. And now Katie tried to urge the horses along faster. Jeremiah did the same until they were going too fast and the bouncing and jostling hurt and I started to cry out from the pain. They slowed a little and continued on as fast as I could stand it.

# Four Sisters and a Friend
# 42

We rode hard about halfway back to Rosewood.

But after about another twenty minutes, Jeremiah could tell that I was getting faint again. I began to slump and collapse in his arms, and he realized I needed a rest.

He slowed. Then he and Katie began looking for a place they could stop for water. A few minutes later Jeremiah led us off the road, down an incline, and across a small grassy field to the river—the same one that bordered Rosewood two or three miles away.

Katie and Jeremiah helped me down off the horse, and I nearly collapsed at the water's edge.

"Water . . ." I tried to say, ". . . thirsty."

Katie jumped to the river, took off her bonnet, scooped it full of water, and hurried back to me. She helped me sit up and held the water to my lips before most of it soaked through the cloth to the ground. But I managed two or three swallows.

She went back, and after a few minutes I had managed to get some water into my belly and Katie had washed my face.

I smiled faintly and said softly, "Thank you."

"Oh, Mayme," Katie said, "it breaks my heart to see you like this!"

She embraced me again. I stretched my arms around her and we held each other for the longest time. Katie relaxed, and I saw Emma and Jeremiah kneeling beside her. I reached toward Emma, and she came forward and embraced me too. My back ached with pain when they hugged me, but the hugging was worth the pain. Then I smiled at Jeremiah, still too worn out to wonder what he was doing with the others.

"We wuz so worried fer you, Miz Mayme," said Emma. "I knowed it wuz my fault an' I'm dreadful sorry what you had ter go through on account er me. Miz Katie tol' me dey wuz lookin' fer me, an' you din't tell 'em 'bout me—I know you didn't an' I don' know how ter thank you. I'm so sorry, Miz Mayme. But Miz Katie, she's so brave, and she said we wuz gwine git you away from dem, but I wuz skeered—"

Katie laughed. "We were both scared, Emma," she said. "I'm not sure about Jeremiah," she added, looking at him, "but God helped us do what we had to do.—Do you think you can ride, Mayme?"

"I feel better now," I said. "I've hardly had anything to eat or drink in two days. I was just feeling faint."

"Then let's get you home."

We mounted again and rode the rest of the way, not

quite as fast but with Katie still pushing the two horses at more than a walk.

When at last I saw the white buildings of Rosewood in the distance, I was so relieved I thought I would burst for happiness.

We had hardly come into sight when a small figure came running and yelling from the house. "Mayme . . . Mayme!"

Katie and Emma jumped down from their horse. Katie steadied me while Jeremiah got down and then I slumped off the saddle into his arms.

I looked toward the house and halfway opened my arms just as Aleta rushed into them and embraced me like I never thought would happen for as long as I lived. My back was screaming in pain from the drying welts, and as she grabbed me it was all I could do not to cry out. But my heart was so warmed from the look in her eyes that I thought I could endure just about anything.

"Mayme, you're back . . . I missed you so much," she said. "I was so worried about you!"

"I'm fine now, Aleta," she said.

Still she kept clinging to me and didn't want to let go.

"I love you, Mayme," she said.

Tears filled my eyes. I looked over at Katie. Her eyes were wet too.

"Welcome back, Mayme," Katie said. "Welcome home."

Jeremiah lifted me in his arms and carried me toward the house. Katie led the way inside and up the stairs. I don't know what Jeremiah thought, but he didn't ask any questions. A minute or two later I was lying on the bed while

Katie and Emma and Aleta were scurrying about fetching water for the tub and talking about getting some food and liquid inside me.

Whatever Jeremiah was thinking as he stood in the kitchen watching all the commotion, he kept to himself. But he couldn't be in much doubt that Katie's mother wasn't anywhere around, or that there wasn't a sign of any other grown-up either. It was clear enough that Katie was mistress of the place.

Once she had Emma and Aleta about their jobs—one stoking the kitchen fire to warm some soup and the other carrying water upstairs for a bath—she went over to Jeremiah and led him outside.

"I don't know how to thank you, Jeremiah," she said. "I couldn't have done it without you."

"I'm jes' glad Miz Mayme's safe," he said, "an' dat I could help."

A moment of silence passed between them.

"Please . . ." began Katie after a few seconds, "you won't tell . . . will you? Someday . . . maybe we can explain what is going on here. But for now, nobody can know."

He stood looking at the serious expression on Katie's face.

"I reckon I can do dat, Miz Clairborne," he said slowly. " 'Tis mighty strange, I gotter say, seein' two coloreds an' two white girls all livin' in a big house like dat together. But I reckon I can keep my mouf shut fer a spell. But you'll tell me someday, I hope, 'cause you got me mighty curious."

"I will try to," said Katie with a relieved smile. "Thank you, Jeremiah.—Do you mind walking back to town? I'd let you take one of the horses, or ride you in myself, but . . ."

"Don' mention it, Miz Clairborne," said Jeremiah. "Dat'll give my pa an' dose other folks in town dat was watchin' us wiff dere big eyes a chance ter settle down an' ferget what dey seen. I'll jes' sneak in a round'bout way so no one sees me."

"Maybe you're right," laughed Katie. "Thank you again!"

# A New Crisis

# 43

MY NIGHTMARE WAS OVER, BUT ITS EFFECTS LINgered for several weeks. I was exhausted and the wounds on my back were so painful I could hardly move for three days. Most of that time I spent in bed, relishing my freedom and never appreciating so much what it meant. The other three waited on me hand and foot. Once she saw my back, Aleta was all the more sensitive and compassionate.

The incident seemed to change us all. We knew this was no game. It was a risky adventure we had undertaken, and we were all in danger. If we hadn't realized it before, we certainly did now, especially now that Jeremiah knew. Katie was deeply concerned about Emma and me and all the more committed to protecting us. Emma seemed quieter and more thoughtful, like she'd suddenly grown up several years in knowing that I hadn't betrayed her, even when my own life had been at stake. I hadn't really thought about it in those terms, but she kept saying over and over, "I can't believe you did dat fer me, Miz Mayme. I jes' can't believe it!"

Aleta seemed most changed of all by what had happened. She didn't seem like such a little girl anymore, but like she was really one of us.

But though the nightmare was past, we all knew the danger was still with us. It would always be with us as long as William McSimmons and his wife were worried about Emma and her baby. I think for the first time Katie realized just how much danger would be part of our lives from now on. But luckily, the man from the McSimmons place asking about black babies and pretending there was some disease going around never came back.

One thing I knew, and it made me sad, was that I could never visit Josepha again.

But though we expected trouble every day, no more trouble came for a time—at least of that kind—and I gradually recovered and got my strength back and began getting up and helping again with the daily chores. And after a while we settled into the old routine from before, though we were all more wary, always watching and listening for the sounds of horses coming.

September came and the crops all about Rosewood were ripening. Katie still had most of the ten dollars left from the gold coin she'd changed to smaller money and the two dollars she'd found in the pantry, and so money was the last thing we were thinking about. To girls like us, ten dollars seemed like enough to last us a lifetime.

And the fact that there was a loan coming due real soon, from when Katie's mother had borrowed against Rosewood, was a fact that neither of us really knew what it meant. We knew that you had to pay back loans, but it never dawned on us what might happen if you didn't.

So we didn't think about it and didn't realize we should be thinking about it, and all the while an even bigger danger to our scheme of keeping the plantation going was sneaking up on us a little closer with every day that passed.

Then a new danger came calling, and we suddenly had a new crisis on our hands that neither Katie or me had any idea how to get out of.

One day a carriage drove up to Rosewood. As soon as I heard it in the distance, I hurried Aleta to the blacksmith's shed and got her pounding on the anvil. Then I hurried to light a couple of fires in the slave cabins while Katie got Emma and William into the cellar with a lantern. When the fires were lit I walked through the yard with the laundry basket we always had ready full of rags and old blankets.

I didn't recognize who the visitor was, but Katie did. It was the man from the bank.

Katie met him outside the back door. He rode up and stopped in front of the house.

"Miss Kathleen," he said in an abrupt tone as he started to get down from his carriage, "tell your mother I am here to see her."

"She's not at home, Mr. Taylor," said Katie.

"What—after I have come all this way?"

He shook his head and let out a frustrated sigh. You could tell he was getting tired of never seeing Katie's mother.

"I *must* see her," he said. "The financial situation since you were into the bank to make that small payment has grown very serious. The balance of one hundred fifty-three dollars on your mother's loan is due next month, and I am being pressured to take action."

"Uh . . . what will happen if the loan isn't paid, Mr. Taylor?" asked Katie.

"I am afraid I will have no choice but to begin foreclosure proceedings."

"What does that mean?" asked Katie.

"It means that the bank will take Rosewood."

"You mean . . . take the house away from my mother?"

"I am afraid so," said the man as he climbed back into his carriage.

"You wouldn't really do that . . . would you, Mr. Taylor?"

"It would not be my decision," he replied. "I don't own the bank, I only work for it, Kathleen. There are policies that I have to follow. Those policies protect the bank's interests and enable it to make loans in the first place. Now I do not want to foreclose on Rosewood. I will do everything I can to help. But if your mother continues to avoid coming to talk to me, there will be nothing I can do . . . or that anyone can do. I am sorry. I will be sending a team of auditors out to Rosewood in a few weeks to valuate all the assets and the house. They will have to look at everything. A public notice will then go out for the auction."

"What's that?" asked Katie.

"When all the assets of the plantation will be sold. It will be announced in all the newspapers. Tell your mother to come see me immediately. These delays are hurting no one but her. If she doesn't do something, and soon, she will lose everything."

He climbed back into the seat, flicked the reins, called

to his horses, then turned the carriage around as they moved off and bounced back in the direction of town.

As soon as he was gone, I asked Katie what he wanted. I could tell from her face that it was serious. She tried to explain to me what he'd said.

"Mayme," she said, "he's going to send people here and announce in the newspapers that Rosewood's for sale! Everyone will find out. The bank's going to take Rosewood away from us. They'll find out about me and Emma and Aleta and you . . . everything."

"Then we have to do something," I said.

"How can we? He said we had to pay back the whole loan. We don't have a hundred fifty dollars. All we've got is what's left over from that one ten-dollar coin. Oh, Mayme . . . what are we going to do!"

"I reckon it's time to start praying again," I said. "God's helped us out of every fix we've been in so far."

Katie's momentary despair was cut short as we both suddenly realized we were hearing the clanking of iron on iron coming from the blacksmith's shed. Poor Aleta—her arm must have been about ready to fall off from pounding the hammer on the anvil!

We turned and ran toward the sound.

"He's gone," called Katie. "You can come out now, Aleta."

# I Have an Idea
# 44

A WEEK PASSED. KATIE WAS REALLY DOWNCAST, like I'd never seen her before. She went through her daily chores hardly saying a word. The thought of us all having to be separated and leave each other weighed her down something dreadful. I think she felt it was somehow her fault because of the loan, and if it hadn't been for that, everything would be fine.

I was pretty well recovered now and feeling good, though my back still had a lot of scabs that hurt if I twisted the wrong way. But we were still being real careful about watching for anyone coming and had a plan to hide Emma and me if anyone from the McSimmons place came snooping around.

One day I went out to the fields. I was just looking about, not thinking of much in particular. I found myself in one of the fields that had been planted with cotton. Cotton was so familiar that I didn't think anything of it. We hadn't been paying any attention to these fields because cotton was of no use to us. But on this day I found myself looking at it. Most of the bolls were bursting open. I recognized the look and knew it was ready to be harvested.

Suddenly my eyes shot open wide. I turned and spun around and around—everywhere I looked, cotton was bursting!

Cotton!

It was the crop that had built all the huge plantations through the South. It was the reason there had been slaves.

They picked it so their owners could *sell* it! Maybe it could be of some use to us after all!

I turned and ran back as fast as I could.

"Katie," I said when I got to the house out of breath. "Maybe there is a way we can make some money for that loan with the man at the bank."

"How?" she asked.

"Pick the cotton," I said. "Pick it and *sell* it!"

"*Could* we, Mayme . . . could we really?"

"We could pick some of it anyway."

"Do you know how?" she asked.

"I know how to pick it all right!" I laughed. "I reckon every black person in the South could pick cotton in their sleep! Well, *most* black folks anyway—I'm not sure about Emma. But I don't know what to do with it after it's picked. What do you do then? How do you sell it?"

"I know how to do that," said Katie.

"You do!"

"Yes—there's a man in Greens Crossing who buys it."

"What about baling it?" I said. "That's another thing I don't know how to do."

"I watched Jeremiah and Mathias do it," said Katie.

"You just put it in the baling box, press it all tight, and tie the baling string around it."

"But the bales are so huge," I said. "I've seen them. They're as big as a wagon. We could never move them."

"I'm talking about small bales," said Katie. "We've got a hundred-pound baler box."

"A hundred pounds is the *small* size! We couldn't lift a hundred pounds either. That's as much as you and me weigh, Katie."

"We could put the box up in the wagon first and do the baling and tying in the back of the wagon so we don't have to lift the bales into it when we're done."

I could tell Katie was getting excited at the notion.

"And you really think we could sell it," I said, "that is, if we *could* pick it and get it into bales?"

"I did it once before," said Katie. "I took a wagon into town for my mama."

I pondered the idea some more. There was an objection that had come to my mind.

"There's one more thing, Katie," I said. "You're going to have to let me do the picking."

"What are you talking about?" said Katie.

"Just what I said. I'm used to it, so I'll do it."

"And I'll help you," she insisted.

"Picking cotton's slave work, Katie," I said. "It's the hardest, hottest, most tedious work there is."

"Mayme, we've got to do something," said Katie. "Mr. Taylor's going to take Rosewood away from us if we don't find some money for that loan."

"It doesn't seem right for you to pick cotton," I said

again. "If it was anything but picking cotton. Maybe Emma could help me."

"There aren't any such things as slaves and masters anymore, Mayme," said Katie. "Everything's changed. There's just you and me and Emma and Aleta. We can't let Mr. Taylor take Rosewood or it'll be like you told me before—I'll have to go to one of my uncles or an orphanage or something. Aleta would be taken back to her father, or taken to an orphanage too if she's not who Reverend Hall was asking about. And they'd find Emma, and what would become of her without us? And what would happen to you? So we've got to do something, Mayme. We can't harvest the wheat to sell. We can't sell the cows or chickens—we need them. And we couldn't get more than a few dollars selling eggs. It was a great idea you had. The cotton's the only thing we've got. And it's my cotton now, Mayme, and I want to pick it."

"All right, you win," I said. "I'll show you how to do it, and we'll pick it together."

"What about Aleta?" asked Katie. "Do you think she could help us too? Is it work she could do?"

"I was picking cotton when I was younger than her," I said. "It's hard work, but I reckon if you're going to do it, she could help too."

"Then maybe it's time we told her what we were doing, Mayme. Maybe it's time to make her part of our plan. If she's going to help us save Rosewood, she's got a right to know."

"You should be the one to talk to her," I said.

"I'll do it tomorrow."

We both sat quietly thinking as everything we'd been

talking about gradually sank in.

"When can we start picking the cotton?" Katie asked eagerly. "There's no time to lose."

"Any day," I said. "I'll go out and check the fields again just to make sure. Then we'll start getting things ready this afternoon."

# Morning in the Field
## 45

THE DAY AFTER OUR TALK, BOTH KATIE AND I got up with a sense of anticipation.

We knew we were facing a crossroads. If we didn't do something, and soon, our little game of trying to make this plantation work by ourselves would be over. People would take us away and all four of us would go our separate ways.

We looked at each other with serious expressions, sort of saying, *Well, I guess this is it.* Then we both went about our business of getting ready for the day.

There was just about nothing in the world I hated more than picking cotton. But for some reason now I was almost looking forward to it. Having it be our *own* cotton, and knowing we *had* to do it to survive and keep going and eat and take care of ourselves and to protect Emma and William and save Rosewood for Katie—all that made it seem completely different. Of course, it wasn't really mine, it was Katie's. But it felt like it was part mine, because in a way it was all of ours. It was *our* plantation now, just like Katie had tried to tell me a while back.

I went out to the biggest field to look over the crop again. It was full of weeds growing as high as the cotton, but the field was full of white too. The bolls had opened and the white fluffy balls were exploding out everywhere. It was the white that mattered, not the weeds.

The field was ready!

Could we do it? Could four girls trying to fend for themselves really harvest enough cotton to sell for real cash money?

How much could we pick? I didn't know. For a field this size a year ago, there might have been twenty or thirty colored men and women. But then the field might all be picked in three or four days. If it didn't rain, maybe it'd take me and Katie two or three weeks, maybe more. I had no idea. If Aleta and Emma could help us, it would go faster. But would that be in time?

I reckon we'd find out. And maybe the whole future of Katie Clairborne's and Mayme Jukes's crazy scheme would depend on whether we could.

I walked slowly through the field, white puffs of cotton all around me. I stopped, then reached down and picked off one of the little white balls from a nearby plant.

I held it in my fingers and looked at it for a few seconds, then again around at the field surrounding me.

*Well, you old cotton field,* I said, *here I am again. But I don't hate you no more, 'cause I reckon the day's come when you're my own cotton now too, just like Katie said, or something like it anyhow. And I'm gonna pick as much of you as I can!*

I tossed the ball of cotton up in the air, watched it float to the ground, then turned and walked back the way I had come. Slowly I began humming the tune we'd sung on my birthday, then started softly singing it as I walked back to the house.

*"We planted this cotton in April, on the full of the moon.*
*We've had a hot, dry summer. That's why it opened so soon.*
*Cotton needs a-pickin' so bad, cotton needs a-pickin' so bad,*
*Cotton needs a-pickin' so bad, gonna pick all over this field."*

While I'd gone out to the field, Katie had called Aleta and Emma together for a serious talk.

"Aleta," said Katie when they were together in the kitchen, "I need to have an important talk with you."

They sat down. Aleta could tell from Katie's voice that whatever it was, it was serious. She looked into Katie's face waiting, and a little afraid that Katie was getting ready to send her away.

"I want you to tell me where you and your mother lived," said Katie.

"Oakwood," answered Aleta nervously, glancing over to where Emma sat quietly waiting and worrying about what Katie would say to her next.

"That's where you were riding away from when your daddy was chasing you?"

Aleta nodded.

"What is your last name, Aleta?"

"Butler."

"Aleta Butler . . . that's a nice name. What is your father's name, Aleta?"

Aleta looked down and remained silent.

"You know, Aleta," said Katie, "we have to do something about getting you back with your father. We must tell him about your mother. Don't you want to live with him?"

"No. I don't ever want to live with him again."

Katie was quiet for a bit, thinking what to say.

"You know, it's real special having a daddy," she said after a minute. "Mayme and I don't have daddies."

"Why not?"

"Because they are both dead."

At the word *dead,* Aleta looked up into Katie's face with a sober expression.

"So you have something we don't have, Aleta," Katie continued.

"But my daddy's mean."

"He is still your daddy."

"What about your mamas?" Aleta asked.

Katie hesitated.

"They are both dead too, Aleta. That's why Mayme and I were here alone before Emma came."

There was another long pause. Again Aleta seemed sobered by what Katie had said, though also a little confused.

"But you tell people that she's not here," she said.

"She isn't here," said Katie. "But sometimes I don't tell them that she's not coming back.—Do you want to keep staying with us for a while?"

"Oh yes."

"Then we will let you, for a little while longer, until we

decide what is best to do," said Katie. "You might have other relatives, like I do, that you might want to go stay with someday."

"Please let me stay here with you," said Aleta.

"You have to promise something, then," said Katie. "I normally wouldn't ask a little girl to keep a secret from grown-ups, but this is very, very important."

"Yes . . . I will do anything you say."

"You have to promise not to tell anyone what we are doing, that we are alone here. No one can know. You know the danger Emma is in from that bad man who wants to find her. And you know what they did to poor Mayme. You saw the wounds on her back."

Aleta nodded.

"So no one must know there are no grown-ups here, for Emma's sake and for Mayme's sake. Some white people want to hurt black people like Emma and Mayme. So we have to make sure they're safe here, don't we? So can you keep our secret?"

"I promise, Katie."

"Even after you leave later, you can never tell."

"I promise.—But . . . are there really no grown-ups? None of them are coming back? I just thought your mama was on a trip or something."

Katie nodded. "We are doing everything ourselves," she said. "We are just pretending that the grown-ups are still here."

"What about that colored boy?"

"Jeremiah? Yes, he knows a little. But we haven't told him even as much as we have you. And he's promised not to tell either. If people knew it was only four girls by themselves on a plantation, they would take us away and do bad things to Emma and Mayme."

"You mean . . . it's all pretend?"

"The work isn't pretend. You see how hard we work to do everything. The only thing that is pretend is that we are alone. And now we have to work harder than ever to pick the cotton to sell so that the bank won't take the house away from us. So, Aleta, if you want to stay, you have to promise never to tell the secret of Rosewood."

"I will . . . I will, Katie!" said Aleta, eyes wide with excitement.

"It also means you have to work hard. Look at my hands. I've never had blisters before. Now I'm sunburned and my hands are rough. Can you do that . . . can you help with all the work?"

"Yes."

"And you promise not to tell?"

"I promise."

"Then you are one of us now. Just like Mayme and I became sisters and then a little while later Emma came, and now you are our sister too. Someday we'll find your daddy, and by then I'm sure you'll want to go with him. But for now you may stay with us."

Then Katie turned to Emma and explained to them both about the loan and what would happen if they didn't get a lot of money, and that they were going to pick the cotton.

"Do you think you can help some too, Emma?" she asked. "That is, when William doesn't need you?"

"Yes'm, Miz Katie. I kin do it. After what you an Miz Mayme done ter save me from dat William McSimmons, I'll do anything fer you, Miz Katie. I owes you my life, an' I's help, Miz Katie. You jes' show me what ter do."

"Good, then let's go find Mayme and help her pick that cotton."

# King Cotton
## 46

We began that same morning.

We hitched up the big wagon. Even with all four of us, we could barely lift the baling box up into the back of it. But we managed it, then drove the wagon to the field closest to the house, where I figured would be the best place to start. We parked the wagon and unhitched the horses and took them back to the house. It would take us several days, maybe a week—I didn't know—to get the wagon full. We got the smaller buckboard fixed up with blankets and water and shade for a comfortable place for William to lie and sleep and for Emma to sit with him when he needed her, but so she could help us some of the time.

Once we had everything ready, we went out into the fields with satchels slung over our shoulders and wide-brimmed hats on our heads to keep us from the sun, and I showed Katie and Emma and Aleta how to do it.

"You gotta circle the fingers of your right hand around the ball of cotton from the top—see . . . like this," I said, stooping down to one and showing them, "while your left hand keeps hold of the stem. Then you squeeze the fingers of both hands together at the stem and the base of the cotton and pluck it out with your right so it comes off at the bottom . . . like this." I squeezed and pulled the ball of cotton off the stem and stuck it into my satchel.

They each tried it a couple of times. It was a little awkward at first. It was something they'd have to learn by doing.

"The main thing is to not get leaves mixed in with the cotton," I said. "Once you know how to do it, we gotta try to work fast. Cotton doesn't weigh much, and we'll get paid by how many pounds we bring in. So stuff your satchels as full as you can, then go dump them in the wagon and go back and fill them again. And you gotta drink lots of water, 'cause the sun can tire you out more than the work if you don't."

Then we started. We each took a row side by side and started out together. At first we were talking and having fun. But within just a few minutes I was moving ahead of Katie, and then Katie started moving ahead of Aleta in her row and Emma in hers. Within fifteen minutes the four of us were scattered apart in the field, and it was hard to do much talking after that.

We picked all day in the hot sun, taking time out for eating and drinking plenty of water and taking a break every now and then. I've got to hand it to Emma, she worked harder than I ever thought she could. She'd stop to check on William, or sometimes feed him, every ten or fifteen minutes. But when she worked she worked pretty fast and after a while was picking twice as much cotton as Aleta could. I dumped about two satchels for every one of Katie's, and Aleta was even slower than that, and pretty soon Emma was keeping up with Katie, even having to stop like she did. They all learned fast. I was mighty pleased and thought we did real good for our first day.

By late afternoon, Katie, Emma, and Aleta were exhausted. And after a whole day, the wagon wasn't even half full. I didn't know how much it would make when we pressed it down and made it into bales. I hoped what we had picked would make a whole bale. I knew a slave doing real good could pick three or four hundred pounds in a day. Master McSimmons used to give his man-slaves a dollar for every day they picked over four hundred fifty pounds. I figured if the three of us together could get so we could even pick a hundred pounds a day, then we would get a lot of hundred-pound bales picked in a month. Maybe we *could* make the money Katie needed, although I had no idea how much you got paid for cotton. Maybe we wouldn't be able to get it all picked. Rosewood probably had forty or fifty acres in cultivated cotton, from what Katie had shown me. But we'd pick as much as we could, and it seemed it oughta help.

The next morning we were all sore and tired. We went out again, but we couldn't put in as long a day. We only worked till early afternoon. Then we went back to the house and slept.

By the third day we started to get used to it, though it was also getting tedious. And we were barely starting on the field. We still had miles of rows to go!

Five days later the wagon was almost up to the top. We had four packed bales of picked cotton. We were all pretty excited to see the full wagon sitting beside the field.

"Shall we take it in to Mr. Watson's?" asked Katie excitedly.

"Let's try to get one more bale," I said. "We'll roll one of the bales on top of the others. That will give us room to pack one more and tie it, and dump it out of the baling box and take the box off the wagon. Then tomorrow or the next day you can take the five bales into town."

"This time I won't even be nervous to take it in to Mr. Watson's," said Katie.

"Do you want me to go with you?" I asked, ". . . or if you want to go in alone, I can stay and keep picking."

"I think I can take it alone," Katie said. "And I'm nervous about you being seen now, after what happened. What if any of those McSimmons men were there? I'd rather take it alone."

Two days later she was on her way into town while Aleta, Emma, and I got started on filling up a second wagon.

A few stares followed her along the streets of Greens Crossing, seeing as she hadn't been to town since the incident with Jeremiah. But she didn't return the stares, and purposefully avoided the livery stable as she made her way through town.

Katie pulled up to Watson's mill two and a half hours after leaving Rosewood, got down, and went inside to tell Mr. Watson she had a delivery. He came out and looked over the load.

"Hundred-pound bales, I see," he said. "Your mama should know I can't pay as much since I have to repack them into quarter tons before shipping them out."

"That's all right, Mr. Watson," said Katie. "She knows."

He jumped up onto the wagon and lifted one of the bales by the straps we'd tied.

"Those aren't a hundred pounds either," he said. "Your hired darkies aren't pressing them none too tight. This feels barely eighty-five."

"Yes, sir."

"Well, it'll all be weighed.—Does your mama want me to credit her account?"

"Yes, sir."

"I haven't seen her in months, maybe a year or more. She doing okay?"

"Yes, sir. But we're shorthanded, and she needs me to bring you the cotton."

"All right, then. I'll get this unloaded so you can get the wagon back to her."

# Dire Notice
# 47

THE WEEKS WENT BY AND WE TOOK A WAGON-load into town every four or five days. Gradually as we picked we got faster.

The man at the mill was a little curious why it seemed to be going so slow when he was getting deliveries from the other plantations by the thousands of pounds. But as long as the cotton came in and looked okay, he didn't ask too many questions.

One day Katie returned from town and came out to the field where I was working. Aleta had gotten tired and gone back in, and Emma had been with William all day because he had become a little sick and fussy for a day or two.

As Katie approached I saw that she was holding an envelope. From the look on her face, I'd have thought somebody was dead.

"This was in the mail, Mayme," she said, showing it to me.

"What does it say?"

" 'To Rosalind Clairborne, Rosewood,' " Katie read. " 'This is to inform you that your loan of $150 is due and payable on September 29, 1865. If not paid in full, foreclosure proceedings will begin immediately.' "

She looked up at me with a forlorn expression on her face. "That's three days from now, Mayme! What are we going to do?"

"We've got to pick as much cotton as we can before then!" I said.

The rest of that day we picked faster than we'd picked the whole time. Katie explained to Aleta and Emma how dire the situation had become.

"I know you're tired, Aleta," she said, "but we've got to keep working together. And, Emma, do you think William could come back out?"

"Yes'm, Miz Katie. I'll bring him out an' den I'll help too. We gotter save Rosewood fer you, Miz Katie, we jes' gotter."

We picked till we were exhausted, then took time out to milk the cows and eat something. After that Katie and I went back out ourselves and were still picking when it was finally so dark we couldn't see the white of the cotton anymore.

"We've got to quit, Katie," I said. "We can start up again tomorrow. It's no use going any more now."

She didn't say a word. We walked back to the house together in silence, completely worn out. Aleta was already asleep. Emma and William had fallen asleep together on the couch in the parlor. We went inside, dragged ourselves up the stairs, and flopped into bed without even washing or getting undressed.

When I woke up the next morning the sun was barely up. I poked my head into Katie's room, but she wasn't there. I went downstairs but couldn't find her anywhere.

I went outside and walked toward the field where we'd been working. There was Katie in the distance, bending down and working her way along a row like she'd never gone to bed at all. I went back into the house and quickly ate something, then packed up some bread and milk for her and went out to join her.

She glanced up as I came. From the pale look on her face, I could tell she hadn't eaten or had anything to drink yet. I gave her the bread and jug of milk. She smiled wearily and ate it, though I think by now her complete exhaustion had made it so she didn't feel hungry anymore.

An hour later Aleta wandered out, hair messy and sleep still in her eyes. Then a little while after that Emma walked out, holding William.

"Katie," I said, "you've been working hard. Why don't you go in with Aleta and Emma, and the three of you have some breakfast?"

"What about you, Mayme?" she said wearily.

"I'm fine," I said. "I'm feeling good. Then you three can come join me after you've had something to eat."

She didn't argue but just turned and started walking toward the house. Aleta and Emma followed her. An hour later we were all four working again in the field.

About the middle of the morning, I glanced up and saw a tall black figure walking toward us. We'd been so occupied that none of us had noticed him.

I paused and stood up, stretching my back. About the same time Katie noticed him too and walked over to meet him near where I was standing.

"You ladies is workin' mighty hard," said Jeremiah. "I been watchin' the goin's on at Mr. Watson's mill," he went on. "It seems t' me dat you could use another couple er han's at dis cotton o' yers."

Katie smiled a weary smile.

"I'm not going to pretend that we don't need help, Jeremiah," she said. "But what about your father? Does Henry—?"

"He don' know where I went. I ain't sayin' he ain't been askin' lots er questions. But I ain't tol' him nuthin' 'bout what I seen here."

"Thank you, Jeremiah. We are all very appreciative of your help."

Katie went back to the row she was working on. I started in picking again too, and Jeremiah fell in beside me, putting his pickings in my bag. He was even faster than me, and we could notice a difference right away in how fast the wagon filled. We found another bag in the barn and now started moving even faster. As we went we talked a little, mostly about how life used to be when we were both slaves. I suppose picking cotton couldn't help but remind us.

We were dumping our pickings into two wagons on each side of the field. By the end of that day, with Jeremiah's help, we had one of them nearly full. I don't know what he was telling Henry, but he came back the next day, and the day after that. We were up every day at dawn. On the twenty-ninth, we worked till about noon, then finally stopped to get ready to take both wagons into town. However much we'd picked in these three weeks, we'd run out of time. But we'd done better than I'd expected. Whether it came to anything close to the one hundred fifty dollars Katie needed, neither of us knew.

We ate some lunch, then hitched a team of two horses to each wagon. To get all the cotton to town, I'd have to drive one of the wagons myself. It couldn't be helped. Katie led her team off along on the road, and I climbed into the second wagon. Jeremiah jumped up beside me. We would take him partway into town, and he would walk the rest of the way by himself. Then I called to my two horses and followed Katie onto the road.

"Y'all hurry back!" said Emma as she and Aleta waved to us.

"And you be careful and watchful," said Katie back to her.

"I will, Miz Katie. Aleta an' me'll stay inside da whole time."

## Payoff
## 48

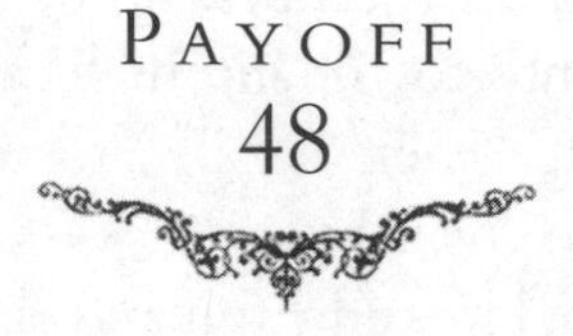

We rode into Greens Crossing sitting on the two wagons, bouncing along the street toward Watson's Mill, Katie leading, me following. Jeremiah had jumped off about a mile from town and disappeared across a field.

These were our fifth and sixth wagonloads since we'd started on the cotton field.

Out of the corner of my eye I saw Henry as we passed the livery stable. I could tell he was watching us a little more carefully than I liked.

"Please, Mr. Watson," said Katie when we got to the mill and his men were unloading the two wagons, "my, uh . . . could you pay us today for all the cotton we've brought so far? My . . . my mama wants me to deposit it in the bank."

"Certainly, Kathleen," he said. "I'll go inside and tally up your account, then we will add today's weight to it. Do you want it in cash or a bank draft?"

Katie seemed confused for just a second. But then she answered, "Cash please, Mr. Watson."

We kept waiting. I tried to sit there looking down as if I wasn't paying much attention. But every once in a while I saw Henry down the street eyeing us.

Ten or fifteen minutes later, Mr. Watson came out of his office.

"Here you are, Kathleen," he said, handing her a small bag. "You'd better take this straight to the bank. Tell your mama I wish it were more, but hopefully she'll get the rest of the crop harvested in a little faster. And here are the scale sheets," he said, handing her a paper, "—two thousand one hundred and ten pounds at sixteen and a half cents a pound, which makes the three hundred forty-eight dollars that's in the bag."

Katie took both the paper and the bag, staring at him like she hadn't heard right.

"Did you say . . . three *hundred* dollars?" she said.

"Yes, three hundred forty-eight."

"Thank you . . . thank you, Mr. Watson!"

Katie turned and ran back to where I was sitting, her eyes huge and a big smile on her face. Then she stopped and turned back.

"May we please leave the wagons and horses here for a few minutes, Mr. Watson," she asked, "while we walk down to the bank?"

"Of course, Kathleen," laughed Mr. Watson. "And don't spend it all in one place!"

I got down. Katie was obviously excited. I tried not to act like I'd understood, but I was dying of curiosity.

"Did he say what I think he said?" I whispered as we

walked down the street toward the bank.

"Yes . . . yes!" said Katie. "There's over three hundred dollars here. It's enough . . . it's enough, Mayme!"

"I had no idea cotton cost so much," I said. "No wonder plantation owners are rich."

Katie laughed. "Maybe we are rich too," she said, "for a few minutes at least."

We walked into the bank and I stopped. "I'll wait for you out here," I said.

"This time you're coming in with me, Mayme," said Katie.

"I can't, Katie. People will stare."

"I don't care. You helped me save Rosewood. You earned most of this money, and so you're coming in with me. We're going to pay off that loan, and with what's left over, I'm going to give you twenty dollars and you're going to open your own bank account."

"Twenty dollars! Katie, I couldn't—"

"I don't want to hear another word, Mayme. If you don't do it . . . I will open an account myself with your name on it."

Katie marched toward the door, with me following.

We walked into the bank, two dirty, scruffy girls, one white and one black. We hadn't even stopped to clean up after our morning's work.

I could see people glance up immediately all through the place looking at us. But Katie didn't seem to mind. She went straight to Mr. Taylor's desk.

He looked up but didn't smile. I think he was getting very tired of seeing Katie all the time instead of her mother.

"Yes, Miss Clairborne, what is it?" he said curtly.

"Today is September twenty-ninth, I believe," said Katie.

"It is. In fact I have just been completing the foreclosure documents right here. Since your mother persists in refusing to—"

Katie set down the bag of money on the desk with a loud clunk. Now even more heads turned.

"Would you please take one hundred fifty-three dollars of this," said Katie, "for the payoff of the loan, and deposit all but twenty dollars of the rest into our account?"

"Well . . . I, uh, yes . . . yes, of course," he said, fumbling for words as he rose from his chair. He pulled the bag across the desk, opened the top, and looked in. His eyes widened just like Katie's at what he saw.

"This is . . . this is, of course, good news. Yes . . . I will see to it, Miss Clairborne!"

He reached down to his desk, picked up some papers, then smiled at Katie. "It appears we will have no more need of these," he added, then ripped the papers in half. "I will process everything immediately. And you say you want twenty dollars in cash?"

"Yes," answered Katie. "We want to open a new account with it."

"I see. What kind of account?"

"Just a regular account, but in someone else's name."

"Ah, I see . . . of course. And whose name would that be?"

"Miss Mary Ann Jukes," said Katie. "This is Miss Jukes with me," she said, nodding toward me. "She will now be your customer.—Mary Ann, I would like to introduce you to the manager of the bank, Mr. Taylor."

I reached out my hand. He looked at it as if he wasn't sure what to do with it. I don't know whether he'd ever shaken a colored person's hand before.

"Uh, I . . . I am, uh—pleased to make your acquaintance, Miss, uh . . . Miss Jukes," he said, hesitating a second, then limply shaking my hand and releasing it quickly.

"You will open the account, then?" said Katie.

"Yes . . . yes, right away," said Mr. Taylor, picking up the money bag and walking toward the counter. I think he was relieved to get away from me!

Katie looked over at me and gave a little smile.

Yes, sir, I thought—she was growing up fast! She had just put a banker in his place who was probably the richest man in town.

When we walked out of the bank ten minutes later, we were both smiling. And I was holding a little booklet that had the words *Mary Ann Jukes* written across the top of it, and that inside on the first line said, *Sept 29, Deposit, $20.*

I'd never been so proud of anything in my life! Now I felt rich!

# Home Again

# 49

WE WALKED BACK TO THE WAGONS.

"That was some pumpkins!" I whispered as we went. I could hardly keep myself from smiling. "Thank you so much, Katie," I said. "This bank account means so much to me!"

"You deserve it, Mayme. If it weren't for you, Mr. Taylor's bank would own Rosewood by tomorrow.—Now let's go home and pick some more cotton, so we can pay off the second loan too!"

"I think we should have a day or two for you to rest, Katie," I said. "Then we'll start in again."

"I'm too exhausted to argue!" laughed Katie.

Katie climbed up on the lead wagon, and I got up onto mine.

"Get'up!" said Katie, flicking the reins.

She lurched into motion and I followed. In the distance, in front of the livery stable, I saw Henry standing talking to

Jeremiah. I couldn't hear them, but it looked like they were arguing.

Just then Henry glanced up and saw us down the street. He left Jeremiah and started walking toward us—taking big strides and moving faster than I'd ever seen him. Before Katie's wagon could turn the next corner, there he was blocking the street.

He walked right out in front of us. Katie had no choice but to rein in and stop. My horses stopped too.

"Hello, Henry," said Katie as he walked forward.

"Aftah'noon, ladies," he said, looking us straight in the face, first at Katie, then over at me. "Looks ter me like you been a-workin' mighty hard."

"Uh . . . we're picking the cotton, Henry," said Katie.

"Yes'm, I kin see dat, Miz Kathleen. Yo han's sho be some ruffed up. I've neber seen yo hands like dat afore, Miz Kathleen. Effen I din't know no better, dese ole eyes er mine'd say you's been a-pickin' dat cotton yo'sef."

Katie said nothing.

"Dat right, Miz Kathleen?"

"I've been helping some," she said.

"An' how be yo mama?"

"Uh . . . fine."

Again he glanced from one of us to the other. He turned back and looked Katie in the eye even more intently.

"Is yo *sho* dere ain't nuthin' you gotter tell yo frien' Henry, Miz Kathleen?" he said.

"No . . . nothing, Henry," answered Katie. "Good-bye."

She didn't wait for him to get out of the way but flicked the reins again. We bounced forward as he stepped aside and just stood there staring at us. Both of us were afraid to look back. We kept our eyes straight ahead until we'd turned a street and were on our way past Mrs. Hammond's.

But then she reined in and jumped down. I stopped my wagon behind hers while Katie ran into the store. She came out a minute later holding a small bag and jumped back on the wagon, and we continued on our way.

I doubt two girls, whatever the color of their skin, could have enjoyed a ride as much as Katie and I enjoyed that ride from Greens Crossing back to Rosewood. What a burden had been lifted from our shoulders! Rosewood was Katie's again! In spite of how tired we were, we were so happy. We had to remind ourselves several times to keep on our toes, especially when we came to the Oakwood junction, in case any men came riding along that we didn't want to see. But even that reminder couldn't dampen our spirits.

When we got back, Katie ran inside to tell Emma and Aleta.

"Is dey gwine take yer house, Miz Katie?" Emma asked, still with a worried expression on her face.

"No, Emma! We paid off the loan! It's still ours . . . and we have money left over from the cotton!"

She gave both girls a big hug.

"Does dat mean we picked enough, Miz Katie?" asked Emma.

Katie laughed with delight. "Yes, Emma—we picked more than enough!"

"Enough for today," I added to what Katie had said. "But we've got to keep picking. There's still another loan."

"But it's not due for a long time," said Katie, "and we're not going to worry about it right now. Today we're all going to rest and take baths and fix something nice for supper. Look," she said, showing them the bag from the store, "I got some treats for us all in town!—and we're going to celebrate. Then maybe in a day or two we'll start picking the cotton again."

For the rest of the afternoon and evening, nothing could dampen Katie's enthusiasm. I'd never seen her so carefree and full of joy, and it was contagious. We all laughed and played together like we never had before.

When bedtime came and we were all bathed and wearing clean clothes, I don't think any of us wanted the day to end.

We were all sitting together in Katie's room. Emma was holding William, who was asleep. Aleta was sitting on the bed all snuggled up to Katie. I was in a chair across the room. I had told one story, and Katie had just finished reading us all another story from one of her books.

She closed it and the bedroom got quiet. I yawned and got up to go to the room she called my room that used to be one of her brother's.

"I don't want anyone to leave," said Katie dreamily. "I'm so happy right now, I want you all to stay with me all night."

Then she seemed to realize what she'd said. She perked up where she sat, awake again and eyes wide.

"And why not!" she said. "All of you, get your things—your blankets and pillows and dolls and come in here and we'll all sleep together for the night!"

"Can we really do that, Katie?" asked Aleta.

"It's my house," laughed Katie. "We can do anything I want! Emma, you and William can have my bed, and the rest of us will sleep on the floor!"

Aleta didn't need to be told twice. Excitedly she

bounded off the bed to the corner across the room where she had been sleeping on an extra mattress we had put there for her.

"But I couldn't take yo bed, Miz Katie," said Emma. "Dat wouldn't be right."

"You *are* going to take it, Emma," insisted Katie, already gathering blankets and pillows to make herself a bed on the floor while I hurried to my room and did the same.

"What if William wakes you all up?"

"We won't mind," said Katie. "We're a family, Emma, and William is just as much a part of it as the rest of us."

Ten minutes later I turned the lantern down and crept under the blanket where I'd fixed a bed for myself on Katie's floor. All of us had one of Katie's dolls with us, and we kept talking and talking until it must have been past midnight. As tired as we were, I don't know how we could stay awake so long, but none of us wanted to go to sleep.

After a while we heard Aleta breathing deep and rhythmically and we knew she was asleep. Emma wasn't far behind and five minutes later she was sound asleep too.

Lying beside me, Katie rolled over and turned her face toward mine. I could just barely see the white glow from the moon coming in one of the windows reflecting off her face. Her eyelids were drooping, and I could tell she was nearly gone herself.

"I'm so happy," she whispered. "I wish it could stay this way forever."

I turned toward her and smiled.

She reached out and took my hand and clasped it tight, then sighed deeply and closed her eyes.

"I love you, Mayme," she said softly.

"Good night, Katie," I said. "I love you too."

A few seconds later she was asleep, her hand still in mine, and I followed soon behind her.

# Epilogue

A TALL, STEALTHY FIGURE CREPT AMONG THE trees bordering a cultivated field of cotton, approximately half of which had recently been picked.

He had ridden out from town after his own work was done, keeping out of sight and making his way closer on foot. And now in the light of the sinking sun, he shielded his eyes with his hand and tried to make sense out of what he saw.

The five workers busily engaged in harvesting what remained on the stalks were the object of the man's attention. What were they doing out here alone? Four of them were girls, one of them far too young to be doing a man's work. The fifth was a slender young man whose skin color and other physical characteristics bore an uncanny resemblance to his own.

"I been wonderin' where he been disappearin' dese las' few days," he said to himself as he watched. "Dat boy's been fibbin' ter me. An' I knew dere wuz a suspishus look in dat girl's eye too. She ain't been tellin' me da whole truf. Sumfin be goin' on roun' 'bout here. Sumfin dat don' mak much sense ter dese ole eyes er mine."

He continued to watch for a few minutes more, then turned and made his way back to where he had tied his horse.

"Me an' dat son er mine's gwine hab a man ter man talk 'bout a few things," he muttered as he went. "And den I's gwine t' pay me a visit ter Miz Kathleen Clairborne an' her young frien's. An' right soon! Matter fact, I jes' might go visit dem termorrow."

Watch for volume three
of SHENANDOAH SISTERS

*The Color of Your Skin*
*Ain't the Color of Your Heart*

Coming Soon!

To share your thoughts with the author,
to receive a complete listing of his books,
or to inquire about
LEBEN,
a periodical featuring writings,
reviews, articles, reader letters, and devotional
thoughts from Michael Phillips,
as well as writings and essays concerning the work of
George MacDonald and his legacy, please contact:

Michael Phillips
LEBENSHAUS INSTITUTE
P.O. Box 7003
Eureka, CA 95502